SOLITAR

By Louise Furley

ISBN 978-1-7349807-0-7

Cover Design by: Pixel Mischief Design

DEDICATION

To Bob- You are my support, you mean everything to me.

To Aaron- I am blessed that you are my brother.

Prologue

"All right girl, you're last, make it snappy," her mother told her.

"Oh no," she whined silently to herself since Mama and Pa did not like complainers. "I don't want to go in. I'm last, they won't wait for me, they'll leave me." She had always been a scaredy-cat her older sister told her. Afraid of her own shadow. Afraid of siblings that were there, and of those that no longer were.

The tiny girl had been petrified of going any further than a few feet from her parents. Last week she was in the department store with Mama, they were looking at greeting cards. Not that she could read at not quite four-years-old but some of the pictures of doggies were cute- then she had glanced up and Mama was gone! *Oh no!*

She ran up and down the aisles in a panic, small chest heaving with the frantic terror of suddenly falling into an infinite void with no hope of climbing out and finding her way home. But she was embarrassed for anyone to know she was lost, that she had been left behind, so she didn't seek help.

Wiping at the flowing tears she ran and ran and looked and searched- there! Mama was in the kitchen gadget section! She raced up to her and stopped abruptly. Standing on wobbly legs catching her breath, dashing at the tears, hiding them, "M- Mama," she stuttered, "you weren't watching for me. You didn't tell me you were leaving."

Mama didn't look at her, just lifted up a juicer and said, "It's your job girl, to watch for me."

A week had passed and now the family was on a travel, one of many, from here to there, she was too young to comprehend geography. They had stopped at a rest stop. There was only one stall in the restroom so the girl had hurried when they left the van, she needed to not be the very last kid in line. She was one of the youngest of the

1

children, and the eldest siblings were already in line. Jostling and joking, teasing and pushing, elbowing and pinching, mocking and name-calling.

The female restroom had a yellow tape across the door indicating it was out of order, both genders of the children were using the male designated room. By the time she sprinted over the blacktop to the restrooms the last of the boys was exiting. She ran in front of her older sister just as their brother was clear of the door, she would be next!

"No." Her sister came up behind her and pushed her back. "I'm going next, runt, you're last." They all called her runt, she was so fine-boned, the tiniest of the litter.

"Please, Cindy, let me go next, I can't-" She tried to move in front of her sister.

"No!" Cindy yelled and roughly shoved her aside then took her place and went in.

So, she was last. She waited so long she was afraid she'd pee her pants. Hopping up and down to hold it off, she rushed inside as soon as her sister exited.

Dropping her drawers quickly she sat on the commode, her toes didn't reach the floor. "Hurry, hurry, hurry," she chanted. She tried to calm herself, they would not forget about her, they would certainly not leave without her. Still...hurry, hurry. She yanked her jeans up, didn't stop to wash her hands, the anxiety continued to build, her breath came tight. She raced outside and-

The lot was empty. She stood, her head whipping around and around searching, maybe- no, not a car, not a soul. She ran around the lot then back inside the restrooms, and back out to look in the rear area, nothing, nothing. Gone. They had left her behind.

An hour later, she was sitting on the curb, her face dirty with unrelenting tears. Maybe a nice policeman would stop and call her mama and pop and tell them to come back and pick her up. Yeah, a nice policeman will come. Another hour passed. It was hot, she was hungry, thirsty, tired. She should have brought her doll, Mimi. She should have-

A big pickup truck rolled into the lot, gravel on the asphalt crunched and spit up under the tires. It pulled up and parked a few feet from her. She didn't move. Sat with her arms wrapped around her knees and watched the vehicle. The truck door opened, a man slid out. Then the passenger door opened and another man got out. He came around the side to join the first man, and they stood and stared down at her.

The first man glanced around the empty lot, squinted up at the vacant restrooms then looked at her. "Hey there, little one, you here all alone? You got lost?" He turned to the other man. They shared a smile, deviancy tainting their eyes, the first man started   towards   her.

Chapter One

Twenty years later

"Okay," he told her, "hold still doll, don't want to get bleach in your pretty eyes now do we?" He snickered at his instructions, like he really cared if she was injured. The woman's arms were bound behind her back and her ankles were tied as well. Nude, forced on her knees as the bitterly cold shower rained harshly upon her, the tape across her mouth made it impossible for her to respond other than the muffled screams she rent against it in her mind-numbing terror.

The man pushed her head forward so the water would rinse the dye from her hair down the drain, along with some of the blood that streaked between her thighs from his earlier savage assault. Running his fingers through the knotted locks he worked to remove all of the bleach.

Satisfied, he sat back on his heels and shoved her. She fell backwards awkwardly landing hard on her rump. Smiling at her frightened glower he snickered and said with a bit of anger, "It's your own fault, doll, if you were a natural blonde we could have skipped this part. Oh well," he shrugged off his annoyance, "onto the next step."

Naked himself, he reached outside the shower stall and picked up a knife. Her eyes grew big over the tape and she scooched back, her butt rubbing and squeaking along the soaked floor until her spine hit the wet tiled wall. Shaking her head frantically, eyes on the gleaming knife, the now white blonde hair flew soggily around her head like scraggly snakes.

The edges of his mouth tipped up in delight. "No worries, doll, this has to be done before the rest," and he leapt at her, his hand slashing the knife across her cheek.

Grinning at the blood that shot out and the shriek against the tape, he sat back and stoically watched the water wash the fresh blood down the drain to join the dye.

Cowering against the tile, the woman shuddered, globs of tears mingled with mucus the water only made messier. Chest convulsing with pain and fraught with raw fear she apprehensively watched him for what was to come next.

Solitar

Chapter Two

He looked about 17, thin, nervous, but his eyes twinkled with rascally merriment. Surreptitiously glancing around quickly and deciding no one noticed him, he snagged a can of beer off a tray on the bar that held half a dozen beverages about to be served. Winking at a girl hovering outside the open door just as skinny as the teen but her timidity starker, he slipped the can under his holey sweater.

Waiting beneath the eaves, the girl wrapped her arms around her body seeking greater warmth than the threadbare jacket gave her while rain drummed behind her spreading puddles wider, joining one muddy pond to another and another. In rural Ruwenstad located outside of Suriname, South America, the rainforest temperature was normally hot and humid but the seasonal rains had lingered and were heavy enough to keep the temperatures unnaturally cold. Closer to the mountains in the higher altitude the temperatures dipped down to the forties. Soon they would rise to normal temps but for now it was near to frigid.

Inside the saloon, local laborers and farmers with grime under their fingernails in sooty sweat-stained clothes, and boots caked with mud lounged on stools hunched over drinks at the scarred, worn bar. The bartender had gone to retrieve a fresh keg of beer.

A barmaid in a black T-shirt with Zuk Zuk's Tavern in white across the chest and a tiny apron tied over her jeans had her back to the door as she set cocktails down on one of the occupied small square tables. Seated at the tables scattered across the faded wood-planked floor were off-duty miners but these men were scrubbed clean.

Grunts and curses marshaled from the slovenly group at the bar counter, a glum foil to the more cheerful tittering at the boisterous tables. A couple of hookers sprinkled amongst the males at the bar, a few female miners and some local girls joined the workers at the tables. Nothing decorated the plain walls under the thatched roof.

Rugged and splintered wood framed the teen as he hurried now mere feet from the exit door, his prize tucked under his sweater. The girl's eyes lit with anticipation of his reaching her when a hand suddenly caught his skinny arm, halting him. The boy froze, his guilty gaze rose in growing fear to the young woman who grasped him.

"You're stealing, Colby McShire," Solitar Lyonne accused. The air damp and chilly, she wore a hooded sweatshirt over a collared shirt and a brown bomber jacket over the sweatshirt.

"I- I- I-" the kid stammered, eyes wide with fright of facing possible arrest. He was inches taller than Solitar but that didn't quell his fear of her accusation.

"Please, Miss Lyonne," the girl spoke softly taking a tiny scared step inside. She and the teenaged boy shared a horrified look. "He- he- it was for me," she lied to help him. "I asked him to take it, please, for our date." She sniffed back a breath, a lock of wispy flaxen hair hung over upraised lashes.

"We- we-" she started again, taking a deep breath, pleading, "we have no money. If- if you tell on him to the sheriff, you know," her gaze flit to the boy and back to Solitar. "He'll go to jail. Please Miss, please, he'll put it back, right Colby?" She blinked earnestly at him.

Colby said quickly to Solitar, "Yes, Miss Lyonne!" Although probably only 6 or 7 years her junior his voice relayed respect. Hope lighting his turquoise eyes, he exclaimed, "I will, right away, here," he withdrew the can from beneath his sweater turned and set it on the bar. Holding his palms up for inspection he said, "There. Okay? All okay, now? Right?" He grasped the teenaged girl's hand. "Me and Lili-Mae will just leave, okay?" Sandy colored hair hung disheveled over his brow.

Solitar's face didn't turn to stone, it was already her normal expression. "You broke the law, Colby." Her rounded cheeks were stained rosy from the warmth of the tavern, she tucked an errant yellow curl back up in the cap that enclosed the rest of her hair. "Besides stealing, you are underage." Her fingers curled around the mug of steaming coffee she'd come inside for.

"Oh let it go, for cripe's sake," a miner interjected from one of the tables. "Not like we all ain't had a snigger before the age of consent, woman. It was a lousy can of beer, what, 65 cents? Here," he stood and tossed a dollar bill on the counter then sat back down. "Done. Move on."

Her small, pert nose rising indignantly in the air, Solitar said, "It's the principle of the thing, Cregg. Stealing is stealing, it's wrong no matter how big, how little." She turned to Colby. "I'm reporting you to the Sheriff." She pulled out her cell, pushed buttons.

When someone answered she said, "Hello. I want to make a report of a theft." Replying, "Yes," she nodded, "at Zuk Zuk's Tavern on Verde near the Gatin de Muur Mine. Ah," she looked at Colby's shocked face and then away. "Colby McShire. He pinched a can of beer. I'll sign a statement." She paused, listening, then said, "That long before someone can come?" her brow furrowed. "Fine. I'm staying at the Cresh Citadel, the police should know where to find me. All right. Goodbye." Clicking off, she stuffed the phone and started for the door.

"Fuck's sake, Solitar," a man at the bar piped up. Dirt clung to the day-old whiskers on his roughhewn face. "A lousy can of beer? The poor indigent kids wanna go on a date and yer gonna toss his ass in jail for that miserly shit?" He spat, squinted a cross of anger and disdain at her. "Yer a piece of shit work girl, you are," shaking his head he turned his attention to the brew in front of him.

Ignoring the annoyed men and the two teens holding hands and staring in tortured shock at her, Solitar lifted the hood of her sweatshirt over her cap, strode out the door and disappeared into the rattling shroud of rain.

Inside, at the back of the bar in the dim light, Kurian van Anastaas muttered, "*Trut*. Cold-hearted as a rock, Rutger."

"*Ja*, you're right, she's a *trut*, a bitch," the man beside him agreed, tossing back a quick gulp of his bourbon. "Welcome to Ruwenstad in the Republic of Kedolamer. Bitch is Solitar Lyonne, one of the civil engineers for the Gatin de Muur Mine. In title she's the project manager. Since Grover Butler was sent back to America with a broken leg and Miles Stewart also left to see to his ill ma, Ms. Lyonne although frightfully young is likely now the chief."

At Kurian's grunt of disapproval, Rutger tacked on, "Lucky for you she will be your equal, not your boss. Not so lucky for the other subordinates under her regime. She is known for adhering strictly to all codes and rules with zero leeway or the tiniest shred of compassion, and as you've just witnessed, she follows the letter of the law one billion percent. She is not well loved here."

Kurian's dark brows arched in disbelief then lowered in contempt. "Hell, Rut, you have learned a lot in the short time since you came on location. You are telling me that sorry excuse for a female is managing the budgets, the resources, acquiring and compiling quotes, the permits all that crap?"

Rutger Martkos nodded. "*Ja*. She's in charge of seeing that the infrastructural elements of the entire dig, testing of the soil, overseeing the design and construction of the mine and the excavating are securely spot-on. At least the digging is on the way. Two main tunnels and three shafts have been established." He signaled the bartender who had returned and finished hooking up the keg for a refill.

His gaze still on the front door Kurian disparaged, "*Hateliijke*, hateful little bitch. Sinking that boy for a can of beer. Teach the lad to try to be romantic. He should have just taken the girl out back and plowed her and gone on his way."

"*Ja* well, never let it be said you were the gentle romancer of the fairer sex." Rutger chuckled and clinked his glass to Kurian's. "And you get to work with the woman. Her name brands her, bro, Solitar. As in Solitairio, Solitaire, solo. Alone."

"I see," Kurian approved with a short nod. "Because no one would want to touch that cold fish with a ten foot pole."

"Actually, pretty much every straight male in town has tried. Under that worn leather jacket and khakis obscures a seriously rockin' hot bod. Hides that beauty behind that stony mien and lowered eyes. But when pressured she shoots men down with one glacial glare, freezes a man's nuts like an ice laser." Rutger gave an exaggerated shiver.

By the door another teenager cautiously stepped inside the doorway. He moved to where Colby and Lili-Mae stood clutching hands. Seeing their pale faces, he asked, "What's wrong? You guys were gonna meet us at the old baseball field. We're waitin' on you, Sammy's got the sandwiches."

"Aw." Colby hung his head in front of his best friend. "I did somethin' really stupid, Richard."

Richard swung his gaze to Lili-Mae whose big brown eyes were brimming with tears. "What? What'd you do?"

Colby squeezed his girlfriend's hand and gave her a meek smile. "I, uh, just wanted to treat ourselves for once to a beer. We're too poor and got no fake ID's to get us one of our own, so, uh," he blinked up at Richard then down at his shoes. "I kinda stole a can and got caught. Miss Lyonne from the mine busted me. She called the sheriff, gonna sign a complaint on me."

"Oh, shit, no way," Richard spurted. "Why would she tell on you like that for a lousy can of beer?" He glanced at Lili-Mae, her big round eyes trained in anxiety on Colby.

Colby shrugged.

Lili-Mae said angrily, "Because she has a black hole where her heart should be. Just a horrid person, Richard." She kissed Colby's shoulder.

Colby smiled down at her. He said to Richard, "I was wrong, can't blame what I did on her just 'cause she caught me."

"But you might go to jail!" Lili-Mae cried breathlessly, a few tears spilled over. Light, wispy blonde hair wafted around her pale face.

"Yeah, well," his voice defeated, Colby said, "let's go to the field and have our little party, might be the last one I see for a while."

As the teens left out the same door as the *trut*, Kurian shifted his attention from the door to his drink. Even with the short couple of days he'd been in the small village Kurian had noticed the lackadaisical if not downright insolent and lazy behavior of the local authorities. It would be hours if not days before one of the police came to address the complaint. He asked his friend, "Why would anyone even attempt to tip the *trut* and risk the prickly frostbite?"

Rutger sipped his bourbon. Ice clinked inside the glass at the movement. "The word is, according to Jamie Orlando, he got in her pants. Said she was granite cold, a frozen tundra. However, per that barmaid over there, Darlayne Tishcott, she claims he's a blowhard liar. Says he gets in his cups and brags to all and sundry he's had her, but that it isn't true.

"But, for some reason Solitar Lyonne doesn't call him on it, doesn't deny it. Still, it's strange, you'll see. Whenever he gets around her she ruffles him off and finds a reason to leave. He just laughs and tells people she wants him as a steady beau but he's a free and wild man meant to taste all the many variety of fruits of the land and won't settle for just one frigid, prickly peach."

Kurian's head swung at his friend, his brows daggered down. "What a bunch of hyperbole bullshit. Who gives a shit anyway."

"Whatever," Rutger responded to his rhetorical statement with a grin. A handsome, broad shouldered man with dark auburn hair and a roguish smile, he said, "Anyway, you really look at that trick? She tries hard to be an uncompromising tough bully, difficult to do when you're built so delicate and soft. Even her voice is hushed femininity and she moves with unintentional grace. You'll see she tries to walk with long purposeful strides and arrogant confidence, steel spine and all but she slips and you catch the underlying softness and elegance, the sumptuous sashay of her rounded hips. Those curves, bro? I'd do her in a heartbeat if she gave me half a notice. Orlando's full of shit, I bet there's hellfire under all that ice and rock. Cruel passion swims fathoms deep in those artic blues."

"Bullcrap," Kurian spat. "When did you become the class poet? The woman is ugly in nature, a thornbush. No matter how pretty, those prickly thorns are lethal and nasty. Like licking the syrup off the tail of a scorpion. I fear you would catch a foul sting if you pressed lips together."

Rutger threw his head back with a barked guffaw. Wiping a mirthful tear from his eye he said with a more serious note, "Can't hate the girl because she plays by the rules, K, even if it's all black or white to her, no grey ground. A law is a law, a rule a rule, you break one and you pay. Like an iron rod, she has no flex, no give. Working with her, you better cross your t's and dot your i's, son."

"Huh," Kurian snorted lifting his glass to his lips. "May have to work with the *trut* but I will be doing my damnedest to avoid her like she was as you say, hellfire. Like a fallen, worm-bitten apple, gorgeous on the outside yet pure rotten to the core on the inside, no thanks."

"Ah." Rutger lifted his glass to his mouth and said against the rim, "Funny you mentioned touching lips, might there be a hint of lusting interest there, *mijn* boy?"

Scowling in the negative, Kurian muttered a vile invective before downing his own straight   bourbon.

Chapter Three

Two days later, standing a few feet inside the main tunnel of the mine, Solitar rubbed the tip of her nose with the back of her hand adding to the sooty smudge already there. Intently studying the clipboard in her hand she wasn't aware anyone had entered the mine. It was after six o'clock and most workers had left for the day. She wore the brown bomber jacket over a flannel shirt and dark brown khakis. The toes of her boots were coated in mud.

"Soli," a female voice spoke. Generated lanterns lined the walls lending spooky dim illumination, turning every rock and crevice into an eerie shifting shadow.

Solitar stiffened in an effort to stunt the anxious jerk in her limbs. Dirt and loose stones crunched beneath her boots at her movement. She paused to clear the tense look creasing her face created by the sudden sound of Camara Bartolo's voice. Her hand tightened around the clipboard she clutched. *Damn*, she thought, would her body ever stop reacting so violently to every sudden sound or motion?

Clearing her throat, the effort to stifle her ludicrous nervous reaction to such a minor act made Solitar sound irritated rather than anxious. "What is it, Camara?" she snapped. Pushing the safety helmet up her forehead she forcefully eased the tightness in her expression, smoothing it to express a practiced blank look as she turned to face the Gatin de Muur Mine's Project Storeperson.

Camara's duties were receiving and distributing parts/goods/materials, maintain all documentations relating to incoming/outgoing materials, ensure all materials were safely unloaded, sorted and correctly stored in the designated locations in the warehouse, coordinate the return of unused parts to suppliers and a myriad of other responsibilities.

Solitar's lips parted with a silent gasp when she noticed the man standing with Camara. It was not just his superior height and muscular build that made him seem so imposing. And it wasn't the hard face and tough bearing that made him appear so intensely formidable. No, it was the angry coldness emanating like censoring blades cutting from his dark eyes that made him come across so…intimidating, threatening, *dangerous.* Solitar had to consciously suppress a shiver of…unease at the daunting scowl he proffered to her. Her startled gaze jumped from the man to Camara.

"Hi sweetie." Camara smiled her apology at the clearly disconcerted Solitar. "This is Kurian van Anastaas, the new Technical Services Superintendent." She turned her bright smile to the superintendent. "Mr. van Anastaas," introducing them, "the current Chief Civil Engineer, Ms. Solitar Lyonne." She beamed between the pair not seeing the wary glares as they studied one another.

At the object hostility radiating from van Anastaas' glower, Solitar ignored the introduction and said to Camara, "Did you receive notification from Esston Technical Supplies of the return of those defective line-belts? And your helmet, Camara, you know better."

Camara's eyes rounded at Solitar's rudeness to the superintendent and scolding of herself. Of average height, the fortyish woman held the safety helmet in her hands pressed against her chest rather than covering the brown curls that bounced on her shoulders. Carrying an extra twenty pounds around her middle, prone to mothering staff as well as Solitar who tried to rebuff her hugs and hot chicken soup, Camara quickly fumbled the helmet over the curls and said, "Uh, um, yes. It's been entered into the CMS. I thought you should meet Mr. van Anasta-"

"Thank you, Ms. Bartolo, just Anastaas." Kurian nodded to the friendly woman. "I leave off the van for convenience. Please call me Kurian." He gave Solitar a brief desultory glance before returning to Camara. "I am sure as we work together the chief engineer and I will have contact. Courtesy and smiles of welcome are not obligatory; I only require professional dialog. Since Ms. Lyonne does not necessitate common pleasantries, there is no need for us to share idle conversation." His deep voice carried an accent, it wasn't the same but it did resemble the accent most of Ruwenstad displayed.

Solitar's mouth dropped. "Wha-"

"Ms. Solitar Lyonne?" a voice spoke from the entrance and the trio turned to it. A male attired in a police uniform of white shirt, charcoal grey slacks and grey hat with black brim stood with his hand raised. He jabbered a slew of words in a language Solitar did not understand although she was assuming it was Dutch as the citizens of Ruwenstad positioned near Suriname, an early Dutch settlement, spoke mostly Dutch.

Anastaas stepped between the women and the officer and he rattled off a string of words that apparently the officer understood because he rattled right back at him.

Solitar spoke quietly interrupting the flow of conversation, "I believe he is here for me. I filed a complaint-"

"He is not," Anastaas snapped at her so harshly she flinched from him. His eyes narrowed at her frightened affect. His voice cooler, he stated, "The *politieagent*, ah, police officer is here to advise of a vandalism. On Wednesday around two o'clock, several autos parked behind Zuk Zuk's Tavern were deliberately damaged and he has been given a list of people that were seen there around that time to interview. Find out if they saw anything. You," he said, nodding to Solitar, "as well as I were both in attendance."

"Oh!" Solitar's golden brows flew up and Camara's gasp was audible. "But I, I mean I was there only briefly to collect a mug of coffee. I'm certain I didn't witness anything so- so atrocious. If I had I would have immediately contacted the authorities."

Anastaas' gaze on her was withering. "I am sure you were too busy throwing some lovesick young fool under the bus to have noticed anything outside of your own vain, perfect, sterile little world."

Solitar and Camara's dual gasps echoed off the dank rocky walls surrounding them. Anastaas ignored them and continued conversing with the policeman.

"Um, can- can you ask him to speak in uh," she pulled the word out hearing it a few times in the months she'd been there, "in Engels?" A small shiver loosened. It was a dank ten degrees cooler inside the musky mine. The earthy smell of soil and rock permeated the air adding to the chill.

Anastaas ignored her and continued speaking in Dutch with the officer. Finally, the officer turned to her, snapped his heels together with a sharp nod and a smile. He spouted a few words, red tinged his cheeks and he turned quickly and sped off.

Bewildered at the situation, Solitar asked Anastaas, "What did he say? Do we need to go to the station to make a statement?"

He stared at her for a moment like she was a nasty bug pinned under a scope, long enough to make her struggle to contain an uncomfortable squirm. "*Nee*, ah, no. I explained who we were and that I was with another fellow that can be verified and I told him you had called in a complaint and left right away. The officer said very large cement blocks had been lifted and thrown at the vehicles. And, well," his indifferent eyes roamed her slight form, "I explained you were too small and weak to have done that."

Her lips bunched in annoyance. "I am not weak, how dare you-"

"Whatever," he cut her off. "He is gone and you are off the hook for any further interrogation."

His look at her was so hard Solitar found herself lowering her head and eyes. It was a protective habit that she just could not break. It was only when she was furiously angry could she maintain eye contact. She forced her eyes up to his jaw and glared at it and asked, "But what did he say as he was leaving? It sounded, and looked like he was making a personal comment about me."

His hard mouth pressed in a thin line suddenly quirked at one end. Whether he was amused at her question or the fact that she didn't raise her gaze all the way up to his eyes Solitar hadn't a clue.

Anastaas replied, "He said, 'Is the cold bitch not a sweet smokin' honeypot even with that bit of soot on her *min* nose?' *Min* meaning tiny." Anastaas reached out and tapped the end of her nose. Before she could jerk back from his touch or produce a scathing retort he swung on his heel and strode off. The rain had suddenly stopped as if to cut a dry path for the damned arrogant liege.

"Oh my God," beside her Camara crooned.

"Yeah," Solitar agreed, "what an offensive jerk."

"Oh certainly not, I think he was quite nice. But the *man*," Camara's voice strained, she appeared to be about to drool.

Solitar turned to the woman. Camara was gaping at the retreating superintendent. "Cam-"

Camara swung her eyes to Solitar and then back outside. "Girl, that man is some fine hunk of prime meat!"

"Camara!" Solitar was shocked. "He is not! He's…just…a rude brute."

A sexy grin lit Camara's almost plain face. "Honey, he wasn't the rude one," she chastised her friend. "And yes, you could call him a brute." She folded her arms over her chest. "A smoldering, fierce, *hot* brute."

Solitar felt her cheeks warm from Camara's outrageous statement. "Really, Cam, he's just a man. A boor, but only a man."

The grin took over her entire face moving into Camara's honey-colored eyes. "Sure, I agree he's a man all right. There is no doubt about that…" She sounded dreamy saying, "Those shoulders, broad damned chest, lean hips in those olive khakis you could just see the outline of his-"

"Cam!" Solitar shouted, her cheeks now on fire. She gave Camara's shoulder a slight push. "Let's get these lights out and the guard fence up. I have a ton of paperwork to do." She moved to the panel that generated the lanterns.

Her bottom lip pushed out, following her, Camara complained, "Work, that's all you do, Soli. There's more to life and you never look forward to all the work involved with this job."

"I don't," Soli responded. "I hate the paperwork and I hate the job. I hate math and graphs and all the analytical stuff and the crap involved working out the contracts, the mud and drilling, the noxious fumes, the digging, the killing of the environment. All of it, every iota of-" She bit her tongue to stop the diarrhea of her mouth.

"Well! That is so unlike you to ever utter a single complaint," Camara said with surprise. "If you hate it so much why on earth do you do it?"

Solitar considered how much to tell her. She stopped so abruptly her helmet slipped forward and Cam almost ran into her. She never talked about her past. Certainly not the very beginning. Hers was the very nightmare all children fear. Maybe she would just give the part of what got her there.

Pushing the helmet back up off her brow Solitar explained, "I kept…failing out of foster homes and eventually the Brightlook Children's Home in Singapore gave up on trying to have me adopted so they focused on academics. They decided I needed a strong career. I was quite…pressured into the field. Actually," her lips twisted wryly, "I was chained to it. Ate, slept, studied, breathed civil engineering, working with mines specifically. The Home received grants from the government for certain mining schools so they weren't hesitant to use corporal punishment if we fell short of their goals. We were used as free intern apprentices; actually we were just unpaid laborers. The school got the money, not us."

"You- you mean they spanked you if you weren't up to par?"

"Huh," Solitar snorted. "More like whipped, beat, and things you couldn't imag- uh, never mind. At least they didn't just toss me out with no education at 18. The kids that couldn't keep up academically to their outrageously high standards ended up selling themselves on the streets for bread. The village where I lived was dirt poor, not as impoverished as this area near Suriname but bad enough. Jobs were very few and hard to come by.

"When I aged out I had won a scholarship to America to intern at Regent & Livingston University, RLU. We learned on the job training, again, free labor. I knew nothing else so I worked at what I was trained for. They gave my name to recruiters from Gatin de Muur and I was hired for this job as Third Chief Engineer because my academics were so high and I impressed the lead trainers at RLU."

"Oh, honey." Camara's face softened with compassion. "You poor thing. But now, surely you can look to something else? Something you *want* to do?"

A mirthless chuckle from Solitar before she said, "Not in the cards. I owe Brightlook so much in school fees this is the only job I can do to earn enough to pay it back. It was supposed to be a nonprofit but we were all charged a fortune to stay there that was a loan to be paid back in full upon severance. Most orphanages don't and can't charge their residents, but Brightlook worked under loopholes. My wages are fully garnished to pay them back for room and board and my education. I got a scholarship at RLU but not a full one and I owe them also for dorm fees.

"Besides, if I do well at this position I could be promoted to full chief on the next job the Gatin de Muur head staff send me to." Still clutching the clipboard, her fists clenched. "I just have to toe the line tight, allow no mistakes, no latitude, don't stir the waters, mind my own business and keep my mouth shut and I'll have the chance."

"Honey." Cam shook her head in sorrow for her friend. "Maybe you could just look into it, try to make a go with something else. Maybe-"

Letting out a held breath, a loose golden tendril fluttered with the blow. Solitar cut her off, "No. This is what I know, what I'm trained to do. I just need to work harder, be harder, get the job done right and quick and smooth. No bumps." She headed out of the tunnel towards the dimming evening light.

Camara traipsed after her. "Well, what about tomorrow? You said you would go with me and the girls to the party. I mean, it's Saturday for crying out loud, you have to give yourself a break. Maybe that hottie Anastaas will be there and you-"

Solitar walked faster announcing, "No time, Cam, I have no time for frivolous drinking and mingling." Her head down as she marched towards her vehicle, she said. "And I sure have no interest in any man, especially that- that boor."

Camara trotted after her. "But Soli, Gatin de Muur's executive director Garrick Miles said all top staff must attend. That includes you!"

Rolling her eyes, Solitar strode faster.

Chapter Four

Kurian Anastaas and Rutger Martkos entered the autopsy room along with Sheriff Artclif Gibson.

Leaning over the body lying prone on the table the doctor looked up and seeing the two additional men he gave Gibson a dirty look.

"Hey Doc," Gibson greeted, ignoring the look and opened a cupboard. He pulled out sets of pale green smocks with booties and masks wrapped in plastic and handed sets to Kurian and Rutger. The plastic crackled as the bags were opened and the wrappers tossed in the trash. Dutifully attired, the trio moved closer to where the doctor was working.

Doctor Sebastian 'Buck' Saccomoto stood up straight and pushed his macro-glasses up on his head. He was attired in a green smock and wore all the mandatory protective gear. A green cap covered his hair that was mostly white yet still thick and combed back off his wide forehead. White brows so bushy they could use their own caps drew down over deep-set intelligent eyes. A bronze tan was odd considering how much time he must spend indoors as one of the few doctors in the area. The village so small, rural, and poor it did not have an actual medical examiner.

"Fellas, this is Doctor Saccomoto," Gibson said.

Put out at the intrusion, the doctor groused, "Sheriff, this is not the line for the roller coaster ride, it's the hospital morgue and I don't need you bringing in hooligans off the street to gawk at the dead bodies. They want a porn show they can head over to the *Paarse Rivier Naakt Nachtclub*."

One of Rutger's auburn brows arched at being called a hooligan. "The Purple River Nudie Nightclub? I take it that it's near a river? Are the girls purple too?"

At Rutger's wisecrack, the doctor glared at all three. "The strip joint used to be called the *Blauwe Rivier Nachtclub*, as in the **Blue** River Nightclub. But now it's a chartreusey purple. Thanks to the mine the river is polluted and the dancers are more likely green with the stench and toxins."

Kurian spoke with a tinge of annoyance, "Not from the mine, Doctor. The reports claim the mine sifts clean."

17

Not hiding his irritation, the doctor complained to the sheriff, "Gibson, what the hell are these two miscreants doing here contaminating my autopsy?" At the term miscreants, Kurian and Rutger shared a glance and Rutger smirked.

Sheriff Gibson rolled his neck until it cracked. He was in his forties, with only a few specks of grey in his short brown hair. He hitched his belt up over his slightly rounded belly. The rest of his body was in good shape from regular workouts, it was just the Guinness he loved that padded his stomach a little. "Wasn't my decision, Buck. I got a call from Interpol of all things and was told to allow this man to be privy to the investigation of this here girl's murder." He nodded to Kurian. He was tall but had to crank his head back to look Kurian directly in the eye.

Buck Saccomoto asked Kurian, "What's this to you, son? You kin or a boyfriend of this poor gal?"

Kurian crossed his arms, his eyes were on the nude body lying on the metal gurney. The scent of antiseptic was so overwhelming it would make a weaker person queasy. The cold metallic appliances, counters and coolers in the room bred a grim gloom that raised a chill over the skin adding to the queasiness. "I got a call as well, Doctor, from someone so high up you have never heard of him asking me since I am stationed here to take a look at this murder case for him, forward a more in-depth report than he would have received through the news or the local authorities."

"Why? Are you a *politieagent,* a policeman?" the doctor asked.

"My name is Kurian Anastaas. I am a technical superintendent at the mine." He spoke in English but his accent landed heavy on the words. He nodded to Rutger. "Rutger Martkos." He didn't give Rutger's title or even where he worked. Kurian went on, "I am just doing a favor, well, it is more than just a favor, nonetheless tell me the results of your autopsy."

Saccomoto glanced at the sheriff. Gibson gave him a short nod. Saccomoto sighed. He turned back to the body and said in an emotionless monotone, "Jennifer Marie Aandersson is, was, a healthy 28-year-old Caucasian female, 5'5, at 135 pounds. No prior surgeries or broken bones. She was sexually assaulted then beaten to death. In that order as the tearing inside her and on her thighs bled." His brow furrowed with puzzlement.

Noting it, "What is it, Doctor?" Kurian asked.

The doctor didn't answer, he motioned to the sheriff with a slight wave of his hand for him to respond to the question.

Gibson remained silent for a moment. He had turned away to stare at the floor rather than the incised victim laid out like a pounded slab of cut pastrami. Severe bruising and lacerations were visible on her colorless skin. She'd been battered to a gory pulp.

He was used to the dead he'd witnessed in the rural village to be men killed in barroom brawls or an accident with a farming machine or a drunken spill off a bike into a gorge. Not beautiful young women who had been brutalized. He wasn't comfortable. It seemed wrong to have the poor nude girl lying there defenseless being ogled by four strange men, it made her appear so…vulnerable. But she was dead and she could no longer feel anything. He muttered, "Someone was really pissed at the girl, really pissed."

"Understatement," Saccomoto agreed under his breath. He leaned over and drew a sheet up to cover the girl to her neck. When Gibson didn't answer Kurian's question, Saccomoto said, "I have previously made my report to the sheriff. I told him that it was odd that it appears she dyed her hair blonde close to the time of her death, there were no dark roots."

"Why is that odd?" Kurian raised his brows, studying the body.

"Well, Gibson here spoke with the poor lamb's family, right, Sheriff?"

"Yeah." Gibson nodded. His gaze rose to the now covered body. A hard gulp rolled over his Adam's apple. "Her parents say she has always been a brunette. Was always disparaging of 'dumb floozy blondes' as she called 'em. We questioned her boyfriend, who has an alibi by the way, and her sisters and friends. They all say she wouldn't get caught dead as a blon-" He broke off with a wry nick to his mouth. "Anyway, I'm thinkin' the perp made her do it or he did it. Doc said her fingers and nails are void of any dye stain and if he was planning to kill her why would he bother to protect her skin? So I think he did it."

"Or she wore gloves. Where was she found?" Kurian asked.

Gibson replied, "A homeless guy stumbled over her in an alley behind a pub. You probably aren't yet familiar with the area. Ruwenstad is touted as a small town, but in reality, the center of the city is small but the neighborhoods and open land sprawl around it for hundreds of miles. There are rainforests beyond the savannas that go on densely for miles and steep mountains further back. There are a few smaller mountains near the town, obviously you know that since you work at one. It would take you years to learn the total map of Ruwenstad.

"Most of us grew up here, and the miners and their staff hang mostly in town. There are shops, a couple of small theaters and restaurants but the miners mostly visit the saloons. I guess a few go hunting and hiking but it's dangerous and easy to get lost if you don't know precisely where to go. And, as you know, decent motorized vehicles are in short supply here. You were lucky to grab those bikes." At Kurian's cocked brow the doctor half-grinned. "Thin walls, I heard the engines when you rolled in."

His hands on his hips, Kurian said calmly, "*Heb je.* Ah, gotcha. So, give me the name of the pub and the general location of where the girl was found."

"All right," Gibson said. "Dracula's Lair is the name of the bar. It's on Bram Stoker Street at the end. You'll find it on the local map. I heard they handed out hand drawn maps to you visitors since there isn't much of a detailed official one."

Rutger chuckled. "Are you serious? They named the bar after a vampire and the street after the guy who penned Dracula? What the hell?"

Sharing his mirth, Gibson told him, "Not a lot to do out here so whenever we create a new street there's a contest to name it. Bram Stoker won. The bar name was only natural. You won't forget the street, or the bar for that matter anyway, right?"

As the sheriff spoke, Kurian moved right up to the table and peered down at the deceased girl. She had been so brutally beaten the bones in her swollen face were broken, smashed in. He commented, "There's a cut on her cheek. What can you tell me about that cut, Doctor?"

Saccomoto's bottom lip pushed out. "Looks like a knife slash. Like a sideways X or a crooked cross or a slanted t."

"Were there any other knife wounds like that on her body?" Kurian inquired.

Shaking his head, "No," Saccomoto responded. "Bruises, broken bones, short jagged cuts made by his nails maybe or gravel as she was thrashed against the ground, but no other indications a knife was used on her. Why do you ask?"

Studying her, Kurian murmured, "Just curiosity. This is the second murder like this?"

Saccomoto stared at him for a heartbeat before nodding with suspicious understanding. "That's why you're here. A possible serial?"

When Kurian failed to respond, he said, "Yes. Another woman with the same beatings, dyed hair, same slice on her cheek was found three months ago. Vic was Martha Zabka." His attention back on the body he stated, "Whatever made the mark was done by a knife, but none like I'd ever seen before. It left an odd cutting, had almost a swirl or something to the line."

Kurian said, "I want copies of the autopsy report, pictures of that vic."

"Ah," the doctor exhaled with a sound of guilt, he glanced at the sheriff. "Well," he hemmed and hawed until the impatient glare from Kurian urged him on. "I only spent a few moments with the body when I was called away. A family emergency." His gaze canted to the sheriff who gave him a slight imperceptible nod to explain.

Clearing his throat, Saccomoto expounded, "My son had been mauled by a puma, I rushed to the hospital. He was critical for quite some time. Unfortunately," his gaze once again canted to Gibson before he went on, "I only have two part time assistants and one was brand new, the other was off as they alternate days. Again, unfortunately she didn't know, and at the pressure of the victim's family she released the body and the woman was cremated. I was therefore unable to do a complete examination of her and the notes are slim at best, and," he coughed into his fist, "there are no photos." He stripped off his gloves and tossed them in a receptacle then stuffed the tips of his fingers into the waistband of his smock pants.

"Any body fluids, semen, saliva on either girl?"

"Not on this one," the doctor answered. "There were traces of spermicide, he used a condom. The first, unfortunately, we didn't collect anything. Her hands weren't bagged or examined for skin under her nails or DNA anywhere else. A complete clusterfuck. But," he sighed, "we can't un-ring the bell. She's ashes now."

Kurian asked, "But you did notice that her hair was dyed?"

Crimson crept over the tips of Saccomoto's ears. "Yes. She was, you know, nude on the table, it was clear she wasn't a natural blonde. And," his head tilted back, "there were no roots showing on the top of her head. I didn't think anything of it at the time of course, many women dye their hair. It was only once I examined this victim," he nodded to the body on the gurney, "that I thought about the other girl and the recently dyed hair and the cut on her cheek."

Kurian stared at the doctor with a blank expression. Then he slanted his head to Gibson. "I need copies of your entire reports on both vics along with all the statements from the family and friends. I want both of their complete histories from birth. Schools, sports, cliques, clubs, church, jobs, criminal sheet if any, all the boyfriends, girlfriends, family members, the phone and computer dumps, everything. And I want photos of the girls as they normally looked before, and photos of this one as she is now, and a sharp pic of that wound on her face." An afterthought he said, "And the brand name if possible, specific color of the hair dye."

One shoulder shrugged. "Sure," Gibson granted. "Gonna take time, ain't no spot on labs here. Don't see the point though. I don't think the murders are really related. I'm looking at the first girl's death as the result of an angry boyfriend. We haven't ruled him out yet. And this one, obviously some sod stumbled drunk outta the bar and put the make on her, she declined, and he didn't take it well. Likely kidnapped her, raped and killed her in his home then dumped her back in the alley behind the bar.

"There was blood in the alley, but not a lot. More like some seepage. Don't need her history for that. Wrong place wrong time. Too poor for a computer but she did have a cell the whole family used, we've reviewed it, it'll be in our report. We interviewed most people in the area where she was found. Unless the doc comes up with some DNA and it's in the system to match, or a wit comes forward or someone confesses gonna be tough to solve."

"Just do as I ask, Sheriff," Kurian responded in a cold voice. "Was she found dressed?"

"Sort of." Gibson stared at the body. "She was wearing a dress but the buttons were buttoned unevenly and a few were torn off. She wasn't wearing undies, no bra, no shoes, socks. Her mother said she would never leave the house unless fully dressed. There was blood on the body but none on the garment. She always wore a necklace with a gold heart from her grandmother, it wasn't found on or anywhere near the body or at home."

"Souvenir?" Rutger looked to Kurian.

Kurian nodded. "Hopefully the killer kept it, help the law to use against him when they catch him. Sounds like he stripped her, did the assault and beating then redressed her. Might be a sign he respected her, or cared that she would be indecent when found. Perhaps he was a prude?"

"So we're looking for a homicidal Dalai Lama?" Rutger quipped.

Ignoring him, Kurian spoke to Gibson, "What about the first victim. Anything noted that was missing from her person?"

Gibson's eyes shut as he reviewed his notes in his mind. He opened them and said, "Yeah. A ring. One of those Celtic things, you know, a Celtic knot. Hers had two emeralds on it. The boyfriend's mother was livid that it was missing. That's why I think the boyfriend did her. He gave her the ring, it had been his grandmother's, she was Irish, and she would have wanted it back if they broke up. I figure he didn't mean to kill her, did it in anger, then took the ring back to appease his ma."

Kurian's expression remained a blank mask. He asked, "Where was the first girl found?"

His eyes sad, Gibson said, "In the fields a few miles northwest of the city."

"Can I assume there are not any surveillance cameras anywhere in the streets, or the neighborhood of the bar or where either vic resides?"

"Ha." Saccomoto didn't hold back his sarcastic snort.

Gibson rubbed the back of his neck brushing up the short hairs to the top of his head. "If you haven't noticed, Anastaas, this area is so impoverished most folks don't know where they're gonna get their next meal from. The mine has helped but only minutely, the company brought in most of their own people," he squinted an eye at Kurian, "like you. The residents ain't got enough money to buy a pot to piss in. Most lack even electric or running water, town ain't got the money for fancy shmancy things like cameras."

"*Oke*, ah, okay." Kurian attempted to speak only English but his native language kept overriding, which was a blend of several languages. He frowned at the sheriff. "I did not ask for a biography of the land. But there are crops? I saw some greenery as I drove in." He was working on his contractions but he had to constantly think about which ones were appropriate to the sentence. English was a big P.I.T.A. But with a mixture of foreign miners and the locals everyone was using the more universal English.

Gibson shrugged. "Few banana plants. They tried coffee but after a devastating weeks-long storm the fields flooded when they were still seedlings, they didn't survive, all washed away. Then a blight killed the orchards, and rice fields didn't take after a fungus choked them out ages ago. A few lucky folks got some scrawny cattle and goats, a few chickens and pigs. Lotta land but no means or way to really produce it."

"Why don't they grow more crops to feed themselves and to sell to bordering countries?" Rutger asked.

The doctor answered soberly, "Seeds and equipment cost money. There just isn't a single extra penny to purchase even one plant. These people are the meaning of the word poor, gentlemen, as in dirt poor. Too poor to even work the dirt."

"*Oke*." Kurian lifted his jaw to the doctor. He said to the sheriff, "I will have someone stop by for the information on the victims. Make sure you include the specific location where the first girl was found."

"Yeah, well," Gibson said, "forensics went over it and with the seasonal rains," he raised his palms with a shrug.

"Sure. Want the info anyway." Back to Saccomoto Kurian said, "*Dank u* for your time, Doctor."

Kurian, Rutger and Gibson exited the building.

Outside, Kurian said to Gibson, "We will give Colby 20 dollars and tell him to come to you at the station and retrieve the files on the victims for me and bring them to the Cresh where we are staying. I got work for him and Richard."

Gibson's head shot up. "Colby McShire?"

"*Ja.*" Kurian stuffed his hands in his pockets.

"I got a report the other day the kid ripped off Zuk Zuk's Tavern. You can't trust a shoplifter with your money, Anastaas. Those boys, him and Richard Garland, two delinquent peas in a pod they are. And 20 bucks for a bike ride?"

Kurian looked down the street lined with white buildings. In wealthier times the structures were built like Dutch colonial three-stories with gambrel roofs trimmed with curved eaves. Bay windows jutted out from the top stories. Balconies laced the second floors and white columns anchored the bottom.

Everything now was weathered with peeling paint and rusted wrought iron. It was worse near the mine and the Cresh where most of the mine staff were staying.

The Cresh Citadel was the only place for outsiders to stay. A palace, it was enormous, built by a man who thought he could create a cartel kingdom for himself in the land rich with coca fields. Eons ago he was assassinated, his dreams of being the King of Cocaine never came to fruition and the palace crumbled and decayed surrounded by bogs and tall grass.

It was now a hotel but brought in little funds to keep it from further deterioration. Visitors were usually hunters and fishermen from other countries looking for exotic adventures. But they kept most of their trekking between the border of Ruwenstad and Suriname leaving the more treacherous rugged plains near the foothills to the locals.

"They are not delinquents, just teenagers feeling their oats. You let me worry about my business, Sheriff," Kurian replied.

"You-" Gibson shut his mouth. "You're right. It's your business if the kid robs you blind. Funny thing was when I sent an officer to take the report of a crime he committed last week the officer came back complaining about ignorant dames that don't know their ass from a hole in the- uh, anyway. Unless you'd like to give me further information on why you need to know about these dead girls, I'm off. I'll see you two chaps around."

"We will be in touch, Sheriff," Kurian said as he and Rutger headed towards motorbikes they'd parked on the street. There were very few vehicles to rent, most had broken down and with no money for repairs or parts they lay rusting in the fields as the encroaching rainforest crept over them like dead wood. It was therefore doubly appalling that the vehicles behind Zuk Zuk's Tavern had been damaged.

Chapter Five

Kurian and Rutger drove out of the city and along paltry crop fields and into the surrounding neighborhoods. The squat, single-story buildings with flat red or green roofs sprawled amongst tall palms separated by curved gravel roads. With sparse electricity, most homes had water tanks to collect rainwater connected to the sides. Broken down farm equipment and other debris littered the unmown grass. They pulled up a dirt driveway and parked the bikes. By the time they dismounted Colby was outside, the wrecked screen door slamming behind him.

"Hey Mr. Anastaas, Mr. Rutger," Colby greeted them cheerfully. Freckles stretched across his cheeks and nose, one of his front teeth was slightly crooked that gave him an impish appearance. Not that he needed any help in that area. Sandy hair flopped over eager turquoise eyes. His jeans were worn through in some spots and his sweater had seen better decades.

"I told you that you can call me Kurian, Colby, and he is just Rutger. You don't work at the mine so we don't need the formality. We came to have you run an errand for us."

"Hey, boy," Rutger greeted the teen with a grin.

"Sure thing, Mister- uh, Kurian, sir." The crooked front tooth showed with his big smile.

Kurian looked down at the teen's boots. They were dirty and one part was held together with duct tape. "Those new shoelaces, son?"

Colby stared down with a grin. "Yessir!"

"You buy them with the money I gave you for the chores you did for me? Washing our bikes and doing our laundry?"

"No, sir." He shook his head, loose hair shuffled back and forth over his brow. He palmed the mop out of his eyes. "I bought Lili-Mae and me supper at the diner with that and got her a new jacket. The laces I earned from another person at the Cresh."

His brow rose. "Oh *ja*? Who?"

The grin faded a bit. "Well, uh, sir, they asked me not to say. So, what can I do for you today?"

His lips pushed out, Kurian pondered the boy. "You're not doing anything illegal for this other person are you?"

The grin disappeared. "No, sir. I only took that one can of beer, never done nothin' like that before and I promised I wouldn't steal again or nothin' like that. I got what they call *penance* to pay for it." The grin returned.

"You dealing drugs?" Rutger asked, his smile gone.

Colby's mouth thinned, eyes darkened. He shook his head adamantly. "No, sir. Me and Lili-Mae want to get married someday and have a family. Someday I might be able to get a good job, maybe at the mines or as an attendant at the Cresh. If I could go to college I would try for an engineering degree, but," the grin fell lopsided, "not much chance of that. Ain't got no university here and I'd be too poor to go anyway. But, still, I don't wanna ruin my record. I did an honest chore, sir, I swear." He looked so abashed and then angry that Kurian believed him.

"How about you tell me what the task was but not supply the name of the person who asked you to do it?"

Colby's brows drew down in a V between his considering eyes. He shrugged. "Sure. I guess that'd be okay on account of it's a amononomous job."

"Anonymous you mean?" Rutger chuckled.

"Yessir. That. Anyways, I brought some paintings from the Cresh to a few of the shops in the city for sellin'. The owners knew they was comin' but not who was supplying 'em. Some of the miners bought a bunch to send home to their families. They're really tops!" he said with enthusiasm.

"What are they, like landscapes?" Rutger asked.

Colby thought for a second. "Some. Mostly were of animals. Dogs and cats. I guess the artist saw some owners and their pets and painted 'em. Sellin' like hotcakes they are!" He added, "One of the store keepers told me the artist don't keep the money but it's donated to that crappy animal shelter off on Dillman Street."

"Huh," Kurian grunted. "*Oke.*" He pulled out his wallet and drew out a few bills. "Here. Go on down to the police station and ask for Sheriff Gibson. He has some files he is preparing for me. Get them and bring them to my room at the Cresh. Got it? There is enough there for new boots for both you and Lili-Mae. You need a jacket too, kid."

His voice had a stern edge as he said, "And I do not want you doing work for us or anyone else when you are supposed to be in school." Grammar, middle and high school were all in one building. There were no buses. Children that lived too far to walk or bicycle and their parents didn't have vehicles just didn't attend school.

Colby accepted the money with a grin and stuffed the bills in his pocket. "Sure thing, Mr. K., sir. Anything you want. I have to do community service at the Cresh after school on Monday, mow the lawn, sweep up and stuff, it's my *penance*," he said the word like he was proud he added a new word to his vocabulary. "But later I can help clean up the area around the mine if you want. I saw a bunch of shit like metal pieces, cut tubing and rubbish layin' around."

Kurian hid his frown. Mine employees were supposed to be taking care of trash and unusable cut pieces and the like. He'd have to look into who was not doing their job. "All right. Tell Richard we can get some pickup work for him too. What about odd jobs for Lili-Mae at the mine? You need anything for your bike? Gas? A part?" he asked the teen.

"No, sir." Colby headed to the old motorbike leaning against the wall of the decrepit house. "You already paid to get it spruced up with a full tank and then some, it's good to go. I don't want Lili-Mae near the mine. It's dangerous and I'm not sure about some of the dudes I seen hanging around. She's in advanced classes in school, I want her to concentrate on her studies." He climbed on and turned the key. The motor turned right over. It was clunky and rough sounding but in relatively good shape. "I even got an extra helmet for Lili-Mae with the rest of the money I got for deliverin' the paintin's."

Kurian was about to ask the teen if he had his parents' permission to do the chores then he remembered he'd been told the boy had no father and his mother was bed-ridden. A gossip at the mine said she was bed-ridden because she couldn't climb out of it after using drugs. These people had no money but many sold their bodies to support their habits. Even the most destitute places in the world still had drug problems. Colby basically had no one watching over him. He fed himself and got his butt to school on his own, most days.

Colby turned the bike to face out the driveway. "I'll get you your stuff and then see you later at the party, Mr. K, and Mr. Rutger," he sent Rutger a grin. "The mining company is paying for the party. They shipped in a bunch of food and drinks and stuff and are paying people to prepare it all. The whole town's goin'! See ya!" And he was off.

The two men climbed on their bikes. "Party?" Kurian asked as he turned on his bike.

"*Ja.* You got the email. Undoubtedly you ignored it like you tend to do. We have to be there, it's a community shindig and since you are one of the head guys at the mine it's a necessary show of good will for you to attend." At Kurian's scowl, Rutger laughed. "Come on, bro, it won't kill you. We can sniff around about the murders. And, might even dance with a pretty girl and haul her back for some lovin' at the Cresh."

Kurian slid sunglasses on and muttered, "Don't need any more attention, Rut. Have to push away the few female miners we have, and the hookers, and the local women, act like they have never seen a man before."

Rutger threw his head back with a loud laugh. "Yeah, small towns are like that, bro, fresh meat. I'm gonna grab up all that's offered. You may prefer quality over quantity, but I'm not so particular. I might even hit that chief of yours, the mean one."

"Not mine, Rut. She is a mean bitch, why the hell would you want a piece of that?"

"Mean with that great of an ass I can ignore the mean. She's not being bitchy, Kurian, just tough. Hard. Like you. Only you wear your hard all over your face and body, she can't much hide her softness though she tries like hell to. She can try to cover fine tits like hers all she wants but they're still there, and they do not look hard, my friend. No, they look mighty soft and friendly to me, wanting a handshake so to speak, right?"

"You are a smacker, my horny friend. Hard is not the same as mean. I could not look past the mean streak. A strong *trut* is *oke*, but mean is unnecessary and a turn off. Come on, I want to take a look at the crime scene."

They took off from the dirt driveway and hit the gravel road back into town.

An hour later they were still scouring the alley behind Dracula's Lair bar. "The crime scene techs went over this, K, what are you hoping to find?" Rutger asked. "At least the rain has stopped, unfortunately it's still mucky in here, damp and sticky." He made a face as he scraped the bottom of his boot off a corner of brick wall.

His head down, with the toe of his boot Kurian pushed aside loose stones and bits of rubbish the CSI had left behind. There was still an outline of the body and smudges of blood on the dirty ground. "I-" he broke off, something caught his eye. He moved to the wall at the edge of a blood smear. A tiny piece of paper was stuck right in the crevice between the wall and the ground. He pulled out a tiny tool case from the lower pocket of his khakis and removed a pair of tweezers. Using the tweezers he picked up the piece of paper. Lifting the paper he squinted at it.

"Whacha got?" Rutger dusted off his pants and moved beside Kurian.

Kurian twisted the small piece of paper to view it better. "It is a bar receipt from The Howling Dog over on Smuggler's Run Road." Sliding the paper into a plastic baggie from his pocket he tucked the bag away. "We need to head on over to the Dog."

"Hell, K, they've got nothing but bars in this sad-sack town. They're that poor how do they afford all that liquor?" Rutger commented heading to his bike.

"I am guessing a lot of it is home stilled and then sold to the bars and liquor stores." They hopped on their bikes and headed out of the alley to the street.

"Ah, yeah…maybe…" The bartender at The Howling Dog, Thad, studied the receipt. "It's stamped Thursday. There were three of us on that night. Two on the floor and one at the bar. The ticket is from the shop out front, the liquor store. Here, follow me." He stepped out from behind the bar and with Kurian and Rutger on his heels he trod across the wooden floor and through an open doorway.

Inside a smaller room with a front window that faced the street, Thad went up to the counter, a woman was stacking packs of cigarettes up on shelves behind the counter. "Hey, Regina," he called out.

The short plump woman turned around, her glance shot to Kurian then Rutger then to the bartender. She set down the packs she held and smiled warily at the bartender.

Thad said, "These gentlemen are working with the police, hon. They have a receipt from Thursday they'd like you to take a look at, see if you remember who purchased the item." He turned to Kurian with a nod.

"*Dank u.*" Kurian held the receipt in the baggie to the cashier. "Leave it in the bag." He belatedly tacked on, "Please."

She took it from him, held it up to a better light and read it silently, her lips moving. The liquor store was small, just three aisles of liquor and wine bottles. The smaller pints and half-pints along with cigarettes, cigars, lighters, matches, rolling papers, loose-leaf and chewing tobacco, and unopened boxes of e-cigs were stowed behind the counter.

The woman had long black hair tied back in a braid, fuzzy escapees crisped around her round face. "Yes," she said, handing the bag back to Kurian. "I recall the sale. It was paid by cash but I remember the brand of tequila. Not as cheap as we usually sell."

Kurian took the bag and slid it into his pocket. He worked a smile, said, "*Dank*, ah, thank you, madam. Do you remember who purchased it?" Most of the country spoke Dutch as did Kurian but he grew up elsewhere so his accent was different and harder to understand, unfortunately his English didn't always come that easy.

She nodded thoughtfully. "Yes," she replied, her eyes hopped around the three men. "He isn't in any trouble is he? I wouldn't want to get anyone into trouble. Is he on probation and not allowed to drink? I mean I don't want him mad at me-"

"Ma'am, just give us his name. There is no reason why he needs to be told who gave us the information. Now, the name. Please." The 'please' came out a gruff addition again. Damn. The people Kurian generally dealt with pleasantries weren't necessary, or expected.

Her eyes cut to him, a blush rolled up her neck. "Uh, um, o- okay. It was Serug Partay. I was quite surprised as Serug is basically homeless and only buys a pint or so when he panhandles enough. The tequila was closer to top shelf, frankly I don't see how he afforded it. There's just not a lot of extra change for folks to hand out around here, you know? Maybe he bought it for one of the miners. Some of them folks are getting paid good dollars. Since the mine opened our sales have increased a bit."

Rutger pointed to the e-cigarettes still in boxes. "Doesn't look like they're a big seller."

She turned towards the electronic cigarettes and smiled wearily. "No. Money hasn't gotten around big enough. The miners purchase necessities but no one really can afford the- the frivolous things. They send much of their earnings home to families. The locals mostly buy the loose leaf and roll their cigs themselves, it's cheaper. Some have hidden tobacco fields they-" She slapped her hand over her mouth and rounded her eyes to the bartender who frowned at her with a short shake of his head.

Kurian said to Thad, "Can you tell us where we can find this...Partay fellow?"

"Sure, sure, well, no, not really." Thad tugged at the collar of his shirt. "Uh, actually, as Regina mentioned, Serug is homeless. Sleeps in doorways of shops in the city, or under a bridge or a tree, or with the group that hangs in that open field down at Marx Street."

"Can you give us a description of him?" Kurian asked, pulling out a small notebook and pen.

His eyes on the notebook the bartender moistened his lips. "Sure, sure." His gaze flicked to Regina and back to Kurian. "Carrot-top, makes him easier to pick out. He's tall, very thin, scraggly, pretty dirty in god-awful garments and smells…bad, if you can imagine. Around, uh, hard to tell," he shot a glance to Regina.

"I'd say late thirties," she tossed in.

"Anyone in particular he normally hangs with? Friends?"

Thad glanced at Regina who shrugged. "Naw, just the other homeless folks and they meander, come and go. Serug flits around like an aimless moth with his hand out. Otherwise he's nodding off somewhere. Check the city stores that are closed. He chooses doorways for his snoozes and looks for ones where no one will run him off."

"*Oke, dank u* for your time," Kurian thanked the pair and he and Rutger headed out.

They were strolling back to their motorbikes when they heard someone talking.

"No, no, stop it, Petey," a woman's voice was saying.

Down the street of broken sidewalk the woman they were talking about earlier had her hand up in front of a dog. Tail wagging, tongue hanging, the dog, at least part yellow lab and the rest mongrel was clearly trying to lick any part of her he could reach. "No, Petey, I have no treats for you, go away." She pushed at his nose to no avail. He hopped around her trying to lick her hands, rub his nose on her legs.

"See there," Kurian muttered with a disparaging growl, "mean through and through. Even with animals." He called out, "Here pup, I got something for you." He shook the coins in his pocket and the dog's head shot up and his attention jumped to the two men. Kurian pulled out a candy bar and crinkled the wrapping. That did it. The dog raced over to him and eagerly sniffed his hand.

Petey got so excited his entire body wriggled. He woofed and whimpered sniffing the candy bar. "*Oke*, good boy," Kurian praised, unwrapping the candy bar. He broke it in half and tossed one half in the air. Petey leaped and snapped the bar and gobbled it right down smacking his tongue and teeth making both men laugh.

Kurian said looking up, "See that, Woman, that is how you treat animals and human be-" Solitar was gone. "*Trut*," he gruffed under his breath and fed the dog the rest   of   the   candy   bar.

Chapter Six

Inside the Community Center the rec room where parties and weddings were held teemed with laughing, drinking, eating, dancing people, young and old. Locals brought food the mining company shipped in and paid them to prepare, everything was laid out on tables for all to enjoy. Drinks were added and a band made up of residents played at one end of the vast room. The atmosphere was bouncing and cheerful. Children chased each other in and out of grownup's legs. On the dance floor people gyrated to the lively song the band was playing.

"*Heer almachtige* save us all, Rut," Kurian groaned as they entered. "A damned hillbilly hoe down, what hell are we to endure here? Can you just pass for me? No one will even notice I am not here."

A huge grin plastered on his face, Rutger chided his friend, "Now, now, God almighty won't save you. I see liquor at that bar in the corner and," he glanced around, the grin widened. "There's plenty of female forms to be found. I'm grabbing a drink, a plate and then a babe in that order. Maybe. Catch you later, bro," and Rutger started for the bar.

Sighing, Kurian slowly followed him to get a cocktail. If he had to suffer it out he might as well do it with a buzz. A double bourbon in hand, he spotted a group of men he worked with and headed to them.

"Hey, Superintendent," one of the men greeted him. Ladio Lafayette was a boilermaker at the mine. He worked with aluminum and steel fabricating of structural, piping, and mining equipment, including chutes, walkways, handrails and a multitude of other things. In his late twenties he was one of the few locals to work at the mine. He had trained out of the country but returned to be with his family in South America. His skin was medium dark and his smile bright white. He gave Kurian a welcome grin.

Kurian lifted his chin to him and nodded to the others in the group. "Laddie," he greeted Ladio with his nickname. To the others he acknowledged, "Siggy, Hubie, Creggar," and joined the loose circle.

"Didn't think you were gonna make it, mate," Shon 'Siggy' Sigmund said. Siggy was a master welder from Australia.

"*Ja*, well, gotta chill sometime, yeah?" Kurian wore black jeans and a black thermal. He'd checked his jacket at the door. He turned his attention to Boris Hubbard. His friends called him Hubie. "Hubie, I heard someone comment today that the river on the east side is polluted. Why would someone say that?"

Hubie turned a confused expression to Kurian. He was a Health and Safety Specialist II at the mine. From Tennessee, his accent was country twang, he had long, dirty blond hair and looked like he was born with a guitar in his hands. Early twenties, he was built strong and lean from hard physical outside work. Creases crinkled around the tanned skin of his blue eyes.

He was an avid hiker and loved kayaking. Plentiful lakes and rivers in Ruwenstad, he was one of the few who made use of them. "I'm not sure what you're saying, Boss. The reports I've seen state everything is P&P and the regular tests show no signs of pollution. Might check with Jamie Orlando, he's responsible for some of that stuff I think."

"Ah, yeah. Thanks." Kurian dipped his head to Hubie then scanned the room. "What does he look like? Is he here?" The name was familiar. Who- oh *ja*, her again. Everything kept coming back to that woman. All beauty and no heart. Jamie Orlando, Kurian had heard was the only guy that managed to nail the *trut* without getting stung by her scorpion's tail.

Tucking long blond hair behind his ears Hubie grinned. "I don't think he's as good looking as he says he is," his chuckle blended with others around him. "He's a Production Supervisor, at the top of the food chain and he likes to lord it over everyone. Bossy asshole."

"Aye," Siggy concurred. "Boy's got a bleedin' head the size of a pregnant sea lion." Agreeing laughs rippled through the group. "Got dark brown hair, and I guess he's over average height. Has neatly trimmed scruff. Look for a flock of fawning ladies, somehow he always manages to nudge his preening way into a gaggle of 'em."

"You're just jealous 'cause he banged the hot chief and she shut you down before you got your full invite out," Laddie scoffed.

"Whatever." Siggy scowled. "Plenty of tail around here for everyone."

"Really?" An offended feminine voice joined the group.

"What?" Siggy sounded innocent.

"Can you say *misogynist* much?" Camara Bartolo stood there with her hands on her slightly plump hips. Her honey-colored eyes flashed at the men. She wore a fuchsia dress that ended several inches above her knees.

Another woman beside her looked just as affronted. A decade younger than Camara's 40 years, Cortnee Rosell added, "Yeah, sexist lot of you cavemen." She tossed her head. With her shoulder-length russet hair tipped with blonde, and longish nose and extra-long lashes she reminded Kurian of a long-legged afghan hound with its fine silky coat. She caught sight of Kurian. "Oh, hi, do I know you? I'm sure I'd remember if we'd met before." She fastened intrigued brown eyes on him.

"This is Kurian Anastaas, one of the tech superintendents. He hasn't been here that long, Cort," Siggy told her.

"Well then," Cortnee flipped the ends of her hair and moistened her lips, her gaze travelling down and back up Kurian's body. A slow smile turned her eyes ardent. "How do you do? I'm Cortnee Rosell. I work with Camara at the store warehouse. You have serious rank over me, I guess that makes you my boss. I look forward to working *under* you." Her innuendo so blatant Siggy made a choking sound. Cortnee sent him an angry frown which he returned with an unabashed grin. She held her hand out for Kurian to shake.

Great. Kurian thought to give her a quick polite handshake but she grasped his fingers when he tried to release them. Using them to pull herself close to him she smiled brightly up at Kurian.

"Ah, my pleasure Miss Rozwell, I need to-" He tugged at his hand, she held it tightly.

"That's Ro*sell*, sugar, but you can call me Cortnee. I would love to take you on a tour around town, show you the sights. We-"

"Well, leave it to you, Cort the wart, to attach your sleazy self to the hottest men in town. Step aside girl, let a pro show you how it's done." A third woman joined the throng.

"Yeah, pro," Hubie snorted, "definitely a professional."

Beside him Siggy sniggered. "Yeah, gal is high maintenance and expects the fella to pay for the action! Crikey, blokes, she wants everything including her rent, electric yada yada for a coupl'a quick tumbles."

"That's your problem, Sig, the word quick." Her nose in the air sneering at the pair of jokesters, the new woman gave Cortnee a not gentle shove aside. Cortnee stumbled ungainly backwards on her long thin legs before catching her balance.

The new woman ran a hand topped with very long, very pointed nails in Japanese manicure complete with sparkly rhinestones down the front of Kurian's thermal as she snuggled into him. Leaning her head back she smiled wide red lips up at him. "Hi handsome, I'm Gizelle Blanca and no one is the boss of me." She cocked her head with a flirty dip and said huskily, "But I wouldn't mind getting under you either." Dark eyebrows beneath a swirl of gold blonde hair arched with incitement.

Shit, Kurian cursed under his breath. Randy bunch. No one ever heard of personal space? He happened to glance over the crowded room that heaved and hoed with constant movement of people mingling, dancing, laughing and damn, he saw her. Solitar Lyonne.

A scattering of tables filled the center of the room while windows dotted all along the walls on both sides. Solitar was standing near the band leaning against a window and looking out. She appeared as unhappy to be there as he was.

The employees of Gatin de Muur had been strongly suggested by Garrick Miles, the executive director of the company that owned the mine, to attend the function and make nice with the residents. The mine brought money to the town as the employees resided there and purchased goods and visited the restaurants and whatever else Ruwenstad had to offer. But also caused it damage and the cash went right back out as soon as it came in.

The shops and eateries were occupied but it wasn't enough to bring the village into the green. They were just too impoverished to climb out of the despair. The gold mine was not that large, it would be played out within a year or so and any meager dollars brought would disappear with the closing of the mine.

"Hi guys, what's going on?" A cheerful girly voice broke into the group. It wasn't interesting enough to pull Kurian's attention but a ripple of pleased male voices greeted the newcomer.

"Hya Brittlyn," Hubie enthused. He gave the girl with the light yellow bob a quick once over. "Where you been, girl? No one had to work today, I looked around for you."

Medium height with an athletic build but not bulky with muscles, just softly toned, Brittlyn Jones favored Hubie with a warm grin. "Hey Hubie," she said with a slightly shy tilt of her head. Batting her lashes at him she replied, "I didn't get around to shopping all week so I had to fill the pantry."

"Well, I'm glad you made it, can I get you a drink?" Hubie rolled his arm around her shoulders.

"Oh for the love of shiny new fucking nickels," Gizelle groaned testily, "no damned gentleman offered to get me drink, huh?" She patted Kurian's chest to draw his attention back to her. "How about it, big guy? How about you fetch me a drink and I'll show you how thankful I can be, real good, huh baby?"

But Kurian's concentration was arrowed across the room.

Solitar Lyonne stared out the window absently sipping her drink. Kurian thought it was strange to see the scorpion in a skirt. Even from his distance he could see she had legs that should have their own zip code. The kind that made a man picture them wrapped around his hips and looked fine walking to or from. The scene from the back was just as good as the front. The girl was blessed with the most perfectly rounded rump in the entire- hell, what was the matter with him?

He did not find her attractive. No. Not at all. Wouldn't stick his wick in her well if she begged him, would be afraid her icy hard vagina would snap it right off. Ignoring the people that called out to him as he left the group, Kurian extricated himself from the hot and handsy Gizelle, tossed back his drink and quickly strode to the bar for another.

"Double bourbon neat," Kurian ordered setting his empty tumbler on the bar. Keeping his back to the corner of the room where the scorpion stood, he drummed his fingers impatiently on the bar while the bartender went to fill his order. Drink in hand, Kurian found himself moving slowly to the side of the room where Solitar Lyonne was lingering. He wasn't going near her, it's just he could hear the band better from that side. Then he saw Colby McShire approach her and Kurian paused.

He expected animosity to spark between the two. They did regard each other with serious expressions but the woman wasn't yelling at him, and Colby was nodding at whatever it was she was saying to him. Kurian slouched closer until he was within hearing distance.

"Now Colby," she said, "you know you have responsibilities to fulfill and conditions you are required to follow."

His face fell. "But Miz Solitar, I just wanted a dance with Lili-Mae. She'll be here in just a-"

Shaking her head she cut him off. "No. You agreed. You go finish that community service scheduled for today and then you can come back. Those church walls won't wash themselves."

"But-"

"No. You must learn responsibility and grow up. Be the man you tell everyone you are. Go now. You drag your feet and by the time you return the party will be over. Do you want that?"

He shook his head, his shoulders fell. "No ma'am." He started to turn then said, "If you see Lili-Mae, she'll be with her parents, can you tell her I was looking for her and that I should be back in a few?"

Before Solitar could respond, Colby turned on his heel and made quickly for the exit.

Still a mean *trut*, Kurian thought angrily. What a piece of work. Well, it was time he gave her a piece of his mind. He started towards her but another man swooped right in. The man was good looking, tall, had dark brown hair cut neatly with a trimmed scruff. Strangely Lyonne sank away from him looking almost fearful. But that didn't deter the male. He moved right into her and gripped her arm. At her wince, it looked like he gripped it hard.

The woman started to move from the man whom Kurian had assumed at this point judging by the description he'd been given of him, to be Jamie Orlando. However, Orlando didn't want her to leave. He appeared to squeeze her harder and pull her up on her toes as he spoke roughly to her. She cowered and turned her head. Grasping his hand she tried to pull it from its painful grip on her arm.

Already moving, Kurian could just hear her whisper, "Jamie, no, please." Whereupon Orlando spewed a bunch of angry sounding words. He had leaned in close and was speaking in her ear. Her rounded rosy cheeks paled and she lowered her head although she still fought to break free of his punishing grasp.

Stepping right over to the couple, Kurian announced loudly, "Hey, there you are, ah, Solitar, you promised me this dance. I have been looking everywhere for you."

The pair froze. She peered around the tall Orlando in confusion at him. Orlando barked over his shoulder, "Shove off, bro, private party here."

Kurian had to hold back from slamming his fist into the back of Orlando's head. At the fright in Solitar's eyes he said softly yet firmly, "Fine *vriend*, but the lady promised me a dance and I have been waiting all night for it." It sounded lame in

Kurian's own ears, the party had only been in full swing less than an hour. But he didn't really care. He found he was itching for a fight and Orlando had about three seconds to back down. As he counted to three he hoped the asshole continued to ignore him.

Orlando turned around and took him in. At over 6'4 Kurian had probably 2 or so inches on the man and that gave Orlando pause. Orlando quickly scanned him checking over the biceps that bulged under the black thermal and the broad chest with wide shoulders that definitely saw a lot of time at the gym and likely boxing or martial arts or both. Scowling, Orlando asked, "Who the hell are you?"

"Kurian Anastaas, tech super at the mine. Guess that positions me above you, making me your superior." Orlando's glower confirmed he got the intimation that Kurian was superior to him in every way, not just at work.

"Don't mean squat outside the job, bro, and I ain't your friend. I was having words with Solitar and you can go fuck yourse-"

"Right," Kurian said. When Orlando had turned, his grip had loosened and Kurian grabbed up Solitar's wrist and quickly strode towards the dance floor toting her with him. Behind them Orlando glowered with his empty hands fisted impotently on his hips.

Orlando could get sacked for brawling at the party, so he stayed put. Kurian didn't care if he was fired, he found he was irritated he hadn't slammed his knuckles into Orlando's nose. But bloodsport in front of staff, and the woman he grasped wasn't politic so he kept moving. Beating the man to a pulp while he held her with his other hand would only make her run from him with fright.

Threading through the crowd, Kurian pulled Solitar to the middle of the dancers and drew her into his arms. Shock lit her beautiful face and she didn't move. "But I don't-"

He jerked her close taking one of her hands and placing it on his shoulder then he caught the other, cupped it and laid it on his chest. He set his hand on her waist and pulled her closer. "Do not talk," he muttered quietly, "I need to chill out for a minute." For some reason he felt rage roiling around his body and he still wanted to go back and introduce Orlando to an uppercut. More than one.

"But-"

"Hush," he ordered yanking her tightly to his front. Enclosing her in his arms wasn't exactly bringing down his heated temperature or securing his control. At least the anger was waning but his temperature continued to rise. Damn, the woman was as soft as she looked and she smelled faintly of wildflowers. Her feminine body tucked into his hard torso was wreaking havoc on his attempt to calm down.

He looked down at her. She peered up warily at him. It was hard to believe with that hot body and stormy passionate eyes that she could lay like a doormat while Orlando banged her. A wave of revulsion rolled through him at the picture of the two of them together.

As they danced gently, rhythmically together, Solitar stopped trying to fight him and her body lost some of its stiffness and she settled more into his embrace. He released the slender hand he was holding to his chest and moved his palm up to cup her nape. His other hand stroked up her back and then down to her waist. His fingers spanning her lower back he tugged her so close her breasts wedged up against his chest.

She lowered her head and rested it on his wide chest and sighed. They moved silently, occasionally bumped by other dancers but he absorbed the jostling protecting her in his arms and continued on as if they were the only ones on an island filled with soft music.

Kurian lowered his head to peer at her. His throat thick, he asked quietly, "Solitar is an unusual name. Was it a fanciful whim or were you named after someone?"

She tipped her head back to look up at him then quickly turned away. "No. It wasn't my birth name."

When she didn't offer more, he started to say, "Why-"

She didn't let him complete his question. Her body grew rigid again and she put her palms on his chest to push him back, but he didn't move. "Mr. ah, Anastaas, I did not come here to dance or make polite conversation. So if you don't mind..." She pushed again but it was like trying to move a brick wall.

A scowl darkened his face. "But I do mind, Ms. Lyonne. I mind a great deal. I want to know what makes you so damned mean. You cannot blame it on hormones because you are like this all the time. Combative and rude. You were a terror to that poor kid, and I rescue you from a prickly situation and rather than thank me you sting me with that vicious scorpion tail of yours." She struggled to get free and he moved his hands to her waist and gripped tightly.

Red spots lit the center of her cheeks. Aghast, she spouted, "How dare you! I was only insisting Colby live up to his responsibilities, be a man. He has no father and his mother is a drug addict that can't get herself out of bed, hers or any other that pays her, to see that he's fed. He lacks discipline and will end up in prison someday if he doesn't get a clue. And I didn't ask you to save me from Jamie. I was, uh, handling the uh, situation just fine. In fact, there wasn't even a situation to handle. You misread whatever you thought you were witnessing. You are nothing but a nosy brute."

His fingers dug hard into the soft flesh of her hips. His grip like a thick pair of pliers held her immobile. "Honey, I misread shit. That prick was manhandling you and you not only did not like it, you were afraid. I saved you from whatever crap he was laying on you, and I saved you from having to suffer an embarrassing scene. There is already talk of you and that jackass getting it on. People say-"

"Oh!" she gasped in horror. Her face flamed scarlet. Blinking wildly at him she cried, "Please, you're hurting me, please let me go!"

Not realizing his own infuriated strength, he instantly loosened his fingers but didn't remove his grasp of her hips. "Listen, Solitar," he said more calmly, "that asshole is causing you some kind of trouble. Talk to me, I can help you. Just-"

She flung her head away from him but he caught the glistening of tears brimming her blue eyes. And they were blue. Brilliant blue. "No, there is no trouble, he isn't bothering me. Please, Mr. Anastaas, just let me go."

He hesitated, staring down at the top of her head. Normally her hair was stuffed up in a hat or hidden by a helmet or a hood. Today she'd chosen to let it hang unencumbered. Her hair was the lightest of blonde, like the center of the sun but he could see flickers of orange flame glinting within the fair locks. The hair fell past her shoulders in fat waves, when she turned from his view some of the silken curls covered half her face. God he did not want to let her go. And that scared the hell out of him. But now he was frightening her just like Orlando had, making him just as big of chump. He opened his hands and she immediately stepped back.

Ducking her head, not looking at him she said through a tight throat, "I, uh, thank you for the- the dance. I'll see you I'm sure at the mine. Good day." She spun and almost raced from him.

He watched her wind her way through the rollicking crowd until she made it to the doorway that led to the front rooms and she disappeared from sight.

"I say, K, you've still got it. You know how to make the fairer sex run from you like a dragon breathing black fire," Rutger drawled beside him. A giggle with a nasty edge to it driveled out at his words.

Kurian merely canted his eyes to see the woman clutching Rutger's arm. The woman, Gizelle, who had brazenly tried to latch onto him earlier was now pasted against his friend's side. She gazed up at Kurian through low seductive lids indicating he could still take his shot with her if he desired to. He didn't. Talk about a she-wolf. All licking chops and sharp teeth. His eyes rose to Rutger who was regarding him with a smirk.

Rutger wasn't a fool, he was well aware what sort of female the femme fatale that was hanging all over him was. The blouse she wore was unbuttoned almost to her navel and a hair couldn't fit between her and her yoga pants under which she clearly wasn't wearing underwear. He smirked at the frown of warning on Kurian's face.

Rutger had seen her make a play for his friend and was now all over Rutger. His grin at Kurian said, 'You don't want the easy bump and dump but I'm not one to leave a free dinner for someone else to munch.'

Shaking his head with a small smile, Kurian said, "I will see you back at the Cresh, *mijn broer*," and he turned but not fast enough to see the dark scowl cross Gizelle's pretty face. She wasn't used to being turned down, and worse, being ignored. It appeared she'd hoped to make him jealous by hitting on his friend and thereby lure Kurian back to her.

But Kurian doesn't get jealous, he's never cared enough. He made a parting shot, "Don't forget to schedule an STD test on Monday, bro." He resisted ducking his head at the castigating cusses hurled at his back in a feminine hiss. He smiled at Rutger's snicker.

Chapter Seven

The man, he liked to call himself 'the Observer' mingled his way through the happy throng partying at the rec center. He moved slowly but never stopped, he didn't want to speak with anyone or draw any sort of attention to himself. He wore glasses and a cap pulled down over most of his head even over his eyebrows. Appearing to be wandering to the bar for a drink, he surreptitiously scanned the crowd and watched with interest the first play between the two men and the female.

The man with the trim beard left standing by the windows staring with vitriol at the tall man that was hauling the gorgeous blonde to the dance floor was as amusing as watching the couple when the song was ending. At first the woman struggled to not dance, then she gave in and melted into the big guy. Then they started talking and she suddenly got fired up and stalked off in a rush with the man staring broodingly after her.

He had seen the other darker blonde, the bawdy blowsy one throw herself all over the same tall man before being shot down. The Observer chuckled as the big man met an equally strapping male with auburn hair at the exit and the ribald bitch was now hanging on him. The two men shared a few words, both appeared to also be sharing a silent conversation. The Observer wished like hell he could have heard the big man's parting shot because the auburn-haired guy had to stifle his grin and the bawdy blonde went bananas with fury. It was hilarious. But watching the play, interesting and funny as it was, was not what the Observer was there for

No. He was already feeling the itch. Feeling it bad. The consuming need to crush a woman, with his bare hands, to death. Assault her until her cries were so hoarse she could barely scream at the savage beat down he favored her with. Then to leave his mark, no *her* mark on the woman's cheek, *damn his body tingled with the rush of adrenalin mixed with the sudden urge for a fresh kill!* Vengeance roiled with excitement through his arousing body.

Straightening his trousers, he stuffed his hands in his pockets to pull the material away from the sudden erection the bloodlust arose in him. No need to draw attention to himself as some sort of perv on the prowl. He desperately needed to find another woman to fill his need. He glanced around, the pickings weren't that great. She had to be the right height, weight, figure, the perfect hair color would be the icing on the cake, but he'd learned as he hunted that was an empty wish.

His gaze moved thoughtfully to the doorway where the first blonde beauty had rushed out. She was petite, too small, curves too lush to be the choice, but...his gaze lingered. The color of her hair was just about...perfect. He could easily dye the hair of another female victim, but he couldn't put height and weight on her. So he chose the girl then changed what he could like her hair color. Once he had cut the tip of a woman's nose off because it was too long to suit his purpose.

The women he took had to be the ideal image, as close anyway as he could get them, otherwise he couldn't get...off. Couldn't get that gut deep, soul ripping explosive ka-boom bomb that would finally clear the fucked-up mudded mess inside his head. But then again, the gorgeous blonde was the reason he'd come to this godforsaken land in the first place. Of course she was the right image, albeit small.

He needed a kill, then he would be crystal clear for a while, the viscous cobwebs exorcized from his spiritual mind and physical body to be cleansed and made whole and pristine again. He could take deep cleansing beautiful breaths. At least until the hell built up again and then he'd have to go back out on the prowl.

Right now the little blonde had too much attention on her between the first man that had manhandled her, then the guy that had forced her to dance, even the teenager he'd seen hanging with her numerous times. There would be time down the road for their reunion. For now, the Observer would seek out easier prey and if he couldn't get what he wanted, well then, his eyes narrowed as he continued to stare at the door. His hand in his pants pocket he drew it slightly out and discreetly viewed what lay in his palm. A necklace with a gold heart, and a Celtic knot ring. Rubbing his fingers over them produced a jagged spurt to his arousal.

Sucking in a deep breath, a grin spread over his murderous face, now was the fun time.   The   time   to   go   hunting.   Oh   yeah.

Chapter Eight

Solitar wiped the sweaty fringe of hair off her cheek. The chilly air from the rains was lessening and the heat and humidity had risen. Staring down at the photos in her hand she rubbed her chin. The piping was going slower than usual, she was going to have to find the master boilermaker and get on him, or her.

She tugged her phone off the clip on her belt and scrolled through it searching the employee list so she would know whom to contact. So many workers had been switched out it was a chore to keep track of who worked where. The owners of the mine had little patience with those that lacked skill or didn't pull their weight. There were too many people waiting in line to take their jobs.

"You look quite intent, Ms. Lyonne," a deep voice rumbled from behind her.

She managed to stop that startle reflex that plagued her. Lifting her head, her stomach dropped. It was that man, the new tech super. Knuckling a spindle of hair out of her eye she acknowledged him with a formal, "Superintendent." She hadn't crossed paths with him since the party. A flush of embarrassment heated her cheeks at the memory. What a slutty fool she'd been all snuggly in his arms against that hard, very hard chest. She suppressed a tingle that threatened to roll through her.

"Do you have a minute?" he asked. At least he was keeping his distance leaving a few feet of space between them. Whether that was in respect for her or that he just didn't want to be close to her because he definitely didn't like her. Outside of the mine, he wasn't wearing a helmet. The light breeze lifted his dark hair. He kept it trimmed but the ends danced in the wind. Eyes under a masculine ridge so dark the color was indeterminable, just hard black pits coldly studied her.

She was confused. Their jobs didn't dovetail, they had their own staff and work to oversee, what could he want with her? Probably a complaint of some sort. People laboring in mines weren't always the most cheerful lot. "Why?" she asked and noticed a quick frown of annoyance tugging his lips down. He had a hard chiseled face, even his lips but their fullness held a hint of sensuality. She blinked and stared at his shoulder. Since when did she even know what sensuality was?

His brows slanted in slightly in a furrow, but he answered amiably, "I would like to check on something and I would like your opinion."

Her lips parted. "My opinion?" Why would the super want anything from her? He'd scorned and ridiculed her for heaven's sake. "I don't see what-"

"Just," his mouth tightened, "just help me out here and come with me."

"Go with you? Where? I don't think-"

But he had already turned away and was starting towards the path that led to the parking area. When she didn't move he glanced over his shoulder. "It is important, Chief, or I would not ask."

She couldn't place his accent. It resembled the Dutch the natives spoke but then again had major differences. With his hard looks and the heavy accent he was quite intimidating. Should she go somewhere alone with him? Hadn't she learned her lesson before?

He stopped and turned around to face her. "Seriously, Ms. Lyonne, if it makes you feel safer you can leave word with someone that you are going with me, I can wait." The lift to the side of his mouth was almost a mock that he dared her to go with him. Or refuse to go and expose her fear.

Well, Solitar wasn't letting him think she was the least bit afraid of him, the big threatening brute. "Okay," she huffed, "fine." She stomped towards him and when he turned around again with a smug gleam in his eyes she almost backed out. Almost. Damn him.

She followed him to one of the business jeeps. He held the passenger door open and waited for her to climb in. She sat down and set her clipboard with the photographs attached on her lap and waited nervously while he rounded the jeep and hopped in behind the wheel.

Sticking the key in and turning it, as the engine caught he looked over at her. "Seatbelt?" he murmured and his mouth twitched at the flattening of her lips. The color inching into her high cheekbones revealed that she had felt like a directed child. She snapped the belt closed as he took off down the path that led to a dirt road that fed to wider gravel roads. He turned south onto another gravel and tar roadway.

When they started on the mine they had paved part of the roads leading to it for easier transportation of the trucks and heavy equipment. The vehicles were shipped in and then transported from the coast over grassy savannas, through thick rainforests and then to the mountains.

Kurian drove amidst lush greenery that toed the edges of the road, creeping across it, the jungle trying to reclaim its gouged terrain. Canopies of large leaves brushed the roof, scraped and flapped along the sides of the truck. Flanking the bumpy road every half a mile fresh dirt lay in piles.

"We're following the pipeline?" Solitar asked with curiosity. Finally, something to talk about, look at, rather than the silence that walled between them and the endless vegetation.

He nodded. "*Ja*, the runoff from the mine flows in pipes we laid."

He wasn't telling her anything, she had been there at the beginning excavation. "Where are we going, Superintendent?"

He glanced at her wryly. "Really, Solitar, my name is Kurian."

Her lips pushed out, she kept eyes forward. "It was you, Mr. Anastaas that made a big deal out of our speaking with strict professionalism, remember?"

Barley stopping himself from rolling his eyes, Kurian let out an irritated breath. "Listen, can we start over, make a truce? I hate to feel as if I am walking on seashells with you."

A giggle slipped out, she quickly covered her mouth. "That's eggshells, Superintendent."

The side of his mouth curved up. "*Ja*? My English idiots are a work in progress."

That brought a burst of real laughter from her. She turned a big grin to him. "I think you mean idioms, Superintendent."

He looked at her, his face softened. "There, that is nice, Solitar, really nice."

Her yellow brows lifted. "What's nice?"

"That smile. First time I have seen one on you. It suits. You should do it more. Call me Kurian." He sounded warmer but the last came across as an order.

The smile vanished, her face reverted back to her normal stony expression. She faced forward again, her lips pressed together.

Kurian sighed. Back to square one. As they drove, the foliage gave way to an old section of town. They had passed the residential area in the valley that was made up of flat, square one-level buildings, and the center of the city were glorious, statuesque white structures with less than a meter between them like row houses. But here, the buildings were large, three stories with the colonial sloping roofs but it had been a hundred years since they'd seen a can of paint. The horizontal planked walls were more brown than white, the gambled roofs with missing patches more peeling than solid red.

They drove down a street then turned to drive behind the *Paarse Rivier Alle Naakt Nachtclub*. Solitar's head swiveled as they passed the building with a picture of a mostly naked female draped over the doorway with one eye closed in a salacious wink.

Her face tinted pink, she murmured, "Is that a…strip club?"

He nodded. "*Ja*. Doubt there is anywhere in the world even in distressed places like this that there is not one."

"What's it called? I don't know the language."

He ducked his head catching it in the side mirror after they passed the building continuing to the rear of the lot. "The Purple River All Nude Nightclub."

"Hmm, Purple River, that's…unique."

Kurian drove behind a series of buildings and the nightclub to an open lot where a few cars were parked and he stopped the truck. Switching the ignition off, he turned in his seat to face her. "*Ja*. That is the reason we are here."

Puzzled, she looked at him then twisted to look out the window. At the very back of the lot was a low, stone wall then some grass, and then water. Wood pilings from broken down piers stuck up from the yellow-brown water. Turning back around she said, "What are we doing here? I am not going into any strip club." She spoke firmly but her voice held a hint of anxiety that he would try to force her to go inside.

"Come on," replying, he opened his door, "let's go." He slid out and came around to her side. She was sitting somewhat bewildered. He pulled her door open and waited for her to get out. He held his hand for her to take.

With suspicion, her gaze went from his proffered hand to the back of the lot and back to his hand. Warily, she set the clipboard on the floor and then put her hand in his. A blunted smile creased his hard face at her giving in.

He gently drew her out and to her feet. When she repeated, "Why are we here?" He dropped her hand and started walking towards the water that flowed up to the back of the lot. After a moment's hesitation, Solitar traipsed after him. He stopped at the edge of the stone embankment that kept the river from overflowing onto the land at higher tides.

Solitar joined him. He pulled sunglasses from his pocket and slipped them on then peered over the expanse of water. Solitar's nose wrinkled at the nasty fumes that rose from the river. "It smells, stinks of rotten sewage or something."

"*Ja*, something," he said shortly.

"I don't understand," she remarked quietly.

"It is not supposed to smell rotten."

"Huh," she made a sound. "And it has kind of a purplely hue. That's strange."

"Not supposed to be purple either."

Solitar offered, "Must be some kind of underwater vegetation that causes the color. I mean they named the strip club after the Purple River and that place looks like it's been around for a millennium."

His mouth quirked. "Not quite that long but, *ja*, it is an old building but the hand painted sign is new. Used to be called the Blue River Nightclub. They changed the name recently when the pollution discolored the water. It was an ironic joke."

Solitar said thoughtfully, "It's not funny."

He turned to her, his expression serious. "No, it's not." His contraction of 'it is' ended sharply exposing his awkwardness with the combining of the two words punctuating his accent.

She raised her head back to look up at him. "Superintendent, why are we here?"

The side of his mouth nicked up at her continued formality. "We are here because before the mine was excavated the river was blue and did not smell rancid."

"Wait, are you saying we're polluting the river? It's been less than a year that the excavation started."

"It is an accusation I have only just been made aware of."

"But- but, all the reports indicate we are cleaning our waste within all federal guidelines. That can't be true, it's not coming from our mine. I mean, I haven't been on site the entire time, I've had to travel back and forth to the offices for meetings and reports and whatnot, but I'm sure I would have heard, ah, at some point." Her eyes on the noxious purple water, shaking her head, she repeated firmly, "It isn't coming from our mine."

"Only chemicals can give it that color, Solitar. There is very little other industrial business here that could yield that kind of damage."

The pair stared for a while at the gooey smelly water. Solitar brushed her palm over her forehead and sighed. "I'll get my testing equipment and conduct an examination of the water. I can separate the elements and trace the chemicals and prove whether or not they came from the Gatin de Muur Mine." She turned and started for his truck.

Kurian strode after her. He reached the jeep first and opened the passenger door. He waited for her to get in and settled before he closed the door and trod around to climb in the driver's side.

He drove out of the back lots around the front of the weathered buildings and turned down the main street. They didn't talk until they reached a narrow lane with three-story row house buildings lining both sides.

Ignoring Solitar's questioning glances at him, Kurian kept on until they reached the business section. He pulled up in front of a building that had a cheerful blue awning and pointed yellow roofing, and shut off the car. Before Solitar could question him, he was out and around and opening her door with his hand out to her.

Eyes rounded, she asked, "What are we doing here?" She looked around. They were on a busy street, well, not actually moving busy, people, mostly men were sitting around in front of storefronts. A gaggle of youngsters in school uniforms scurried by with laughter. Their clothes were well worn as were the books they carried, but with the optimism of youth and the thrill of being out of classes they seemed unconcerned.

"Lunch," Kurian stated, grasping her hand when she didn't move, he pulled her out and closed the door.

"Wait, we can't-"

"*Ja*, we can. We have to eat and I am starving." Not taking no for an answer he set his palm on her lower back and moved her forward. The place was more of a cantina. As poor as the village was the restaurant was in pretty good condition. Since the weather was more temperate warm today, not hot but dry and sunny, they sat outside enjoying the soft breeze. Solitar ordered the shrimp soup with spicy green curry and noodles, and Kurian had the pom kip with fried rice and green peas.

A round loaf of warm bread on a cutting board was set on the table along with ramekins of herbed oil. Kurian took the knife that came with the bread and cut off a slice, laid it on Solitar's bread and butter plate then cut a hunk off for himself. Ignoring the oil, he cut a slab of butter off a small plate and slathered it on his piece. The plates were faded and chipped, everything was served family style, nothing wrapped in packages. The fresh local milk came in small pitchers not tiny, packaged creamer cups, the sugar in bowls not packets.

Kurian drank beer and Solitar spooned sugar into her iced tea. They didn't talk. Solitar hadn't been into the city but once and never in that area. She couldn't stop looking at everything. Some of the buildings were designed like the Caribbean with bright bold colors and dancing cutout figures on the fronts. Tall slender palm trees swayed when a stronger breeze whooshed by. The servers wore bright colors as well although their clothes were as worn and faded as the buildings.

Solitar was busy watching the passing pedestrians and Kurian was busy watching her.

When the server set the check on the table, Solitar stared at it and swallowed awkwardly. "I…I don't have any money on me. I didn't think to grab my purse."

Kurian pulled out his wallet and removed a few bills, he laid them on the check. "I think I can handle a simple lunch bill, Solitar. Just say thank you graciously." A grin hovered at his lips at her annoyed frown.

"I know my manners, Mr. Anastaas," she said with a haughty lift to her chin. "Thank you. The lunch was lovely. Now, I can't wait to come back and draw some samples of the horrid water."

"Ah, I guess that indicates the end of our date," he said sagely.

Her head popped up, then her eyes narrowed at him before lowering to his shoulder. "This was certainly not a date. I assume you think you are amusing. Trust me, you are not," and she shoved back her chair to stand.

The ride back to the mine was uncomfortable silence for Solitar. She took a chance at a quick glance at Kurian, and her lips pushed out in a surly pout. She could swear he was stifling a grin at her expense. He wasn't uncomfortable at all. The rude brute. She nestled back in her seat, crossed her arms and glared out the front windshield.

When they arrived at the mine, Solitar hopped out before Kurian could get around the jeep and help her out. She immediately started towards the shanty that was near the mine. It served as an office and held supplies. Kurian sauntered after her. Following her inside, he watched as she made her way to a connecting room. Inside the room there were shelves of beakers and rows of containers. Solitar went right to them and started picking up several jars.

"Ah, Solitar," Kurian said coming up next to her. "What are you doing?"

"What do you think?" She picked up a case and tucked the items inside it. "I need to prove it isn't the mine causing the pollution."

"What if it is?"

She stopped and stared wide-eyed at him, then her brow knit. "It can't be, we take every precaution. I've read every report, it just can't-" She shook her head. "I will prove it."

"It is too late tonight, Solitar." They'd had a late lunch and with the drive back the sun was waning.

"I need to go, I have to, I must find out as soon as possible. If it's us we have to stop it immediately and begin reparation."

"You cannot go tonight, it is too dangerous. You will not be able to see what you are doing in the dark. There were no parking lot lights and the stores will be closed. Illumination might as well be zero in the dark, you could fall into the river by accident. Besides, there is a dangerous element that hangs around that area, you would be vulnerable to attack. There is no one around to go with you and I have to be somewhere. You need to wait."

"I'll take a flashlight. No one will even notice I'm there."

He gave her such of look of stupefied derision. "Are you crazy or just plain stupid? A lone female in the dark in one of the grungiest most unlawful sections of town, behind a strip joint for Pete's sake? Hell, girl, they could rape you and toss your body in the river where you would disappear forever." He shook his head. "Stupid. Plain stupid."

Her lips pushed out angrily. "Listen, you don't have to call me names. I have a job to do. It's too important to put off. My God we may be poisoning the entire village!"

"I get it, Solitar, I do. Waiting until tomorrow morning is not going to make that much of a difference, now will it?"

She noted the lengthening shadows through the dusty window, and conceded. She wasn't that familiar with the roads which would be dark, she could easily get lost even with the makeshift maps they were given. "You're right. I'll go first thing tomorrow." Then she frowned. "Darn, we have a meeting first thing, I'll head out right after."

Having the grace not to look smug, he said, "I have some pipeline I have to review along with some heavy equipment to check out in the morning. I'll try to get most of it set before the meeting, I can finish the rest right after it. When I am done I will take you."

Picking up the case, she stood back from him. "I don't need a guard. I can do this just fine on my own."

"Do not- ah, don't be reckless, Solitar. A woman like you is not safe alone in the city. Especially wandering around the back of a lot near the river." He stepped close to her, towering over her.

"What? Don't be ridiculous. A woman like me, what's that supposed to mean? Are you calling me weak and stupid again? That I can't take a few samples of the river without toppling in?" She held her ground, she wasn't going to allow him to intimidate her.

"No, don't be absurd, that is not what I meant. Accidents can happen."

"Oh," she snorted. "Now I am just an incompetent female who can't find her way to the river and scoop out a cup of it."

"Come on, I did not say- don't put words in my mouth. I meant you are…ah, well," his voice lowered. "Hell woman, you are soft, naïve, I can tell the way you don't notice what is going on around you. The looks men give you, you glance back blankly with a vague frown. And you are…" he broke off awkwardly. "Beautiful. A woman that looks like you cannot just wander aimlessly around a dangerous section of the city. If you cannot wait for me, then take one of the other men with you. Siggy or Hubie or whoever is free to go."

Her eyes widened, mouth dropped. "Are you kidding me? I can't believe such baloney is spilling from your sexist, troglodyte mouth!"

His hands' clasped behind his back, Kurian gazed at her with cool eyes. "Whatever. Just don't be foolhardy and go alone."

She leaned into him, her lids slit low over her eyes she sputtered angrily, "You can't tell me what to do! Who do you think you-" She stopped speaking because Kurian suddenly grabbed her, bent and slapped his lips on hers and ate at her like he was a fat man who hadn't eaten in weeks. Solitar didn't have time to react, not to protest, not to fight him, not to scream, not to…respond and he released her so abruptly she had to grab a hold again to steady her from stumbling backwards.

The back of her hand over her lips parted in stunned disbelief, she stuttered, "You-you- you-"

"*Ja,*" Kurian muttered. Wiping his mouth with his hand, his dark eyes daggered on her lips, then rose to her flushed face and wide shocked eyes. He said coldly, "My point. You are alone, defenseless, you live too recklessly. Your father should put his hand to your ass and teach you female safety."

Her lashes flew up in astonished anger, the words sputtered out, "How dare you! You animal! A gentleman wouldn't take like that from an unsuspecting woman! I should be safe where I work, I should be-"

He stepped into her. Her shoulders turned rigid, fear struck the color from her face. He didn't smile at the effect he had on her. "Again my point, Solitar. You should be but you are not. Just like you will not be safe tomorrow if you go alone. So," he tugged his shirtsleeves down under the jacket and scrutinized her calmly beneath low lids. "You will wait for me. As I said, I may have to finish a job right after the meeting, it will not take long. I will text you when I am done and we can meet at your jeep." He turned towards the door but she called out to stop him.

Her face raging with red anger, she threatened, "I'm going to report you to- to Mr. Miles! You can't assault me like that and walk away! I will go-"

Kurian spun around so fast she staggered a step backwards. The lids lowered further hiding his deepest thoughts. He rounded on her and said, "You will not say a word. You have kept mum about whatever went on between you and that jackass Orlando." His eyes narrowed at the white that slapped the red right back out of her face leaving her pale as Casper. Her lips trembled, she raised her arms and crossed them protectively over her chest.

He paused, then moved back. He said thoughtfully, "*Ja,* some shit happened between you and that jerk that you did not want. We will talk about it at some point, but for now," his gaze lowered to her mouth again, his own lips twitched, "just be ready for me tomorrow. Goodnight." He swung around and strode out before she could fire off a retort.

She left the office and Kurian stood in the shadows watching her wend her way along the trail that led to where the business jeeps were parked. Two dogs and a cat bounded from the bushes and raced towards her. His muscles tightening, Kurian prepared to rush to rescue her from their attack, when instead of pouncing on her with barks and bites and snarls and claws, the animals nuzzled her, vied for her attention, licking, bussing her hands, her legs.

Giggling, she pushed at them. "No guys, come on, quit it, I have to get home and take a shower." But the animals persisted and followed her as she strode to her jeep. She inherited the jeep when the other project managers had been forced to leave the site. When she opened the door, she bent inside, then stood back and handed each of them a cookie. Laughing as they chowed down, she slid inside and drove off.

Off to the side, concealed in the darkness of the shadows, Kurian stood watching, perplexed. That wasn't the stone icy bitch that he was used to. Did she actually have a heart under all that stone? Maybe he would find out tomorrow. He touched his lips recalling the kiss he'd shocked both of them with. Soft, at least one part of her was not made   out   of   stone.

Chapter Nine

The dawn was on the verge of piercing the night clouds when Solitar was in the kitchen of the Cresh. The would-be cocaine king had designed the palace himself, and assuming he would have a kingdom of soldiers to rule, he had the commercial kitchen installed. The owners of the mine kept it supplied with food staples and toiletries, the employees were to feed themselves. They purchased anything extra they wanted and they were expected to clean up after themselves, and any violations of laziness were squealed to the house manager, Dozi Shunnar.

Dozi was the iron maiden of the fort and no one, not the toughest most weathered miner dared to ignite her ire. She wasn't an Amazon, but she was stalwart with a helmet of iron-hard grey hair and a harsh lashing tongue. And she kept notes, made demerits. When the good food, pastries, cookies, liquor, sheets, pillows, anything decent that was trucked in, if someone had desecrated her regime, took what wasn't theirs, left a pigsty behind them, well, she was in charge of it all. If someone tried to thwart her, they were on her shit list and that meant they didn't get shit. Including toilet paper. So, the line was toed. Mostly.

Anything anyone prepared had a label on it. Taking someone else's food had led to quite a few brawls already. Many of the miners couldn't cook and relied on frozen, packaged food, or restaurant meals which got expensive, and they hungered for homemade. Some of them were bold enough to snag someone's homemade feast and if caught, that meant war. It also meant demerits in Dozi Shunnar's notebook. And that was worse than a black eye.

It was not normally what Solitar made for breakfast, too rich and calorie heavy, but, thanks to her nerves she hadn't been eating well for a while and it was starting to show. She was moving into the unhealthy side of thin. After sautéing peppers, onions and mushrooms she folded them into the scrambled eggs in the skillet and then checked the gravy. She had even put sausage and more mushrooms in the brew, she leaned over and inhaled deeply. "Ah, heavenly, spicy, nice," she smiled.

The biscuits already on a tray in the oven, she turned it on then moved to the mug of hot chocolate sitting on the counter. Her ponytail flopped over the back of the green sweater she'd tugged down over black jeans. Wiping her hands on the apron she'd tied around her waist she reached for the hot chocolate.

"Damn, woman, I'd give my first born for a plate of that grub."

She couldn't stop the startle reflex. Gulping down the alarm, she pressed her lips together, took a deep breath and turned around. A man was leaning against the doorway, his eyes, thank goodness, weren't on her, they were on the stove. Beside the bubbling gravy, sizzling bacon sputtered and popped adding its own fragrance to the delicious smelling room. "Um…" Solitar cupped the mug and sniffed the dark chocolate. The man's eyes shifted to her then to the mug.

The aroma of the rich gravy and now the baking biscuits filled the kitchen merging with the frying bacon, along with a hint of dawn's candlelight stroking through a window and over Solitar's light hair made the large room appear soft and cozy.

Dark auburn hair hadn't yet met a comb this morning, his gaze flicked over her and a slow smile lifted the corners of his mouth. His arms and ankles were crossed and he leaned one broad shoulder against the doorframe. "I'm asking permission to come in, darlin'," he said, the smile growing friendly. He had caught her nervous jolt when he'd first spoken and softened his voice. "I don't want to alarm you, you have the right to the kitchen and I'll go on my way if you say," his gaze traveled to the empty coffee pot and the smile turned forlorn.

Solitar couldn't help but smile at his desolate look. She padded across the tiled floor in her socks and handed him her untouched mug of hot cocoa. "Here," she said, grinning at the surprised look on his face as he took it. "That should hold you until I get the coffee going. In fact, you'll find out that's going to beat a cup of coffee hands down."

He grinned down at the mug steaming up at him, tiny marshmallows melting on the chocolatey surface. "Hey, wow, thanks. I really wanted this but wasn't about to ask."

"Uh huh." She traipsed back to the stove and turned the oven off. Opening the door, the scent of the toasting biscuits wafted out and she heard his involuntary moan. Pulling on a mitt, she removed the tray of biscuits and set it on the counter. "You go ahead and have a seat at the table and I'll fix you a plate."

"Wow, really?" The hungry excitement jumped out even as the sound of his stomach growled loud enough she heard it across the room. He said politely, "No, I really couldn't," his words lacked oomph. His stomach growled again.

"Go on, it's fine, I've made enough to feed half the people staying here. I thought I'd leave it covered in the fridge with a note to people to help themselves. Lucky you, you won't have to heat it up. Do you want toast?"

He was already pulling a chair from the long farmer's table. "Are you giving me some of those biscuits and gravy?" he asked.

"Of course, unless you don't want-"

"Oh, yeah, I want. And yeah, I'd like toast too if you don't mind. I mean I can toast the bread if you want. I'm into carb loading." He glanced at the table, Solitar had already laid out butter and cream and sugar for coffee. A carafe of orange juice and a glass sat on a towel on the table. She retrieved another glass and set it beside the carafe.

"Well, if you don't mind," she said while tipping the biscuits into a bowl and then grabbed a pair of plates from the cupboard. The kitchen had been built many years ago but held all the amenities. Green tile splashed behind the sink and the walls were wallpapered with a mix of green and blue. Curtains at the large window were a match of gingham.

"I'm Rutger by the way," he said as he pulled slices of bread out of the sleeve. "Will you marry me?"

Just down the hall, raking a hand through his hair, Kurian was hungry. He hadn't eaten dinner last night due to the late lunch he'd shared with Solitar, and he needed a cup of java ASAP. He could hear gentle laughter wafting down the hall and it and the aroma of food had lured him quickly to the kitchen. He stood in the doorway and frowned. Solitar was sitting at the big wooden table with his friend Rutger and they were eating, and laughing. Something in his gut tightened.

"Yeah," Rutger was saying, laughter in his voice, "you shoulda been there. Big ol' lumberjack craggy Creggar was so cocky, his name was at the top of the dart competition's list and he was jeering Brittlyn something bad. Said a bit of a skirt couldn't come close to beating him. He couldn't even blame liquor for mucking him up when she creamed him, he'd only had a few sips of his draft."

"Another piece of toast, Rutger?" Kurian heard Solitar ask. "Some just popped."

"Sure, great, thanks," he said. Then, "So, anyway," Kurian heard crunching sounds as Rutger chewed and talked. "She beat the loving pants off him, Sol, it was great! The entire bar was hysterical. Poor Cregg sulked over in a corner with his nose in his beer. I heard Cortnee felt compassion for the hit to his manhood and she threw herself on the altar, saving his masculinity and made out with him the rest of the night, but he didn't play darts again!" Solitar's soft laughter joined his. She was back in her seat.

Kurian stepped into the room. "How cozy," he commented drolly. The pair at the table paused, forks in the air, words on their lips and looked to him. Solitar suddenly appeared flustered, and Rutger, his friend, smirked at him.

Rutger scooped up a biscuit drenched in gravy and laid it on a piece of buttered toast. He folded the toast over and was aiming it at his open mouth when Solitar scolded him mirthfully, "Rutger, carb on carb, you sure you want to do that?"

He winked at her and took a huge bite. Speaking out the side of his mouth he said, "Oh yeah, good, darlin', so good," and he grinned at Kurian.

Shooting him a glare, Kurian trod over to the where the coffee pot was steaming.

"Mugs are above on the left," Solitar tendered.

With a grunt, Kurian removed a mug and poured some coffee then went to the table. He glanced pointedly at an empty chair with a raised brow.

"Go ahead, *broed*," Rutger told him, "take a weight off. You can be the first to congratulate us on our engagement."

Kurian's gaze slashed to his friend then to Solitar when she laughed. She said, "He likes my cooking."

Kurian sat with a grunt and eyed the mug in front of Rutger. "That is some harsh looking coffee, Rut."

A grin split his handsome face, Rutger said, "It's hot chocolate, my man, Sol makes the best." He grinned at Solitar who smiled briefly at him then wiped her mouth daintily with a napkin.

Kurian's rapt attention on Rutger's plate that still contained remnants of eggs and bacon emboldened Solitar to offer, "Would you like a plate, Superintendent?"

A frown emerged across his forehead at the formality she still used for him. Hell, he'd bought her lunch yesterday, she could be a tad friendlier. But the food looked too good and smelled too awesome to quibble over a name, he said, "I would be obliged, *Solitar* if it is not too much trouble." Damn, he sounded like a harsh robot. He needed to concentrate on making his English come out more smoothly.

He watched her as she rose and swiftly fixed him a plate piled high with scrambled eggs, bacon, biscuits and gravy, buttered toast. She set it in front of him then went to the refrigerator and returned with two jars of jam, one Concord grape the other raspberry and placed them within his reach. While she was up, she refilled his mug that he had already emptied.

"*Oke, oke*, please, Solitar, I am not helpless, you don't need to wait on me," Kurian said with a glower.

She returned to the counter and started putting food into containers. "It's nothing, Superintendent, I prepared it, I love to cook and serving it is all part of the process." She shoved the leftovers into the fridge, wiped her hands on the apron and returned to the table where she looked down at Kurian who was shoveling the food in like he hadn't eaten in a month.

Solitar then took note of his attire. He wore different clothes than she'd seen him in last night when they'd parted, but there was dirt on one sleeve and his boots. "Have you been out already today? The sun isn't even up yet."

Biting a piece of bacon in half, Kurian replied, "*Ja*, I told you I have a project I am working on. I wanted to get as much done as possible before the meeting so I can be ready to leave with you as soon as possible after." He crunched the smoky bacon complimenting, "Damn, this food is the shit, Solitar, girl you can cook," and he gobbled the rest and reached for his fork.

"Forget about it, she's marrying me," Rutger informed him. He laughed at Solitar's rolled eyes. "You didn't eat anything before you went out, K?" Rutger asked, watching his friend devour the food with amusement.

Food pushing out the side of his cheek, Kurian slurped coffee washing it down then said, "*Ja*, had a piece of toast."

"Ah ha!" Solitar crowed. "That was you that left the plate with bread crumbs and the butter knife on the counter." Her eyes thinned at him. "Haven't you heard of Dozi's wrath? You have to clean up after yourself or you'll regret having her on your back."

His head down, Kurian's eyes turned up at her. He said calmly, "Female warriors don't scare me, Solitar, it is the mean little ones that put fear into my soul."

Rutger threw back his head with a loud bark of laughter. Kurian glanced at him with a crooked grin then continued to attack his plate.

"Uh huh," Solitar murmured. "Well, I saved your skin, I cleaned it up so you are safe for now, but I warn you, Dozi is not someone to sneer at."

His fork in his hand, Kurian sat back against the chair and looked up at her. "I have plenty of women to see to my needs, Solitar, I am not worried about one domineering female."

"You-"

"Hey!" Two teens entering the kitchen interrupted her. Colby and his friend Richard burst into the room. "That bacon?" Colby asked, salivating before he even got to the counter where the bacon was on a plate under plastic wrap.

Solitar smiled warmly at him before she flattened her lips. "Yes. There is plenty of food there for you boys. Help yourselves, but when you are done make sure you seal everything up and pop it in the fridge and clean your dishes, all right?"

"Yes Miss Solitar." Colby was already plucking the plastic wrap off the bacon.

Richard stood back. Solitar coaxed, "Go ahead, Ritchie, make yourself a plate."

His eyes flipped from the food to her and right back to the food. He didn't move. "But we aren't staying here, Miss Solitar, and we don't work for the mine."

"It's okay, boys," she told them. "There's plenty for all, take as much as you want, no one will care."

"Make sure you do as she says," Kurian's deep voice rumbled over them. "Eat and clean up then get yourselves to the mine. You have the work list I gave you?" He had stirred himself after hearing the boys call her Miss Solitar, not Miss Lyonne, and she called Richard Ritchie. Where was the cold scorpion lying in wait to sting an unaware person with her poisonous tongue?

"Yessir," Colby said, filling a plate he had taken from the cupboard and passed one to Richard.

"You do not go into the mine, you hear me?" Kurian said, the deep voice deeper, sterner with warning.

Colby's turquoise eyes switched to him then lowered to the floor. "But Mr. K, we thought we could, you know, maybe just slip inside a little ways, just to see some stuff."

"Yeah," Ritchie joined in, "we wanna ride in those cars on the tracks. We-"

Kurian set his mug on the table with a slight bang. "I said no. It is too dangerous, you boys stay outside, you do not go inside. You do and I will whip your hides and you will not be able to do anymore clean up. You hear me?"

In his seat Rutger pulled at his lips to hide his grin. The two teens looking abashed stared down at the toes of their boots. They nodded their heads, and muttered together, "Yes sir." They held their pose for a second to show they were serious, then when Kurian said nothing else they turned back to the food and loudly chatted about what they were eating and what they were going to do once they hit the mine. And what they were going to do with the money they would earn for doing the cleanup.

Their attention on their food, Solitar whispered to Kurian, "You didn't have to yell at them, Superintendent."

His brows drew up at her chastising him. Where was the *truf?* This woman appeared to care about the teenagers. "'Tis none of your business, Solitar, how I talk to the boys. You just make sure you wait for me after the meeting."

Her lips bunched and eyes tapered, but she said nothing. Untying the apron, she tucked it into a handle on a cupboard and said with a smile to Rutger, "I guess I'll see you around, Ruger, since you don't work at the mine. Maybe we can share a coffee sometime and you can tell me what you do here at Ruwenstad."

"Sure, darlin'." Rutger glanced quickly at Kurian before giving her a big grin. "I'd like that, we all need all the friends we can get."

She didn't say a word to Kurian as she rather flounced out of the room.

His jaw flexing, Kurian turned a glare to his friend. "Friends?"

Ruger shrugged and reached for his glass of orange juice. "Yeah, you should try it sometime Mr. Huff and Puff," and he downed the juice in one swallow.

Picking up his empty plate Kurian carried it to the sink. "Here," he said, handing it to Ritchie. Both teens were gangly and moving into their adult height which would be near six feet. Where Colby had straight fair hair and light eyes, Ritchie's mop was dark curls and his mischievous dark eyes glowed with desire for fun.

"See that everything is perfectly spic and span, boys, and make sure the food is covered and put in the fridge. Rake a broom here and there to make sure Commandant Dozi does not catch an errant crumb. And I want to see both of you have a glass of OJ and take an apple for a snack." He pointed to a bowl on the counter containing apples, oranges and bananas. "I will see that extra dollars are in your pay for today's work at the mine and for the spotless kitchen you will leave behind this morning. *Oke,* gentlemen?"

"Yessir!" Ritchie grabbed a juice glass and saluted Kurian with an impish grin.

"When we get done, Mr. K.," Colby said cheekily, "you'll be able to see your face in the floor!"

"You mean my reflection, boy?"

"Yeah!" The teens bent over laughing.

"All right." Kurian ordered them, "Get to work, see you at the mine." He glanced at Rutger who took a last sip of his hot chocolate and got up. "I have a call into the sheriff to see if they got a brand on that hair dye. We might be able to track down the store where it was purchased, the clerk might remember something."

Outside as they reached their motorbikes Kurian said quietly, "Rut, I have to go in to work, you go try to hunt down that homeless guy, Serug Partay."

Climbing on his bike Rutger replied, "Planning on hitting the regular spots I heard these blokes gather and make my way to Marx Street. The sheriff said the guy hangs out in the field there most of the time when not panhandling but it's far out. I'll catch up with you later."

Kurian nodded and mounted his bike. They started their engines and turned the bikes to face out. As Rutger started to pull away, he said over his shoulder, "Now, don't mire in jealousy today, *mijn broed*, my brother, just because your hot mean girl likes me more than you!" He burst away before Kurian could shoot off a retort.

As Kurian followed him, he muttered, "She is not my girl."

Chapter Ten

The staff piled into the weathered wooden shanty, a large shack they used as an office near the mine. People sprawled on chairs, some stood and leaned against plain plastered walls. Chattering ceased when Solitar entered the main room. She kept her eyes lowered to the desk in the center rear of the room.

She set a file down on the old cracked desk and took a deep breath. Public speaking was not her forte. She was an introverted private person and this was just one more part of the job she despised, she hated attention on her. She'd spent the formative years of her life trying to be invisible, meld into the woodwork, be no more noticeable than a potted plant. Gaining attention only led to pain, blood, heartbreak, and soul devastation.

Then Camara and one of the only other people who pushed her to be friendly, Daniela Picola, moved to stand in front of her, between Solitar and the crowd. Both women gave Solitar a cheerful grin and encouraging nod.

Although Solitar rebuffed their efforts to be friends, they persisted. Both women had seen the isolation bleeding in her soft face and the haunting fear blanketing her eyes. Although she worked constantly to suppress all thought and emotion, still, the wrenching anguish that lived carved deeply in her bones sometimes wavered visibly before she could quickly mask it.

Camara had told her she could see Solitar's essence had been burnt so badly there was little left but chars of black cinder and she needed sweet warm butter to heal it. She believed the soul could be healed through a happy belly, therefore she persevered in bringing Solitar cakes and scones fresh from the oven. She and Daniela prodded and poked at Solitar, pushing her to go to the pub once in a while on country dance night and made her learn to line dance with them. A few times they'd shown up at her room at the Cresh on their days off loaded with nail polish and cold cream, wine, gossip and giggles for girls' night.

Solitar struggled to keep them at arm's length but they just laughed and ignored her efforts to remain in her own isolated little bubble where she could stay...safe. And alone. Now, at her silent contemplation, conversations were building up again.

Sucking in breaths of strength and poise, she squared her shoulders and spoke, "All right, let's get on with the meeting, everyone, come to order please." She kept her eyes away from the far corner of the room where Kurian Anastaas leaned a shoulder against a wall, arms folded over his chest and crossed one ankle over the other, a cool look of nonchalance. She felt his eyes boring his contempt into her but she looked only to Camara and Daniela when she spoke.

"Mr. Lafayette, can you give us a briefing on the third shaft? How close to completion are we?"

Laddie Lafayette nodded to her. He said, "Done, Miss Lyonne. We are at plain rock now, there is no indication of more gold so we won't need to dig any deeper." He wore jeans that were stained with chemicals and grease, a flannel shirt tucked in over a t-shirt, and boots that although he'd scrubbed were still grubby. He lifted his helmet off his head and palmed a hand with square fingers over his dark wavy hair and replaced the helmet. His complexion the bronze-olive of his compatriots, dark eyes friendly yet professional.

Solitar looked at him then back to Camara who smiled brightly at her. Solitar said to Laddie, "Are we ready for another tunnel?"

Laddie glanced a few feet away to Creggar Trent.

"Ah," Cregg answered Solitar, "yes ma'am, the breakdown of the drill has been repaired and we can get started. I have your design and calculations, we can start first thing tomorrow."

"Good," Solitar replied. "Mr. Trent," she said to Cregg the vent officer, "I have a report of a broken fan that per an electrician equipped with a methane gas device used to measure the gas claimed the fan had been broken long enough for gas to build. We all know how deadly a gas build up can be. Besides poison there is danger of an explosion. Can you tell me how this could have gone overlooked for the day or so before it was discovered?"

Cregg's lips bunched, his hands clasped behind his back he rocked on his heels. Blowing out a heft of air, he said, "It was in a haulage area where the gas can be quite high overhead and difficult to detect." A thick man, his pock-marked face scrunched in embarrassment.

"That is not what I asked, Mr. Trent. It's not the gas detection I am referring to," Solitar commented with an arched brow. She forced herself to look him straight in the eye.

He shuffled his feet uncomfortable with being put on the hotplate. "Yes ma'am. The fan. Ah," he scratched the top of his head, he wasn't wearing his helmet. "I, uh," he looked back to where Jamie Orlando leaned against a wall. "It just wasn't noticed right away. There was no one working in that area for a few days."

Solitar's gaze flashed to Jamie then down to the floor. "I see." Then she made herself raise her head and scan the room touching on all of the senior staff present. "Everyone must be one thousand percent diligent in safety procedures. From now on I want check lists marked off at the beginning and the end of every day and brought to me to sign off. Any questions?" There were some hems and haws, a bit of mumbling and grumbling, feet shifting, but no one spoke up. She didn't need to look at Jamie again to know he was regarding her with disdain and mockery, and anger at the subtle jab at his lacking in his duties.

She went over more business then she paused and let her gaze roam the room landing on almost all of those present spare the two males she preferred not to make eye-contact with. Inhaling quickly, she looked around again and said with emphasis, "We have rumors of pollution." Over the collective gasps in the room she went on, "The river behind the, um-"

"Purple River tittie club," Jamie Orlando provided for her. Snickers rolled through the room. At Solitar's stern glare they quickly died down.

"Hmm," Solitar murmured then said, "funny you should mention that location, that river, there are many others around and I've heard no rumors about them." She was taken aback by the black scowl Jamie suddenly sent her. Goose bumps prickled up her arms at the hostility in his glare. Purposefully straightening her shoulders she stiffened her spine then lifted her chin and looked directly into his eyes. "I have your reports, Jam- uh, Mr. Orlando," she lifted up a file. "Everything in here states we have properly cleansed our waste with all federal guidelines and procedures adhered to."

Jamie stuffed his hands in his pockets, he wore khakis and a button-down shirt. His tone insolent he replied, "Of course, most are my reports. So then what's the problem? Our scheduled examinations indicated there is not a hint of pollution. You know these natives, they don't give a shit what they throw into their own lakes and streams. It isn't us, *honey*," his voice derisive, his words disrespectful, "don't blame their lazy slovenly habits on us."

She had to bite her tongue to keep from lashing out at him. Her hands fisted at her side, holding the file in one of them she tapped it against her thigh.

"Hey, you shut your mouth." Laddie rounded on Jamie, his own fists clenched. "We love our home, we do everything we can to preserve it. We didn't bring the mine here, we were against it for environmental reasons."

"Yeah well, *native*," Jamie sneered, "didn't stop you from reaping your own financial benefits by working for Gatin de Muur."

"You sonofabitch, I'm working it to be close to my family! It's here anyway, I might as well feed my parents and siblings you asshole." Laddie inched closer to Jamie, his fists and anger rising.

"Okay injun, don't get your feathers in a snit," Jamie mocked. "Just be thankful we white folks are here to help put food on your table and you don't have to hunt your dinner and cook it in your wigwams-" He jumped forward as Laddie went at him. The two men started hurling blows.

"All right, knock it off," Kurian ordered, grabbing Jamie from behind, and Cregg and Siggy grasped Laddie's flailing fists pulling him back from Jamie.

When the two men went at each other Solitar automatically stepped back and still just missed getting her chin clipped by one of Laddie's flying fists.

"Hey, ya'll look out!" Hubie grabbed her and jerked her clear out of the way. His long dishwater blond hair swished across the back of his neck as he hustled her to safety.

The rest of the throng started shouting and backing away from the scuffling men. Finally Kurian held Jamie still with one hand wrapped around his bicep and the other arm strapped across his chest. Jamie was laughing and still hurtling insults at Laddie but the red in his face advertised his own rage. "You're gonna regret that attack you-you redskin," Jamie taunted. "I'm turning you into HR and you're outta here, boy!"

"Shut up you asshole, or I will tell Cregg to let Laddie have at you," Kurian spoke roughly moving his thick forearm up to a hard crushing squeeze across Jamie's throat. He pressed until Jamie could barely suck in a breath.

A few feet separated the fighting men. Laddie grunted and roared like a bull wanting at the red cape, spittle flew from his enraged mouth, his chest heaving with the strain of struggling to break free from the now three men that held him. His dark skin darkened further from the fury that gripped him.

Hubie still held Solitar but she pushed from him and moved to stand between the belligerent men. She held her hands up. Inserting bravery and boldness into her voice she ordered, "Okay, that's enough. You," she said to Jamie, "will not make a complaint since you instigated the whole thing, and you will refrain from that disgusting name calling. And you, Mr. Lafayette," she turned to address Laddie, "you will calm down right now, get yourself together or you can get on the next plane out of here. Do you both understand me?" She glared from one to the other.

Hubie came up to stand beside her as if he was her new protector, grinning at the two pugnacious men. Her hands on her hips, Solitar said, "If I have to count to ten both of you will be off the job. Bigotry will not be tolerated. Now, stop it." She tried to not look behind Jamie at Kurian but her eyes lifted briefly, she couldn't read his expression, his enigmatic dark eyes were on her.

A few seconds passed and Laddie made the supreme effort to stop fighting. He closed his eyes and muttered, "I'm good, guys." Cregg let go first then the other two released their hold on him. They all watched Jamie. He stopped struggling but smirked at the still infuriated Laddie.

Laddie spat, "He ain't worth it." Glaring at Jamie he said, "You and I will talk later," then he pivoted and strode out of the shack.

Jamie called out to his retreating back, "Yeah, we already got a pow-wow scheduled, buddy, we'll chat then. Okay big man," Jamie said insolently to Kurian, "you can let go now."

Face a hard mask, Kurian didn't release him, his gaze on Solitar. She looked up at him then quickly lowered her eyes to his shoulder. "Mr. Anastaas, let him go."

With a grunt, Kurian released Jamie but gave him a negligible shove when he did so.

Her exhalation loud, Solitar said to Jamie, "I am going out today to collect samples of the river. We will see how accurate your reports are." She leaned in towards him with narrowed eyes, her finger pointing. "There had better not be an iota of a hint of anything from this mine in the water or you will answer to Garrick Miles and the EPA as well as the Republic of Kedolamer's environmental agency."

Jamie's face lost the comical smirk and his own eyes squinted at her. "Don't you fucking threaten me, Solitar or I will- *oof*." His words barked off as Kurian slapped the side of his head. Jamie swung around with his fists raised. "You motherfucker, I'll kill you if you ever touch me again you fucking gorilla!"

"Oh *ja*?" Kurian stepped between Jamie and Solitar, his chest swelled. "You want to rethink your pussy words, boy?"

"Boy?" Jamie was flabbergasted. "You aren't any older than I am, you think to belittle me by calling me that? You-"

"Enough!" Solitar shouted. Geesh, she was gonna suffocate with all the testosterone throwing around in the room.

"Yes, quite enough," said Camara moving through the crowd to Solitar. "Come on, you have to sign off on some paperwork before you do anything else. Come to the warehouse with me." Her calm voice cut through the seething emotions in the room, everyone took a breath and the agitation in the air settled albeit warily.

Without looking at anyone else in the shack, Solitar allowed Camara to lead her out. The sun was bright, striking them in the face as soon as they stepped outside. Thankfully it was still a bit on the cool side so the humidity was slight and the breeze more refreshing than biting.

"Lord, girl, what a freakfest that was!" Camara remarked with a short relieved laugh.

"True that." Solitar drew in several long deep calming breaths and let them out slowly. She was trembling. It had taken everything she had to stand up to the men as she had. But she was in charge and she couldn't stand back cowering in the corner, she would lose all the respect she'd worked so hard to build. "I need to-" she started in the direction of the warehouse then stopped.

Near the mouth of the mine were several women and half a dozen small children. The children were playing with discarded riggings.

Solitar stomped over to the group. One of the tiny children jumped up and toddled over to her. "Solly, Solly," the three-year-old sang wrapping her chubby arms around Solitar's thigh. Wispy blonde hair clung to a sticky rosy cheek.

"What the hell is going on here?" Solitar demanded giving the toddler a nudge. "No, Bonnie bee," she said pushing her away.

The adults turned suddenly anxious faces to her. One of the women, Laurie, said, "Hey Ms. Lyonne, how're you doing today?"

Solitar's lips compressed, her jaw ground, she snapped, "What is wrong with you people?" Bonnie stumbled back from the anger in her voice. Another child had hurried over and took Bonnie's pudgy hand. The seven-year-old scolded her, "Miz Soli, you scarin' Bonnie bee, you mean today." The boy was almost identical to the little girl, both blond-haired with huge blue eyes.

60

Her throat working, Solitar glared down at the boy. "Bobby, this is adult business. You put that wire down, all of you kids," she looked to each of the children. Each had ahold of a wire or tube or nail. "Put those things down, and you," she snapped at the women, "get them out of here. You all know very well they aren't allowed to play here. What were you thinking?"

Laurie shared a look with the other mothers and frowned at Solitar. "Jeeps, sorry about that, Ms. Lyonne, but our men worked late last night and came here before dawn this morning. The children just wanted to say hi to their fathers. I brought Bonnie and Bobby along because I'm babysitting them today, their parents are busy on their farm. It's not a big deal, the children-"

"Out," Solitar commanded. "All of you. Go home now and don't ever think of doing something so dangerous again. This is not a playground. You are all well aware of the rules. Children are not allowed within 500 yards of the mine or the heavy equipment." She schooled herself from the angry and hurtful looks the women and kids gave her. Quickly, the women gathered up the children.

"Miss Solitar, don't be mad at them it was our fault."

Solitar turned to see Colby McShire and Richard Garland approach with sheepish expressions on their young faces. Colby spoke again, "The kids here ain't got much to play with, Miss Solitar, so we kinda," he bunched his lips at his friend Richard, "me and Ritchie are cleaning up the trash for Mr. Kurian and we thought, well, that is…" His eyes widened at Ritchie seeking his help.

His voice super quiet, Ritchie said, "Yeah, uh, we just wanted to- to give them something more than just rocks and branches to play with, you know?" The teens stood close to each other, shoulders hunched, heads down they peered up at her under the brims of their ratty baseball caps.

One hand on her hip, the other holding the file, Solitar tossed her head to fling a few loose hairs out of her eyes. She had tied her long hair back in a ponytail, it fluttered along her back. "Well, I will certainly have a word with Mr. Anastaas about allowing you boys to hang around here. He knows better, this is no place for children." She started to turn away but Colby spoke stopping her.

"Please, Miss Solitar," he said. "Mr. Kurian told us we weren't allowed to enter the mine, he's paying us to clean up outside and gee," he glanced at his friend from under the brim of his cap. "We can really use the money, we didn't mean no harm with the kids, we only wanted to help. Please don't tell Mr. Kurian we got in trouble. We never went inside the mine, he told us not to. Please." His eyes lowered and his shoulders sagged.

"Please, Miss Solitar, don't tell on us," Ritchie implored.

But Colby sighed and said, "Never mind, we know you're gonna tell 'cause you have no heart, Miss Solitar, just…" he hit Ritchie's arm. "Come on, let's go, it won't do any good to beg her."

The mothers and children had been watching and now Laurie tugged little Bonnie and Bobby away. The children glanced back at Solitar. Tears slipped down Bonnie's plump cheeks and Bobby glared at Solitar.

Solitar hardened her heart. She was not there to appease the children, play with them, make them happy, that was their parents' job. Solitar's job was to ensure there was zero probability of anything bad happening at the mine. She didn't care if their feelings were hurt, they'd get over it, just like she had. And Colby and Ritchie needed to adhere to the laws and rules. Give them wriggle room, give them an inch and the next thing they'll be off robbing stores and selling drugs. They needed a firm hand.

"Well, so far you're batting zip, honey," Camara said next to her. "I think they're a bit miffed at you. Maybe you could have softened your orders just the tiniest bit?" She raised one shoulder, the side of her mouth pulled in with a gentle smile. The rest of the people that had been at the meeting were starting to filter out of the shack, most headed to the mine, others went to attend to other duties. The roar of heavy equipment sounded in the distance behind a thick patch of wide-leafed trees.

"I am not here to make friends, Cam. Come on, let's get that paperwork done, I have a task to do."

"You're going to the river?"

Solitar started towards the warehouse. "Yes. The second I'm done with you."

The women walked side-by-side along the path that led from the mine around the bend to the warehouse they'd built to accommodate all the supplies and equipment needed to work the mine.

"You're not going alone are you, Soli?" A tinge of concern came out with Camara's words.

"Of course. I'm a big girl, Cam, I can take care of myself." Their footsteps were soft on the dirt trail. Camara waved at employees they passed, Solitar kept her face blank and gaze shuttered.

"But, Soli, honey, I don't think you should go a-"

"I'll be fine, let it go," Solitar said, and hurried her step.

Kurian answered his phone, "*Ja*, Rut, what did you find out?"

Rutger answered, "It took all day yesterday to hit the places I was told Serug Partay hung out. Should have gone straight to Marx Street where the homeless camp is located nearby."

"*Ja* well, the sheriff said he would likely be there."

Rutger's heavy sigh came through the phone. "Yeah, I know, but it's way on the north side almost to the mountains, quite a trek on the bike. Don't know how all those homeless folks get from there to the city to panhandle. Actually it would be easier on foot, the trails are steep, rocky and pitted with holes animals dug. My back is still aching from the jarring ride."

"*Oke*, you poor thing, you have endured a lot worse. What about Partay? I take it you found him? Did he tell you who he bought the expensive liquor for?"

"Ah…" Rutger paused and Kurian had a bad feeling. Rutger confirmed it. "I had to search a ton of boxes and shit the people had made for their homes but yeah, I found him. He was as described, talk, skinny, smelly, orange hair. The gash separating his neck from his head was new. His throat was slit. Sheriff Gibson and his boys are out there now."

The men were quiet a moment. Then Rutger said, "I searched his, ah, box and crap, bunch of stinking sheets and shit but there was nothing to allude to who paid him to purchase the liquor. I mean it might even mean absolutely nothing. Could be just a local with a bit of money and couldn't shake the wife long enough to come to town to buy his own booze."

"Hmm," Kurian murmured. "Maybe. I don't know, the receipt being there, and there was a speck of blood on it. Gibson told me, it was the vic's blood. Where I found it, it was not lying in any blood, it was stuck in a corner. Apparently one of the part time assistants at the morgue has wealthy folks that live in Sweden and they supplied her with lab equipment. She came out here to be with one of the miners and got a job with the doctor. She loves to study blood. It appears the killer probably was unaware he even lost the receipt. It likely fell from his pocket or stuck on his shoe and came off when he deposited the girl."

Rutger grunted. "Uh huh. So, Partay bought the booze for some high roller, maybe Partay kept the receipt. Suppose he dropped it in the alley, he could be the killer."

"Maybe." But Kurian doubted it. "I talked to people who knew the guy. He was a downer drinker, depressed, barely ate, would not have the stamina to do what was done to that girl. People said they had never seen him ever show a spark of temper or impatience, spent his days drinking and sleeping and panhandling, could not get it up if offered a million bucks. I do not, ah, *don't* think he would have the strength to carry her down the narrow alley. And, he had no vehicle to transport her to the alley. Besides, he is now murdered, he did not slash his own throat. No, we need to find whoever he bought that tequila for."

"All right. I'll go back and interview more of the homeless. A bunch weren't at the site, they had been out when businesses were open, better chance of dumpster diving and panhandling, and stealing. They'll be back at the fields now sleeping it off. Gibson also said the hair dye was too common to locate who bought it. What are you doing today? Working at the mine?"

Kurian nodded with the phone at his ear, it bumped his helmet. He was striding down a dark shaft to finish the project, he would lose his signal shortly. "Unfortunately, *ja*, I have work here that must be done. As soon as I can break away I plan to meet Solitar and take her to the river to get samples. I need to hurry, I don't think she will wait for me." *She'd better or-*

Rutger's rumble of an amused chuckle came through the phone. "Okay. Guess you got over our private tête-à-tête where the beauty made breakfast for me, huh?"

Kurian snorted. "Sure, dream on, *broeder*. She was already making breakfast when you horned in on her."

Rutger laughed. "Didn't take you a split second to jump right in yourself, my man."

"Food's food, Rut, and hers was especially good." He rounded a corner where a group of men wearing helmets and rubber boots to their knees were working on a machine. "I have to go and get this done before Solitar leaves without me. I don't want her running around alone in that area of town, and knowing her, she will not ask anyone for help. Later," he disconnected and joined the miners.

Chapter Eleven

There was no way Solitar was hanging around waiting for Kurian Anastaas to escort her to the river. She has taken care of herself all these years and she doesn't need some overbearing brute bossing her around. All she needed was a few containers of the water, it will take longer to drive there and back than it will to obtain the samples. She tightened her ponytail and pulled the emerald green sweater down over her black jeans.

For all her strong talk, she snuck out the back door of the warehouse when she was done with the paperwork Camara had for her. Kurian was a big bold man that she knew would override her objections to him coming with her and she would be unable to force him to stay out of her jeep. Brawn outweighed arguments every time. And once again, she didn't dare complain to her superiors, they would see her as a weak female and replace her without a blink of an eye. She peered around the corner of the building. The coast was clear, she sprinted across the tall grass taking a short cut to where she'd parked the jeep.

Fast shallow panting ratcheted her pulse to triple digits as she made her escape. In moments she was tearing hell for leather over the gravel road and onto the asphalt heading towards the city. Glancing anxiously in the rear view a dozen times, she didn't take a calm deep breath until she was well out of sight of the mine and ascertained there was not an angry superintendent hot on her heels.

Relaxing the death grip on the wheel, Solitar sat back and forced herself to drive slower. There were all sorts of hidden dangers along the road. Any kind of wild animal or even a dog or cat could run out from the bushes, potholes made by the heavy equipment were abundant as were big rocks. The natives had dug out the larger rocks for their banana crops, and the mine staff left dug-up earthen debris all along the road.

Using a copy of the hand drawn map they had all been give upon arrival she found the way to the city. Although the village was horribly destitute, the small city still bustled, everyone trying to make a buck. Even the government employees only worked part time and were paid a pittance.

Solitar located the river on the map and trailed it to the Purple River Nightclub. Huh, she grunted with disparagement as she exited the car with the case of containers. Nightclub, a high class moniker for what was really just a basic strip joint. Where the men came up with the money to visit the club she had no idea, likely mostly miners and the few hunters and fishermen that came in by helicopter from other regions.

Large predatory fish like anjoemaras, tukunari, and pakusi, a big brother to the piranha drew those loving to catch fighting fish to the rural area. Of course the same types of fish were available in Suriname and other areas, but the more hardcore hunters came to Ruwenstad where the land was rugged, tougher, more unforgiveable and there was much less competition for bites.

Solitar removed the containers from the bag and unscrewed the lids. She very carefully knelt on the short seawall and bent over gingerly scooping up several samples of the water. Her nose wrinkled at the nasty smell that reeked from the river. Placing the containers in the bag, she cautiously picked her way back to the jeep. The ground was slippery where the higher tide had slicked earlier in the morning. Last thing she needed was to slip and plunge into the smelly river, or worse, fall and break a bone.

The backdrop of the raunchy club as well as other rough and tumble dilapidated buildings remained quiet, nothing but leaves on branches stirred and a few vehicles chugging by out on the front roadway. There wasn't a sign of life, no shrieking rapacious mob racing out to molest her as she made her way back to her jeep.

Setting the bag on the floor of the jeep, Solitar drove out of the back lot of the strip club with a smile of satisfaction on her lips. See, she complimented herself, easy peasy. No problem. No nefarious males had fled the strip club to chase her down and do heaven's knows what Anastaas had thought they'd do to her.

A frisson of devastating memories, old and new zapped down her spine. Once upon a time she'd been left out there in the open on her own and hell had been paid. She pushed the shattering thoughts out of her mind. She was in charge of her safety now and she'd be damned if she let her life be led by fear.

She got her samples and was already making her way back to the mine. Except, after she'd traveled several miles a frown wrinkled her smooth brow, her head swung back looking behind, was that the road she was to take? There were so many unmarked partial gravel, tar and dirt roads leading like spider webs winding through the tall grass, and few landmarks. She unclipped the compass from the dashboard.

"What the…" the front of the compass was smashed in, the needle was missing. It was useless. "Was that an accident or- no," she told herself, there would be no reason for someone to destroy the compass. Someone must have accidentally broken it and put it back hoping no one would notice. Great.

The forest stretching like a dark mass beyond the open savanna all looked the same to her, the grass looked the same, in fact, she bit her lower lips as she peered all around, everything looked the same. She must have happened onto the wrong road at one of the crossing junctures. There wasn't a building, vehicle or person to be seen.

Nothing except trees and grass and- "Oh no," she cried at the suddenly odd sputtering sounds the jeep made.

"No, no, please don't do this to me," Solitar begged as smoke rose from the hood. The arrow on the engine icon on the dashboard was reeling into the red, and…the jeep rolled to a stop. Steam whooshed from under the hood with a loud whistle as the vehicle wheezed as if dying, and then it died. "You have got to be kidding," Solitar muttered. Sitting in the seat she contemplated what to do.

Glancing around she again noted there was nothing but grass and trees that seemed to sprawl on forever. She peered down the road she'd been traveling. What were the chances of someone coming along any time soon? Someone trustworthy that is. Damn. Wait until Anastaas finds out she broke down, she'd never hear the end of it. That's if she makes it back. "Okay, Solitar," she gave herself a pep talk, "life hasn't always been very kind to you, make that never been kind to you, but," she sighed and opened the door, "no evil God would throw me under the hades' bus now, would he? She?"

Stepping out of the jeep she pulled out her phone and held it up. No stars. Zip. No service, of course not, what did she expect?

Locking the door, she wondered if that would deter anyone that might happen by. Undoubtedly, as poor as the people were, few would pass by without breaking a window to see what they could steal. She debated grabbing the containers, but decided to leave them. It would be tiring walking as it was without carrying extra and if someone stole them she could always get more. Sucking in a deep breath, she let it out with a groan and set upon treading along the mostly dirt road.

She should have hit the paved roads the mine staff had made by now. After a mile or so of still trekking on hard dirt Solitar deduced she had not driven on this particular road on the way to the city which meant she was totally lost without a clue which way to go. She considered heading back the way she'd come but she had driven for miles after the last juncture before the jeep broke down, it would be nightfall if she managed to find her way back to there, so she might as well continue on forward and hope to come across some civilization.

Gazing over the thick grass, Solitar prayed she wouldn't come across any wild animals. What had she heard lived in the jungle? Monkeys, sloths, creepy looking anteaters, but they were harmless. The dangerous critters, she thought back to what Laddie had told them. Her stomach pitched as she recalled him telling them stories of panthers, boa constrictors, and a man had been torn apart by a jaguar, someone else had perished at the jaws of a puma. Making her feet move faster, she thought even wild dogs could present a problem.

Fear caught and lodged in her throat as her head toggled back and forth searching for any movement between the trees. "Great, scare yourself to death, you idiot," she scolded herself. Thinking of being an idiot reminded her of Anastaas and his mixing up idiom with idiot, it brought a shaky smile to her mouth tightened in fear. It helped calm her racing heart, she laughed at herself.

"Dolt, all grown up and still afraid of your own shadow, Solitar. You- oh!" The breeze ruffled the grass and rippled leaves on trees, but the direction of the wind changed and it surged in from the south bringing sounds with it. Human sounds. She stopped walking and saw in the near distance a grove of large-leafed trees lined up almost like a rambling orchard.

She paused and studied the trees. "Banana plants," she determined out loud. "Well, I'm guessing that's what they are. Maybe there are some farmers that can help me get back home." She pushed her way through the tall grass keeping alert for an animal napping or even a snake basking. It was warmer today, she was probably going to have a nice sunburn by the time she makes it back. Unclipping her cell she held it up again, still no service.

The closer she got to the tall stalky plants with long wide leaves the louder the voices. "Hello!" she called out but the wind blew her greeting back at her. Plodding right into the grove, Solitar pushed branches and broad leaves aside and made her way through the copse of green stalks, her boots stomping on rougher grass and dirt. The voices were clearer, males and females chattering. She proceeded making her way through following the voices, when, the plants changed.

Instead of the thicker stalks with long broad leaves, she now found herself amongst small shrubs with thin branches lined with small oval leaves. Clusters of red berries were visible in some of the plants. "Well," Solitar mumbled to herself, "I thought they said the only thing that was growing out here was the banana. I wonder what these..." she bent and more closely examined the bush.

"Hey you!" someone shouted, and she heard heavy boots thumping over the hard soil coming towards her.

Solitar stood up straight and smiled with relief at the approaching huge male. "Hey there, hi, uh, perhaps you can help me, I-" And her body recoiled at the pistol that was suddenly aimed straight at her head. She raised her hands. "Wait, I- I please don't shoot, I don't mean any harm!"

The man stomped closer, one eye squinting at her. An immense man, he wore a wide brimmed straw hat over messy fair hair, overalls and a t-shirt covered his thick chest. "What're you doing sneaking around our coca plants, girl?" he growled, waving the gun at her. "Talk fast, honey, I ain't got no patience for spies."

"C- coca plants? You- you mean like co-*caine*?" Solitar stuttered in shock before clamping her mouth shut. Had she stumbled onto an illegal cocaine operation? Oh shit.

He clomped to a stop and waggled the gun at her. "Speak, woman, what the hell are you doing here? I aughta put a plug in ya, ya nosy bitch. You work for Simón Bolívar? Huh? Spyin' for him?" He sneered, "Yer dead right where ya stand before I let you run back and tell him where we are."

Her heart clutched, Solitar thought she'd pee her pants. "N- n- no, I- I-" words failed her in her abject terror.

"Jared, what's going on?" A feminine voice sounded and a woman appeared. She wore old jeans and a T and the same wide-brimmed straw hat. Her skin like his was darkly tanned, slight lines spidered from her eyes and around her mouth. She stood next to the man staring at Solitar.

Solitar thought for sure this was her last day on earth. Drug dealers. Oh God, she'd stumbled onto their illegal crop of coca. Her hands in the air her eyes flit from one to the other. More voices and then several people emerged from the cover of the trees and plants.

"What the hell, Jared? Who's she?" a man asked.

"A spy," Jared answered aiming the gun at Solitar's chest. "I'm gonna kill her. We can bury her by the gorge, the animals will take care of her eventually, no one will ever find the remains."

"N- no!" Her legs trembling, Solitar's body swayed, she couldn't catch her breath, she was on the verge of blacking out from the fright of the gun in her face and the man's threat of death.

"Stop it, Jared, you're scaring her to death." The woman put her hand on the man's arm pushing it so he lowered the gun. She smiled at Solitar and took a step to her. "Hi, my name is Marlie, and this here is my husband, Jared DiCello." She turned to one side and said, "Brandon, Gregor, Beth-Ann," then the other side as more people appeared. "Thomas, Cesar, Jims, Coral and Frankie," she introduced the rest of them. They ranged in ages early twenties to mid-forties.

A few more people peeked at them through a cluster of wide leaves behind a thicket of brush and trees. Solitar recognized Laurie and the children she had been babysitting, Bonnie and Bobby. Solitar had had contact with the tow-headed children on many previous occasions. They both looked the spitting image of Jared DiCello. The children grinned and raised their hands to wave but Laurie grabbed their arms and with a rustle of leaves they were gone. Solitar could hear the children's small voices asking why they couldn't play with Soli, then there was silence.

Solitar didn't know what to say, what to do, she just stood wide-eyed, lips parted with her rapid breaths.

"What's your name, hon?" Marlie asked. She looked around mid-thirties, her brown hair tied back in a low ponytail, she was very slender, thin. Her big brown eyes were kind. "Don't be afraid, we won't hurt you, I promise." She turned to Jared with a frown and ordered, "Put that away, Jar, you're scaring the hell out of her."

Jared snarled, "She's here spyin' for Simón Bolívar, Marlie, doncha know, we can't let her go tell him about the farm, for fuck's sake." He still held the gun but it was aimed at the ground.

"N- no, I don't know who- who that person is," Solitar squeaked out with a frightened gulp. Her wide eyes roved around the group, they were all staring at her, most with angry belligerence like Jared, along with curiosity.

"Then what the hell are you doing here?" the man Thomas asked. His hat rode low half covering his dark eyes narrowed at her in distrust. He was covered with dirt head to toe.

"M- my car broke down, back- back a mile or so," Solitar told them. "I heard voices, your voices, I thought someone might help me. I didn't know you were breaking the law."

At that, many of their curious looks turned threatening. "You see?" Jared raised the gun again. "She's gonna turn us into the cops, we can't let her go."

Solitar's heart sank at his words and the violence that screwed over his face dark brown from years toiling in the sun. Sweat popped around her body, rolling down between her breasts, beading along her hairline. Frantically she scanned the area, she needed to run. But they were surrounded by nothing but open savannah dappled with thick clusters of trees. Of course there also was the coca crop hidden magnificently by the blowsy banana plants. The illicit farmers would catch her before she fled a few feet.

Observing her eyes jerking around broadcasting her plan to run, the motley group tightened around her obstructing any avenues of escape.

"Wait." Marlie stepped between Jared and Solitar. "She wouldn't do that, would you, Miss?" Her brown eyes pleaded, her smile friendly. "You see, this land, our people, we're poor, so poor we can't afford to purchase seeds or plants to grow good crops. These coca fields were planted by a drug lord ages ago. When all of our other crops failed and everyone was starving, Jared came across these old fields and we propagated them. The banana trees weren't viable enough to help us survive, but the coca, well," she raised her hands sheepishly.

"We know it's wrong, Miss, but watching our children starve or die of illness we hadn't the money to pay for medicine, well," her smile turned flat, eyes flared with righteous motherly anger, "that's wrong too."

The group stood glaring at Solitar, they inched closer, fencing her in. She could smell their sweat, the soil that clung to their hands, their clothes, even their hair. Heavy breathing and muttered curses oppressed her from every angle. She wasn't a good liar. Her intent scribbled clearly across her face she still tried to deny she would rat them out. "No, uh, I wouldn't uh-"

"Yes she would," Jared snarled. Pushing Marlie aside he came within a foot of Solitar and raised his gun. "We let her go she will run straight to the sheriff and not only will they destroy our crops we will be arrested. What will happen to our children then? Orphans in this shitty land? Starving and alone they'll be taken and forced into prostitution in the streets like the other unfortunate ones."

Mixed emotions rode over Marlie's thin tanned face. She wiped perspiration that gathered over her brow. She read the truth in Solitar's pressed lips, her evasive eyes that traveled the land before connecting uneasily with Marlie's.

Seeing the grief flash in Marlie's deep brown eyes, Solitar's brows hopped up as alarm rang through her body, they were really going to kill her! "No! Wait! I won't-"

"You will." Jared grabbed her arm. "I'll take her out by the ravine. I can bash her head in with a rock or break her neck and toss her down the gulch. If they find her body they will think she left her car, got disoriented and fell, hit her head. Let's go." He started to drag her.

"No, please, wait!" Solitar tried to fight but he was a mammoth man and he easily hauled her. "Marlie, please, don't let him do this!" she begged, her stomach shriveled at the look of defeat and sorrow Marlie showed before she turned away. Solitar had no choice, Jared had her up on her toes, he would just drag her if she dropped to the ground.

"Don't do this," she pleaded with the suddenly deaf Jared. He trudged through the group, they all carried the same expression that Marlie had as they stepped aside to let them pass. "No!" Solitar screamed, struggling in his grip, but Jared just dragged her.

A gunshot rang out!

Jared stopped so abruptly Solitar stumbled but he held her upright. They turned.

Kurian Anastaas was standing a few yards away. No one had seen or heard him approach. He wore dark green cargoes and a dark green t-shirt, boots planted akimbo, and he held his own weapon out aimed at Jared.

"Let her go," Kurian demanded. His granite gaze harsh on Jared making no illusion that he would not shoot him. The first bullet had gone into the air to get their attention.

"This is none of your concern, mister. You need to ghost right on outta here before I do to you what I plan to do to her." Jared pointed the gun now at Kurian.

Kurian fired, the blast so loud everyone's ear rang. The bullet blew Jared's hat right off his head. "The next one is between your eyes, let her go." His face a hard mask, his eyes all lethal blackness with promise.

Very slowly, Jared's fingers unwound one-by-one from Solitar's small arm and he stepped back careful to keep her in front of him. Lowering his gun he said, "I was only going to scare her into silence, bro."

His weapon aimed at Jared's head, Kurian ordered, "Solitar, come to me." He held the gun steady on Jared but his eyes flicked around at the others and swept the land surrounding them searching for surprise hidden danger.

Her legs were shaking so badly Solitar had to keep her knees locked or she would topple right over in sheer fright. The look in Kurian's eyes as they flicked to her was just as deadly as when they swung back to Jared.

"Mister," Marlie said softly to Kurian as Solitar moved within feet of him. "Jared is all temper and bluster, he never would have hurt her." She gave Solitar a faint smile of apology. "He was only trying to frighten you into keeping quiet about us. Next he would have taken you to our homes, the shacks we live in, show you how little food we have for our children, no running water, electricity. I swear he wouldn't have harmed you."

"Now we don't need to find out if that is true," Kurian replied and nodded to Solitar. "Follow the tramped down trail, walk in front of me."

She looked down, there was a distinct trail in the smashed down grass. She hurried to it and swiftly followed it out of the coca then the banana fields. She was afraid to turn around to see if Kurian was behind her. Either way she was almost as afraid of him as she'd been of Jared. Jared wore his danger on his sleeve, Kurian was drowning in it.

When she reached the road, she sucked in a deep shaky breath and paused. A heartbeat later Kurian stepped from the trees and tall grass to join her, the gun still in his hand but the barrel was pointed to the ground. "This way," Kurian growled and started walking down the road towards the direction she'd left the jeep.

Only a few minutes and they came upon a motorbike. Kurian stuffed the gun in the back of his belt and said, "Get on."

Her legs still barely able to hold her up she stood blinking at him. "I- how did you find me? Were you looking for me?" Maybe he had been involved with the drug farmers and just happened to be there. The suspicious thought took flight and she stepped back from him, her head whipping around again looking for somewhere to run to.

A dark anger rose up his neck. "Stop. Get on the goddamned bike, Solitar, I have zero patience left for your foolishness."

Still glancing in all directions for an escape from the clearly furious man, she said, "You can go on, I will walk...ah," where could she really go? Her words made the darkness spread over his face.

His hands on his hips he threatened, "You get on that bike right now or so help me God I will paddle your ass into tomorrow and put you on the bike and tie you the fuck down."

Her cheeks paled. He could and would do it. "You don't have to swear at me Mr. Anas- eek!"

He stomped to her, grabbed her around the hips, lifted her, turned and dumped her on the bike. She landed with a huff knocked from her lungs. Without another word he snatched the helmet off the handlebars and dropped it on her head. Before she could protest he clipped the chinstrap closed and tightened it under her jaw.

"Really, Mr. A-"

Kurian swung his leg over the seat and started the engine and took off letting the wind slam the words out of her. He grabbed her arm and jerked it around his waist as he sped down the bumpy dirt road. She didn't want to touch him, but Solitar was forced to wrap her arms around him to keep from falling off. After a bone-jolting mile she let herself lean against his strong back for support.

Chapter Twelve

Instead of going to the mine or the Cresh, Kurian drove into the city and parked the bike under a shade tree in front of the pharmacy. Peeling red paint over the front window that was crossed with protective bars read, "Paul's Medical Supplies."

Kurian climbed off the bike and pointed a finger at Solitar. "You do not get off the bike. You do not move." He suddenly reached to her belt and snatched her cell phone from it.

"Hey! What do you think you're doing?" Solitar yelped. She had hoped to secretly dial for help while Jared the coca grower was distracted hauling her through the brush on the way to bash her head in. She knew she hadn't had much of a chance of getting away from the brawny farmer, yet she still had to try. Except there was no satellite service when the jeep had died and none along the road so the chances of her using the phone while in Jared's custody had been slim to none anyway.

She had thought maybe she could topple carefully yet quickly over the cliff if it wasn't too steep before he broke her neck or cracked her head open and safely roll down the hill without him managing to pursue her. Of course he'd only need to lean over and put a bullet in her brain as she cascaded down. Besides, if she could roll safely down he could just as easily hike down after her.

Breaking into her ponderings that she no longer needed to worry about, she now had a new enraged aggressive male to deal with.

"You have caused enough trouble for the day," Kurian told her, his posture rigid with anger. "You stay put or I swear I will put the fear of the devil in you." He gave her a hard warning glare then turned and tramped into the pharmacy.

Not wanting to learn what the fear of the devil entailed, his face was frightening enough, Solitar didn't move a muscle the few minutes he was gone. When he returned, one of the pockets in his cargo pants bulged slightly and he climbed back on and didn't stop driving until they reached the Cresh.

After he stopped the bike, without waiting for him to shut it down, Solitar awkwardly stumbled from it. "Well, uh, thank you for-" She broke off as he turned the key killing the engine, jumped off, and moved past her to the huge stone building.

Tearing the helmet off, she hung it on a handle bar and hurried after him.

The broad set of steps led up to a brace of red double doors. Three-stories of grey stone were lined with vertical corners made up of white stones that also arched over the front door and many of the large cathedral shaped windows. Several wings jagged on both sides of the main structure with A-framed roofs gabling various sections. Chimneys poked up from the stone shingled roofs.

More stone staircases arched around the Cresh Citadel, and a two foot high, white-stoned barrel fence roped around most of the structure. Solitar moved more slowly following Kurian as he entered the hotel. He marched to the stairs and moved up them as if he ran up and down three floors all day long without taking a breath.

Solitar however was panting by the time they stopped in front of her room. He stood waiting for her to catch up. "Um," she drew in a deep breath, "well, uh, thank-"

"Key," he snapped with his hand out.

"What?" Her hand covered the pocket of her jeans where she'd put her keys. "I don't need-"

"Give it to me or I will take it," he ordered.

She shook her head. "No. I am going inside, alone. Thank you for-"

He grabbed her arm, roughly turned her sideways, stuck his hand in her pocket and drew out the room key.

"Hey-" She was speaking to empty air. He'd opened her door and was inside. "Great," she muttered and followed him in. She didn't close the door, no way was she going to stay inside alone with him without a way to get out-

He closed the door and locked it then he started pacing. His boots stomped over the planked floor.

The rooms had been built for lavish opulence but still had an open-air, rustic jungle feel to them. Thatched fringe swathed over part of the large window to the balcony, wooden slats made up the ceiling with cross beams overhead matching the headboard to the bed. The furniture was wood and wicker with blue and green mosquito netting draping from the ceiling. Ambient amber lights gave everything a golden glow, the glossy planked floor was covered with a few colorful scatter rugs. Outside the window the jungle flourished wild and green

The nightie Solitar had worn last night lay across the foot of the bed. She watched his eyes draw to it, and stay there. "Uh, listen, Mr. Anastaas, you don't need to-"

He turned on her, dark eyes blazing with fury. "You stupid, stupid woman," he snarled. "Standing behind the door when the angels handed out brains?"

She jerked back. "Huh? What?" Her brow furrowed. "You can't-"

"I told you to wait for me, goddammit," his voice snarly and fierce. "I told you it was too dangerous for a lone woman to be wandering around out there."

"Well," she blanched, he was right. Nonetheless she responded, "I was perfectly safe getting the samples. You-"

"Oh *ja*?" He gave a mean chuckle. "And where are they now?"

She paused, her eyes flickered guiltily, then she stiffened. "They are locked safely in my jeep."

"Ah, and where is the jeep?"

"Well," she repeated inanely, "it broke down. I thought it best to leave it and hike out. It wasn't my fault it broke down. Nothing nefarious happened that-"

"Ah," he rudely cut her off for the tenth time. "Nothing nefarious you say?" His hands clasped behind his back he started walking a circle around her, his eyes a black stabbing glare. Her shoulders rigid she tried not to flinch at his penetrating calculation and clear fury.

"Um, well, no, the car just, you know, died. They do that, especially here. The vehicles are all old and-"

"Are they? It just...rolled over and died? And the samples are safely tucked inside?" His sarcasm not even slightly veiled.

She fisted her hands, straightened her shoulders. "Yes, of course. Stop doing that, stop cutting me off. You-"

But he did it again. "*Chief*," his lip curled on the word making it an insult. "As soon as I realized you had so gleefully snuck away without waiting for me, I hopped on my bike to chase after you. You were not at the river so I took the road back and came here but you had not returned. So, assuming you had gotten lost," his sneering look raked her up and down letting her know he had assumed correctly. She struggled not to cringe under his accurate assessment.

"I went back out. It had rained last night so fortunately there were very few tire tracks to trace. I easily spotted where you turned off onto the wrong road. Then I found your jeep. You will be distressed to learn the samples are not there, tucked so carefully inside the locked car. You know, the jeep with the driver's side window broken." His eyes slit at her, he said, "One wonders what could have happened to you if you had stayed with the jeep? Would the thieves have helped you...or?" He left off the end of the insidious suggestion.

Just what she'd feared. If only someone other than this- this arrogant ass hadn't been then one to find the jeep. "Really, Mr. Anastaas," she sighed with impertinence, "it could have happened to anyone. Cars break down all the time. It wasn't-"

Again he stepped over her words and said, "It did not break down by accident, *Chief*," again the title came out in a snide sneer. "I checked the engine, there was a hole jabbed through the water pump. Wasn't by mistake, the hole is the size of I would say a screwdriver. Someone wanted you to break down. Whether they wanted to harm you or just steal the samples, who knows?" He shrugged. "I would guess both. You must have wandered off before he or she could track you."

"But why? I can just retrieve more samples."

"That is why I think it was to bring harm, or fear, to you. Someone wanted to stop you from reporting the river becoming polluted by the mine, if that is true. If you disappeared, as you almost did," he leveled his eyes at her, "the whole check into the pollution thing might have been dropped if you were not there to pursue it. You even made it easy for them by dropping yourself right into an illegal coca production. That big guy was about to do someone else's dirty work for them without even knowing it. Two stones, one dead bird."

He was right. Who knows if Jared was going to kill her or not. She had been in deep dark shit and she knew it. Solitar moved on legs so weary from shaking in fright they felt wooden to a rattan chair and she plunked down, her shoulders slumped. She looked up at him in confused despair. "But who would do such a thing, Mr. Anastaas?"

Kurian raked a hand through his dark hair making it spike. He moved and crouched down in front of her. "Who has something to lose if you prove we were polluting the river?"

Her eyes rounded in confusion, then she turned her head.

"Solitar?" Kurian prodded.

She shifted her attention to his jaw. He reached out and wound his hand around her neck, his thumb under her chin, he lifted it so she was forced to look directly at his eyes. "Who, Solitar?" he asked again.

Her neck arched, her head fell back. She dragged the band off her hair and let the thick locks fall around her shoulders. Kurian gently stroked her neck with his thumb. It passed over her pulse in a caress, a soft sigh slid out as the motion oddly relaxed her. Her chest rose with a heavy inhale, she let it out with a muddled sigh. "I can only think of Jamie. Jamie Orlando." She sat up and Kurian was forced to drop his hand.

She said, "He even said he was responsible for most of the reports indicating the water was clean. Unless someone was giving him bad info, but, still, it was his job to check the sanitation procedures." Solitar tried to hide the quiver of dread that roiled through her, her lips twisted, the brilliant blue of her eyes dulled. "At best he is in trouble if he took someone else's fact checking without checking it himself per procedure, at worse, he fudged his reports." Her eyes rolled up to Kurian then quickly dropped away. "Unless the river was polluted from another source, then we are all in the clear."

"But you don't believe that, do you? You know Orlando is capable of…wrongdoing."

The color leeched from her round cheeks, she bit her lower lip to still the trembling.

Kurian sat back on his heels, his knees spread. "It is important, Solitar, that you tell me what is, or was going on between you two. I have seen you together. You are…frightened, you avoid him when he comes around. When he tries to speak to you, you make sure someone else is present, you practically pushed Camara between you two the other day. Did he…hurt you?"

As she swallowed, her throat flexed roughly with blatant distress. "It's," she looked away, her voice strengthened, "it's none of your business, Mr. Ana-"

He gripped her knees and pushed so he was kneeling between them, still sitting back on his heels. "It is my business. And if you call me Mr. Anastaas one more damned time you will regret it. My father is not here, I am. Kurian. Now," he moved his hands up and pressed his fingers into her thighs and watched her eyes widen. "I am not leaving until I have the truth from you. You don't tell me and I will contact Garrick Miles right now and tell him there is some crap going on here and he needs to replace some of his key players, and by that I mean you and Orlando. Now, talk."

Solitar moved until her spine was flush against the back of the chair, she looked down at the man's large hands splayed over her thighs, his thick fingers pressed into her jeans, into her flesh. He had maneuvered until he was between her spread legs effectively holding her captive. "Mr. Anas-"

"Kurian, goddammit," he cursed in an irritated growl. "Just tell me, tell me about you and Orlando."

Her chest fell with her resigned sigh, she laid her arms on the chair arms, her fingers curled tightly over the sides. "All right. But," she leaned forward and said, "you have to promise what I say will stay between you and me. You cannot tell Mr. Miles or anyone, no one, promise me."

His fingers tightened as he looked into the blatant shame and fear in her eyes. "Fine. *Ja*, ah, yes, I promise I will not tell the law or Mr. Miles."

She raised her gaze to see the sincerity in his hard eyes. If anything she didn't think this man ever lied. He wouldn't think he ever needed to, who would he ever be afraid of? Squelching a morose chuckle at the divergence between them, he was brave and strong and she was just a weak puddle of nothing. She tried to turn away again but his enigmatic eyes held her like black chains.

"Solitar," he warned, his patience was waning.

"Okay, I'll tell you, but you need to let go of me and move away."

"No," he said flatly. "You got one allowance from me, the rest you will do as I say. Go on."

She couldn't look at him as she spoke, she turned her head slightly so her gaze streamed towards the balcony with the pretty greenery ruffling softly in the background. A bird swooped in and settled on a thick branch, it cooed.

Chapter Thirteen

Speaking to the bird, Solitar said, "He, Jamie Orlando," she drew in a deep breath, shame etched sharp angles in her soft face, pain bled in the haunted blue eyes. "He kept asking me out, and I kept saying no. It wasn't just him, I have no interest in dating any man," her gaze skimmed across Kurian's broad shoulders but didn't meet his eyes.

"But," she sighed, the tension grew more tautly in her neck, in her voice. "He stalked me. Relentlessly. Everywhere I went he would insert himself. Whether it was working in the mine, or the office in the shanty, or the small diner at the outskirts of the city, he would pop up and would not leave me alone even though I insisted, demanded, begged." She took a shuddering breath.

Kurian's hard face revealed none of his thoughts. He said coolly, "Did you tell anyone? File a complaint?"

She shook her head with a wry, humorless smile. "No." Now she looked directly at him then quickly away, back to the bird that tilted and cocked his head, listening for the sound of a cricket in the brush, a beetle scraping along the wood, anything to wet his whistle.

Solitar explained, "I am young, a female in a man's world, I can't ever show a hint of…weakness, or let my femininity be an object of contention. I am only the chief here because the two senior chiefs had to leave for personal reasons. Mr. Miles told me if I do an exceptional job with no, I mean zero problems he might promote me. Last thing I could do was whine about a pushy male harassing me. And, Jamie deduced this so he persisted with bold audacity."

His mouth a curl of repugnance, rank acid in his voice, Kurian said, "So, the prick stalked you. But, I am thinking that wasn't all he did?" His fingers stroked her legs, she didn't seem to notice. She went on.

"No. I…" she paused and glanced back to the window where the bird chirped happily with no worries but where the next bug would be. The bird was gorgeous, flamboyant in his yellow body, scarlet head and colorful beak. Turning back to Kurian, she leaned forward, her eyes firm, she said, "Remember, you gave me your word, you won't tell the police or Mr. Miles?"

Kurian nodded. "I swear, Solitar."

Her shoulders drooped as she sat back. "Okay. One night, I was working late in the office shanty and Jamie came in." Kurian opened his mouth, she said quickly, "Yes I locked the door but as a senior he had a key. Anyway, he pressed me again to go out with him, come to his room for a drink, talk only, he promised."

"You did not-"

"No, of course not," she said with a self-disparaging smile. "I'm not quite that stupid, that gullible. No, I refused again and had to shove him out of the way to get out the door. He followed me in his jeep. Then he cursed, begged, threatened me when we reached the Cresh where I thought I'd be safe."

"Did you ask the front desk attendant to walk you to your room?"

"Ha," she snorted, with sardonic elegance. "There is only one attendant at the Cresh as you should know by now, and Gordy is usually sleeping off his marijuana high in one of the empty rooms. Anyway, I hurried to my room but Jamie was right behind me. I stopped at my door and told him if he continued to harass me I would file a complaint. He laughed at me. He understood my precarious situation only too well."

"Bastard," Kurian spat. He stroked his palms over her thighs, softly caressing in a soothing manner.

"Yeah, worse than a bastard, that's being kind." She snorted again. "He pretended he was walking away, I opened my door. One foot inside the door and he crashed through behind me, knocked me down to the floor. He closed the door, grabbed me off the floor, he..." her face bloomed a ghastly red in remembrance, she plucked at her sweater as the anxiety crept through her bones, her punished brain cells. "I...fought him, kicked, punched, screamed, he...he hit me...a few times until I almost blacked out. Then he..." Tears sprung and rolled down her cheeks, her chest rose and fell rapidly as her distress deepened.

"Solitar," Kurian murmured, his fingers pressing her thighs as he felt her anguish mangling the air in the room even though a window was open letting in the flow of fresh crisp air and the incongruent cheerful song of the bird.

Her head dropped forward, her palms pressed against the falling tears as if she could stop them. "I was scarcely conscious when he tore off my clothes, and he kept hitting me to keep me...unable to fight back. He pinned me...then he...raped me." Her words hung in the air. Then they rushed out with a hideous gasp. "Brutal, Kurian, he was so...violent, he brutalized me, left...bruises and..."

She shook her head to clear the image although the physical pain and shame that lingered in her mind manifested in her shaking hands, quivering lip. She reflexively tried to pull her legs protectively together but Kurian's large body was in the way.

Kurian made no comment, just carefully stroked her to remind her she wasn't back in her nightmare, that she wasn't alone. He said, "Solitar, he assaulted you. That surely superseded any vague minor trouble that could upset Garrick Miles. The fucker belongs in jail for shit's sake, girl." His voice grew louder, rougher in his rage. "You need to-"

"No!" She jumped up forcing him to shuffle back. "I can't, I told you." Solitar stepped away from him as he got to his feet. The bird flew off with a sweep of wide colorful plumage and a squawk.

"You are being ridiculous, Solitar, he fucking raped you!" He shouted in her face then moved a few feet from her as she folded into herself at the sudden fear of his obvious hulking strength.

"What's done is done, Kurian, it's over. I need to work here." Her hand clenched in a fist over her pursed mouth.

"It is just a job, woman," Kurian said angrily, "you are talking fucking *rape*! He beat you-"

Her lips jutted, shoulders rose to her ears, she shouted at him, "It's not just a job, it's my life! I owe money, I can't do anything else. I was put through school for this. Besides," her eyes grew glassy, she suddenly rambled, her voice vague and hushed as repressed memories of horror rose, "it's not like it's the first time. I'll get over it, I-"

"What!" He yelled and grabbed her upper arms. "What the hell are you talking about? Has he done it again? I will fucking kill him!"

Her eyes pinned wide open when she realized what she'd said. "N- no, I have been so very careful since to never be caught alone."

"Then others? Miners? Here? Who? Tell me!"

She tried to break his grip but it was futile, she hadn't a quarter of his strapping strength. "No, Kurian." The wind seeped out of her, deep sadness filled, carving lines in her forehead, her limbs hung limp. "It was a long time ago. Forget about it."

He squeezed her arms in disbelief. "Forget about it? Are you insane? You are young now, you had to be very young when-"

"Stop it!" Her scream so piercing, her suffering so great, Kurian had no choice but to release her.

"Solitar, you cannot let Orlando get away with this. He could assault another woman." Kurian tried to beseech her compassion. Was he their serial killer?

"No, no one else is in this...untenable position. I told him if he ever touched me again I would bring charges...but, he said he would claim it was consensual."

"Huh," Kurian grunted, dragging his fingers angrily through his hair. "Were the bruises from his beating consensual as well?"

She turned away to hide her shame. "He had lost control that time, he said if he did it again he would be more careful and not leave...evidence, drug me perhaps. So, I just need to stay clear of-"

"Oh my God, Solitar!" He grasped her arms again. "Are you hearing yourself? You are going to run and hide so this man, this- this monster does not assault you again? No," he shook his head, his face dark with wrath. He declared, "I will take care of it. Of him."

She tipped her head to look at him with protest. "No, absolutely not! You said you would not tell anyone that includes Jamie."

"Oh baby, talking is not what I am planning." He smoothed his ruffled hair back with his palms as he struggled to shove down the riled beast that raged for a kill.

"Stop, Kurian, just stop." She sighed, the strain evident in the tightness that pinched her eyes and mouth. "You can't do anything, I am begging you, stay away from him. I can deal with this."

"Deal with it? Are you fucking crazy? You have to get out of it. *Dios* woman, he can come after you again, you must-"

"No!" she exploded and the tears broke loose. "Just," she heaved in a ragged breath and turned her back to him. "Please leave."

"No way, Solitar, I am not leaving you in this condition. Talk to me-"

She faced him, face ravaged with tears and shame. Her voice quieter, she whispered, "Please, just do as I ask, Kurian." Already regret flooded her for revealing her secret. What was she thinking telling someone? And a stranger, a co-worker for that, a man she didn't even like, or trust, she must have lost her mind like he said.

His dark gaze rolled over her, the torment so crushing Kurian could not bear to be part of making it worse. "*Ja oke*, I will leave you. For now. But, Solitar," he waited until she raised her eyes to him. "You will trust me with all of your horrible secrets. It is time you let someone else shoulder them for you. Sharing that agony may lessen it. At the bare minimum you need protection."

He watched her, he could now understand just the tiniest bit why she was so cold, so hard, so mean. She had learned to follow the rules at some point, in a likely vicious manner, and could not veer from them or risk losing the weak strands of strength that held her fragile psyche together. Orlando's assault was merely one more rock on top of her, folding her into so many pieces until there was little left of the woman Solitar, and holding her down.

He reached in his pocket and pulled out the small package he'd bought at the drug store. "It is aloe for your sunburn. At least take care of part of you." He set the package on the desk and stood in front of her.

"Keep your doors locked and make sure you are never outside alone. Call me if you are. Call me if he comes anywhere near you, here, at the mine, the office. Call me if you just need," he took a breath and brushed a few tendrils of hair off her wet cheek, "if you need to talk. Anything. Call me." He bent and gently kissed her forehead, felt the tremble roll through her at his touch then left quietly.

Solitar didn't hear his footsteps leave until she latched the door.

Chapter Fourteen

He found her in the kitchen early the next morning, she was anything but alone. From the doorway he observed his traitorous friend, Rutger chowing on a plate stacked high with pancakes along with the teens Colby and Ritchie with equally filled plates sitting at the long farm table. There was a large dining room in the building but most of the people just hung in the kitchen to eat.

Additionally, Kurian noted drily, Laddie and Hubie were both lounging against the counter, one was gnawing on an egg sandwich, the other sipping a mug of hot chocolate. Kurian could see the marshmallows swimming in the dark potion from where he stood and he bet dollars to donuts Hubie hadn't prepared that hot chocolate himself. For some reason Kurian felt a frizzle of...something. Jealousy? No, that was an emotion he had never possessed. The ache he felt in his gut must just be hunger.

"Hey, Mr. K!" Colby greeted him with a crooked toothy grin and a wave of pancakes on his fork. "Come on in, Miss Soli made tons of food, enough for the whole country!"

Her cheeks tinted pink from the heat of the oven and the memory of how she'd spilled her guts to Kurian last night, she peeked over her shoulder briefly at him then addressed the pancake she was flipping in the skillet. "Have a seat, Superintendent, I'll make you a plate. Butter and syrup are on the table."

He hesitated, the boys returned to their raucous ribbing each other, Laddie and Hubie continued their conversation. Rutger's smirk made Kurian take a chair and join him at the table, albeit with a frown at Solitar's returned formal addressing him.

Shoveling a huge pile of blueberry pancakes into his mouth Rutger spoke around them. "You're gonna love these, K, light and fluffy as sin. Mmmm," he groaned, gobbled and forked for more.

"Here." Solitar set a plate in front of Kurian and a steaming cup of coffee.

"Thanks," he muttered. Taking a sip of coffee, he asked her, "Have you eaten yet, Solitar?"

She nodded to his shoulder. "Yes. I'm just going to clean up and then I have some paperwork to get to before I go to the mine."

82

"The guys will clean up, you go put on some sweats and sneakers and meet me downstairs in the gym. The paperwork can wait an hour." Kurian plopped a huge dollop of butter on his stack then poured a liberal amount of maple syrup over them.

Solitar halted abruptly. Surprised, she stared at him in the eyes. "What? I don't-"

"The guys will clean the kitchen, you are going to meet me in the gym and you are going to start your self-defense lessons."

Shaking her head, Solitar brushed back a lock of hair that escaped her ponytail with the back of her hand. "Are you crazy? I have work to do, I can't be-"

His fork poised in front of his mouth Kurian squinted one eye at her. "You be there or I will get involved with that...our conversation of last night."

Her brows dashed up in horror. "You promised you wouldn't tell! You-" She glanced around, the males had all stalled what they were doing and were gawking at the couple. Solitar's face splashed beet red, she gave Kurian an 'I'm gonna kill you,' look.

His head down, attention on his food, Kurian replied, "I am not telling anyone anything, but I will get involved in a physical way." He rolled his eyes up at her. "I don't think I need to spell out what I mean by that. And the rest of you," he glared around the room, "mind your own business. Now," he stabbed a sausage, "meet me downstairs, I will be there in ten."

Solitar's eyes flit around the room, the males quickly diverted their attention from her and zoomed swiftly back to what they were doing. "Ooo," she huffed snatching off the apron. Throwing it on the counter she snapped, "Fine," and stalked out of the room.

"Good," Kurian muttered, "angry is good." He spoke quietly with Rutger. "I need you to get me a gun, one for a small hand."

"She in danger?" Rutger asked with concern.

Nodding, Kurian popped a blueberry in his mouth and said, "I plan on giving her as much protection as I can until she leaves this godforsaken hellhole but I cannot be with her every second. You can help but you have work as well." When he finished he went and gave Solitar her first of many lessons in self-defense.

Chapter Fifteen

A few days later and Kurian had given Solitar several lessons in self-defense and a couple with the gun. Now he took her out for target practice. He had showed her how to clean and load the gun he bought her and they were on their second day of lessons in shooting it.

His arms rolled around her, he covered her hands with his and said in her ear, "*Oke*, like you have been doing, squeeze slowly, but this time keep your eyes on the target, don't close them. You are still closing them when you fire." Helping her hold her arms up and steady he let her pull the trigger. The boom was slightly muffled from their earplugs but they could still clearly hear the gun discharge.

"*Oke*, good, that is better, you hit the can," he praised her. He had lined up empty cans on an old stone fence a mile into the woods behind the Cresh.

Solitar lowered her hands and moved from the circle of his arms. "Kurian, I have to go to the police about the coca field," she started. They had been arguing for days about her filing a report.

"Solitar, we talked about this, you need to wait. There are things to check first, give us time to get-"

"What do you mean, us?" She raised her gaze to him quizzically then lowered it to his jaw.

He looked away before answering. "Ah, I cannot go into it, I just need you to wait until I give you the go ahead." Seeing the ambivalence flicker in her face he said, "I will not let them get to you, hurt you."

"It's not that, I don't think they would try to come out here and go after me. It's…" she sucked in her lower lip, her chin dropped. Then she raised it and looked him in the eye. "I mean, I see their profound poverty. Marlie said the coca was the only thing keeping the people, the children from downright starving to death. But still, they are breaking the law and they need to be held accountable." Her soft voice firmed she said, "I simply can't look the other way and pretend I don't know they're out there breaking the law. That man, Jared, was going to kill me, hurt me at the very least." She held the pistol out for him to take.

"No," he shook his head, told her, "it is yours to keep."

Her mouth opened in surprise then her brows drew down. "What? No, I can't accept this."

"*Ja,* you can and you will. Besides possible retribution from the farmers if neither I nor any of my men are around to protect you, I want you armed in case that bastard Orlando comes within ten feet of you."

She stared at the gun in her hand. "I...don't think I could shoot someone, *kill* a person, Kurian."

He folded his hand around hers that held the weapon and with his other hand lifted her chin to gaze into her pretty blues. "*Ja* you could if they were trying to hurt you, or kill you. We will have more lessons and you will soon feel more comfortable. We will practice with role play using cutouts and dummies so you are shooting at people not cans." Scenes of caricatures jumping out at her and popping out from behind trees ran through his head. Kurian planned on scaring the beejeesuz out of her so she would shoot first ask questions later. One second of hesitation could cost Solitar her life. "Put it in your purse, little scorpion."

Her brows arched at the moniker, she tucked the gun and a box of ammo he handed her in her purse. Yesterday he had come to her room early in the morning with a cleaning kit and had taught her how to clean and load the weapon, he left the kit he'd bought for her there. "Nevertheless, I am calling the police today," she stated firmly. The tip of her nose and cheeks were still pink from the sunburn of the other day and a sprinkling of freckles not there before traipsed like tiny ants over her nose. Kurian kept staring at them as if he thought they were cute or something. Solitar almost giggled at the thought.

He took a step closer to her. "Sol-"

They both looked over as the sound of an engine distracted them. A jeep was rumbling, bouncing over the uneven grass towards them. Kurian saw Rutger at the wheel.

Rutger pulled up and stopped. He rolled down the window. "Got another one, K, hop in."

Ignoring Solitar's curious look, Kurian opened up the back door and said to her, "Get in."

"Kurian," Rutger said tersely.

"But I-"

Kurian gave Solitar a firm push until she was nestled inside the back of the jeep and he climbed in the front passenger side. He said to Rutger, "I am not leaving her out here."

"Kurian," Solitar said, "I can walk back it's only a mile or so," she put her hand on the door handle to get out.

"Go, Rut. You stay put, Solitar," he ordered. "There is no one at the Cresh and your repaired jeep is at the mine, too far away for you to go on foot."

"That's because you grabbed me at the mine making me leave my jeep there and brought me back to the Cresh on your motorbike. If you could just give me a quick lesson on the bike I can drive it to the mine."

Kurian and Rutger shared a look but said nothing.

While Rutger drove, the two men spoke very quietly in a language Solitar wasn't familiar with. She tried to break in, "Rutger, I haven't seen you around the mine, so I guess you're a local?"

The men kept speaking, not answering her.

She tried again. "Maybe you have a business in the city? Or you're a hunter on vacation?" She fumed in frustration when neither deigned to answer her.

They ignored her and continued speaking almost inaudibly for her to hear for the next forty minutes. Then Rutger turned onto a two-lane blacktopped road where up ahead they could see the flashing red and white emergency lights swirling against the leafy green backdrop of the lush jungle.

Rutger pulled up and parked behind a row of law enforcement vehicles and got out. Kurian opened his door then turned around and said to Solitar, "You stay here, do not leave the car."

"Humph," she grunted her response. Kurian gave her a stern eye before hustling after Rutger.

Solitar waited approximately six minutes before she slowly opened the door and warily climbed out. She trod past the row of marked and unmarked cars and closer to where an ambulance and a firetruck were parked. All of the vehicles were decades old. She could hear the rumble of voices where dozens of people were gathered. She quickly spotted Kurian and Rutger as they were both well above average height.

The clustered group was looking down at something they were half-circled around so no one saw Solitar quietly approach. She crept up to the back of the group and wormed a little until she could poke her head in and see what they were all looking at.

"Oh!" She slapped a hand over her mouth but not quick enough to cover her gasp.

They were all staring at a body. A young woman lay unmoving on the side of the road. Two paramedics stood close to her, a man with white hair in green smock pants and shirt was crouched beside her.

Fortunately because of the mellow chatter no one heard her gasp and she inched forward. *Poor thing*, she thought, must be a car wreck. She glanced around puzzled, the only vehicles were behind her. Must have been a hit-and-run, jerk, she thought. Who could hit a person and flee to leave them to die? Clearly the woman was deceased as she wasn't moving and the paramedics were making no efforts to put her in the ambulance. She crept closer. "Oh no!" This time she'd cried out so loud heads turned.

The black eyes of Kurian lasered right to her. Blanching, she covered her mouth again, but her eyes were glued to the body. Kurian muscled through the small crowd making his way to Solitar. When he was in front of her he scolded, "Goddammit, Solitar, I told you to stay in the car. What the hell are-"

"It's- it's-" Solitar swallowed hard. "It's Brittlyn Jones, Kurian, it's Brittlyn! Oh my gosh, is she going to be okay?" She already knew the answer to that but her head was suddenly spinning when she realized she recognized the body.

"*De hel*, Solitar," Kurian cursed and moved to block her view. He grabbed her arm and spun her around then pushed her until she was away from the crowd.

When they stopped, she cried, "Kurian, that's Brittlyn Jones. What happened to her?"

"Listen, Solitar, you-"

Suddenly she froze. Her body turned to a block of ice but it suddenly felt like her scalp was on fire from her brain burning inside out. "Wait, wait," she uttered, her hand splayed against the bottom of her throat. She started to walk back to the scene but Kurian grasped her arm to stop her.

"No, Solitar, you cannot corrupt the scene. You don't belong here. I will take you back to the car and you can-"

"No," she protested, yanking her arm from his grasp. "You don't understand, her face, her face," she murmured in an odd voice. Her breaths came rapid and frantic, she felt tears sting the backs of her eyes. Her palm to her forehead pushing back her hair, she said, "Let me see her."

"What are you talking about, her face?" But now Kurian's voice held an inquisitive note along with the edginess of the gruesome scene.

"The mark, Kurian, let me see the mark," she insisted still trying to break his grip.

"Tell me-" He started but she broke away and dashed back to the crowd and pushed through people until she was feet from the body.

Brittlyn Jones lay twisted on the ground. Her dress torn, blonde hair mussed. She was on her back, her arms bent with palms up, legs curled to the side. Bruises marred every exposed part of her body. The doctor looked up at the whimper Solitar made.

"Fuck, Anastaas," Sheriff Gibson cursed seeing Solitar gaping at the body. "This ain't no fucking art show man, get her the hell outta here," he commanded.

Kurian grabbed Solitar's arm again but he didn't try to pull her away. Instead he said in a low voice, "What about her face, Solitar?" He had seen something in Solitar's ravaged expression, heard something in her cracked voice. She wasn't just experiencing the terrible demise of someone she knew. There was something else going on.

Solitar clutched at the collar of her shirt in front of her throat and she pointed at the body with the other. "That mark, that crooked X," she said, "I know it." Everyone there had stopped talking and watched Solitar. At her words they followed where she indicated and looked at the mark on Brittlyn's face. What appeared to be an imperfect X as if it lay on its side swimming with one side longer than the other was lashed on her right cheek.

Kurian wrapped an arm protectively around Solitar and asked, "What do you know about it? Do you recognize it? Have you seen that mark before?" He had, on Jennifer Aandersson.

Her body shuddered under his arm, he wrapped his other arm around her waist enclosing her in a safe embrace. The crowd grew completely silent waiting for her answer, only the wind nuzzling the leaves at the tops of the tallest trees made a sound.

"Yes," Solitar answered so quietly she barely made a sound, "on my mother." Collective gasps rang around the group and murmurings started up while others shushed people, they waited for more. But, Sheriff Gibson stalked over to the couple.

His face red, steam pouring out of his ears he snapped, "Do you mean your mother had cuts on her face that resembled that one? It's a fucking X or cross or someshit, hardly a unique cut. Listen Miss, you don't belong here, you need to get the hell out of my murder scene," he gave Kurian a nasty look for bringing her.

"No, Sheriff, the exact, precise mark, the one line longer than the other, the other side deeper than the first, you look carefully you'll see an almost undetectable hook at the end of the long line, the line almost curls. There are no other cuts on her face but that one. It would have been made by a...an unusual knife blade. It's called a-a Jagdkommando, it's a knife named for something to do with a manhunt command or something in the Austrian Armed Force's Special Operations. It's a three-edged blade that twists to a point." She paused, everyone there was gaping at her.

Solitar's voice shook, she explained, "My father had a knife from his grandfather from WWI and in one of his rages he made that identical mark on my mother. On purpose. He laughed when he did it. I read it all. That cut there," she blinked at the dead woman and quickly looked away, "it wasn't made by an accidental...ah, slash. It was done deliberately with that special kind of knife. It's a signature. Literally."

Gibson glared hard at her then glanced to Kurian who was also studying Solitar. Her face was wreathed in horror and grief, and fear, she wasn't making it up.

"Artclif," the man with the white hair in the blue smocks said to Gibson, "it's the same as on the other two vics. Jennifer Aandersson and Martha Zabka."

"You sure?" Gibson asked the doctor.

Saccomoto's lips pulled in, he nodded, let out a labored sigh. "Ayah," he muttered.

Gibson snarled at Kurian and Solitar, "You two, come with me, now."

Solitar's haunted eyes shown bright in her face, huge blue circles in a pale oval moon. She burrowed into the brace of Kurian's big arms.

"All right. Rut, bring the jeep for us there," Kurian told his friend as he and Solitar were hustled to the back of a police car.

In the car, Solitar whispered, "Sheriff, I need to stop at the Cresh, I have to get something."

"You don't need shit, girl," Gibson snapped from the front passenger side of the vehicle. Another officer was at the wheel. "You're just coming in to answer some questions."

She said, "No," shook her head and shivered. "You will need to see this. You must."

"Just do it, Sheriff," Kurian ordered.

Solitar couldn't tell how long it took them to get to the police station, she was in shock and her brain had stalled. In the back of the car Kurian kept his arm wrapped around her, holding her close to his chest. The warmth of his strong sheltering body helped with the chill that had taken her over. She bit her lip to stop her teeth from chattering but failed. She knew the driver could hear her, his shoulders were hunched up to his ears, all three men were stoically silent.

Kurian rolled both arms around her tucking her against his hard torso and he murmured things to her in his own language. She couldn't understand the words but the sound of his deep rumbling voice soothed her, subconsciously anyway. Her hands clutched the book in her lap that she had insisted they stop at the hotel and retrieve.

She scarcely registered the car stopping and Kurian helping her out. He and the sheriff flanked her as they entered the station. The building was large considering how poor the town was but it had been built long ago when the original town had flourished with ripe farmlands, prolific fishing and herds of roaming wild animals. In the beginning the gold mines brought the money and Ruwenstad soared. But the mines played out after years of excavating and they all slowly shut down starting 50 years ago until in the last 20 years there wasn't a nugget to be found. That was until a miner associated with Gatin de Muur ventured out and made a hit. Unfortunately it is a small hit. Beneficial to Gatin de Muur but less so for Ruwenstad and its people.

They passed through a metal detector. Solitar gaped as Kurian set the metal detector off. He said calmly, "I am armed."

The guard at the detector looked to Gibson who nodded for Kurian to proceed on through. She was surprised the sheriff allowed him to enter the station armed. The trio strode across a lobby, their boots studding over beige and white diamond tiling with gold specks that was polished but showed its age.

Solitar and Kurian followed the sheriff down one hall then up some stairs then down another hallway. He stopped in front of a door, pulled out keys and opened it. He held his arm out indicating for them to go in.

Inside, the faded brown carpet had bald spots and the pale blue walls were scraped and pocked. A large desk took up the back half of the room, it was piled with files and books and a laptop, landline phone and other essentials. A window was behind the big office chair looking out over the jail located behind the station. Books piled on shelves, and a cabinet lined a wall, to the side of the room was a round table and four chairs, Gibson motioned to them.

Kurian pulled a chair out for Solitar then settled on the one beside her. She sat stiffly with the book clasped in her lap. Gibson removed the police hat he wore and hung it on a rack by the door then he plodded over and dropped down with a grunt in a chair at the table.

"All right," Gibson said with a harsh sigh, "what is so bloody important about the book, Miss? And," he leaned in and squinted fiercely at her, "you better explain quick what you were blathering about in hysterics at the scene back there." He sat back and crossed one ankle over one knee, folded his arms over his chest and glared at her.

"Lose the aggressive attitude, Sheriff," Kurian growled and the two men glowered at each other.

"Yeah, sure. Okay, Miss," Gibson leaned in again to Solitar and said, "first off, who   the   hell   are   you?"

Chapter Sixteen

When Kurian opened his mouth to admonish the sheriff for his roughness, Solitar held up a hand and gave him a sad smile. "It's all right, Kurian." She lifted the book and very carefully set it on the table then looked down at it, her expression warped with misery. Drawing in a long breath to steady her nerves, she let it out slowly and began. "This is my mother's diary," she said, and set her palm on the book. The pages in the book were yellowed; the blue, fake leather cover was tattered. Across the front MY DIARY in white letters had peeled and turned grey with age.

Gibson blinked hard a few times then blustered, "What the hell? Who gives a shit? I thought you had the mystery to the goddamned killings in there, girl. Shit," he pushed his chair back and went to stand up. "I am too busy for this waste of time."

"Take it easy, Sheriff, hear her out. Sit down," Kurian ordered. The sheriff glared at him, then obeyed with a huff of annoyance as he plopped back down. The two men turned their gruff attention from each other to Solitar. Kurian gave her a short nod.

She found she was holding her breath as the men had their battle of wills, she let it out. "Okay." She stared at the book as she spoke. "I've never told anyone this, but, ah, when I was, oh, not yet four-years-old, I was traveling with my parents and my siblings. One day they left me at a rest stop and never came back."

"What the fuck?" Gibson barked, sitting up straight in his chair. "They left a little girl alone? I mean," the confusion gouged a deep vertical line of angry disbelief between his eyes. "They did come right back for you, right?"

Beside Solitar, Kurian had stiffened.

Shaking her head with a dour laugh, Solitar said, "No, they did not. Ever."

The sheriff's rough face paled. In his forties, he was still buff except for the tiny beer belly. He rubbed one of his broad shoulders then forced himself to calmly clasp his hands together and set them on the table. Dread in his voice he asked, "What happened to you?"

With the men's stunned attention on her Solitar shrugged. "The worst thing that could have happened, did."

"Huh," Gibson snorted mirthless, "you aren't dead, girl."

Kurian shot him a glare telling him to shut up. "Go on, honey," he said quietly to Solitar.

She couldn't look at them, she stared at the book. "Sometimes Sheriff, there are things worse than death."

Gibson blanched, his lips clamped together and his fingers tightened their grasp. "You're right, Miss, uh, didn't get your name?"

"It's Solitar Lyonne," she stated with no affect. "I am employed by the Gatin de Muur Company."

Gibson shot a glance at Kurian before he asked, "Your name is quite unusual, is it...uh, your original birth name?"

"Actually, no," Solitar replied with a wan smile. "I...well, I don't really remember my real name, it's been so long. After I was brought back to Brightlook Children's Home in Singapore the second time the foster care liaisons named me. They chose Solitar because I was obviously not wanted, and Lyonne because they said I fought my foster fathers...and brothers," she laughed unhappily, "like a little lion. Before then they placed me under only one name. The men who had taken me called me Poppet. That was the only name I was called until foster care legally had me named Solitar Lyonne."

Kurian and Gibson's eyes shifted to each other then back to her.

Gibson said with a husky sound in his voice, "The men who took you?"

Her shoulders sagged with an exhaled plague of memories she'd never told anyone before and had struggled to bury deep, so deep inside her shattered soul they couldn't climb out and strangle the life out of her. "Yes. At the rest stop. No one came for the longest time, then these two men, Barron and Grant, grabbed me and forced me into their car and took off with me." She sat silently contemplating the book under her palm.

Gibson cleared the thick discomfort from his throat and said, "Did they, uh, hurt you?"

She made a small dismal sound, her eyes misted. "Yes. Barron hurt me. Grant took the pictures."

Gibson coughed and repeated, "Pictures?" His first inclination was disbelief. The story was too...traumatic, unbelievable. Parents just don't dump their child out...there...for anyone to take? But, he peered harshly at the young woman. No, despair shrouded her like a vacuum of emptiness she kept nailed down under steel armor. Exquisite suffering performed in her unceasing nightmares like a rolling movie in those pretty agonized eyes. Gibson winced and shuttered his own eyes protectively against the visceral pain that lashed from her to him. She spoke the truth, and the truth was vile.

Solitar nodded. "Yeah, they'd dress me in tutus and princess outfits and bikinis and put me in poses, then undress me and do things to me...while...they...took pictures, videos. Their favorite was me standing and lifting my dress up to show my Little Mermaid panties. Before they removed them. Grant took the photos because he wasn't into little girls. He liked his women fully developed. Usually." She peered up at first Gibson then Kurian. Both men stared at her. Gibson's eyes were pinched, his mouth compressed.

Kurian's expression was a harshly carved blank, but his eyes burned black fire. This was what she meant by Orlando's assault of her not being the first time. She couldn't fight against Orlando because as a tiny child she couldn't fight against the perverts who hurt her. The mining job be damned, she was frozen in helplessness as her mind was still that captive, powerless child. She was a victim trapped in her past.

She said, "They, um, put pictures on the dark web so they could sell them and videos of…me."

"How long did this…atrocity go on, Miss Solitar?" Gibson asked. His voice held a slight tremor, he couldn't hide the effect her words had on him. He was devastated for the kidnapped, assaulted, exploited, *unwanted* child she'd been.

Solitar shrugged one slender shoulder. Her face and eyes were blank. She had suppressed the sordid memories for so long behind the practiced veneer, she hadn't brought them forward before now because she knew she couldn't go on if she did, she would have been irrevocably broken. She would have just laid down on the ground and…died.

But something bigger than her was going on now, women were being murdered, and she couldn't keep quiet about what she knew. She had to tell her secrets as grotesque as they were. She moved her hands to twine her fingers tightly and placed them in her lap.

"I think it was around, um, two years or so. They didn't let me out much, sometimes Barron would let me walk in the backyard when it was dark, with a leash around my…neck like I was his puppy." Her eyes closed, she made a tortured sound in the back of her throat. "Eventually someone in our neighborhood saw me and thought the way Barron and I interacted was weird, unnatural. They took a chance and called the police. Barron and Grant went to prison and I was put into the Brightlook Children's Home."

"So, uh," Gibson asked slowly as he digested her story, his face was red, he had a hard time looking at her. It didn't matter because her eyes were lowered in shame. "Did you get adopted?" his tone hopeful.

Her features bitter, the look in her tormented eyes came with a gruesome chuckle. "No. They tried three foster families, huh," she grunted glumly, "you would have thought the prior complaints from other kids would have deterred them, but," she shook her head. "Made no difference, they told me, there were too few places to place orphans they had no choice but to disregard accusations of alleged abused little girls."

"You were abused there as well?" The creak in Gibson's voice revealed how her story was souring his stomach and crazing his mind with sickness and rage. He dragged a sweaty palm down his face as if he could dispel her horrendous words.

Kurian reached over and clasped her two clutched hands in his one and gave her a gentle squeeze. She couldn't look at him, at neither of them. "They tried. Fathers and sons. Crept into my bed at night. But I had learned," a devious smile lifted the wretched corners of her sad mouth. "I hid all my cutlery. A butter knife isn't much yet still makes a nasty wound when slashed across skin, a fork in the hand even with the meagre strength of a child, they backed off quickly.

"They thought they could have sex with me and no one would find out, but they knew they couldn't explain copious bruising and such they would have produced while fighting and overpowering me and my weapons so they were forced to back off. But they were angry, so off I was shipped back to Brightlook. After the third time the Home gave up sending me out for foster so I stayed there until I aged out. We were schooled at Brightlook, however I was sent to apprentice at Regent & Livingston University for a Civil Engineering degree. As I earned my degree, recruiters solicited me for Gatin de Muur thus I ended up here at the mine."

"Fuck me," Gibson muttered, then frowned at the wording. He shot a glance at Kurian, but the dark man's stare was on the woman who sat with such desolate misery wrought in her face, the fingers tangling so hard they were white. Kurian worked to soften their clutching, their sadistic twisting. The slope of her drooping neck, eyes watered with the pain of the past that could never be erased.

Gibson mumbled, "Yeah, so, the book?" He needed to move on, his heart had taken a huge hit from the delicate, fragile young woman he would have to excuse himself and leave the room to get a grip if she went on with any more of her lovely past. She was right, sometimes there are things worse than death.

Solitar's eyes shifted to the book. When she moved her hands, Kurian moved his from covering them. She wanted to tell him thank you for his support, but the words caught in her throat. Sentiments were not a part of her make up. They had been eviscerated from her core a long time ago. "Yes," she said, "the book."

Both men forced themselves to sit back in their chairs to give her breathing space. She explained, "After I left Brightlook, I had dreams. I think they were suppressed memories of before I had been taken. When I still lived at home with my...loving family," the laugh was pure pain. "Anyway, pictures flashed in my head. A street sign, a church, a school, a house draped in beautiful lavender wisteria. I decided to try to trace where I came from originally. The street sign was the best clue."

"What was it?" Kurian asked if only to break his silence and a bit of the tension.

Her head slanted to him, she looked briefly then away. "Brandiwood Road. I remembered it because every time we traveled and were forced to return my mother would grimace and grouse, 'Ah there it be, that damned Brandiwood fucking Road.' I Googled it of course. There were three in the States. Somehow I had ended up in Singapore but when I returned to the United States for my apprenticeship it felt...familiar. I was sure I was originally from somewhere there. I mean," she laughed cynically, "I didn't look or sound like a native of Singapore."

The men nodded in unison at the blonde with the large blue eyes.

"So, I visited all three Brandiwood Roads. One in Avon Ohio, another in Denver Colorado, neither of them was it. The third in Magnolia Arkansas was the hit. I drove around the area until I found the church and school of my dreams, the wisteria was still on the big white house at the end of the street. I researched real estate listings and found the house we had lived in."

"That's uh," Gibson sat forward, his hands on his thighs, "good investigative work, Solitar." She nodded blankly. He said, "Did you find, uh, were your folks there? Siblings? It had been years since you…ah…"

"Since they dumped me?" She made a disparaging sound. "We had traveled from town to town but apparently the house was my grandma's and the family often returned to her when they ran out of funds. Which was constantly. They weren't happy times either. Grandma hated us and we hated her. I recall a few vicious slaps for spilling juice or something else. Anyway, my mom," tears welled, she dashed at them as they fell, "she was the only one there when I knocked on the door. My pop was briefly in the hospital, had emphysema. I think he's in remission and back home now. Judging by her black eye he still has the energy, and temper, to beat her. And," Solitar shrugged with a grimace, "she still lets him. Still…likes it."

"Did you confront her?" Gibson asked.

"Huh," Solitar snorted. "Tried to. She freaked out when I told her who I was, she hadn't recognized me of course, I was barely beyond a toddler when…well. She yelled, cursed at me, kicked me out. I came back a few days later and waited until no one was home and I broke in. I…needed to know who I was." She lifted her eyes to Gibson but he shrugged. Like he cared she broke into their home. She could have killed the bastards and he would do nothing. They deserved a lifetime of torture for what they'd done to their child.

"The only thing I took was her diary. I thought there might be a glimpse in there, a mention of why they…deserted me, left me like I was just a piece of trash. Had I done something so egregiously wrong they couldn't forgive? I mean, I was not even four, how bad could I have been? The least they could have done was adopted me out. Left me with the police, a neighbor, a relative, anything but what they did. Barron had told me when I reached an age that I was no longer, uh, desirable to him he would pimp me out. How's that for a future to look forward to?"

They were all silent for a few moments as the tears broke and streamed. Not only dumped, she had been unlucky enough to be picked up by two criminals. Worse yet, one of them was a sadistic pedophile. No policeman or kind couple found her, no, she was found by the worst of the worse. At least she'd dodged being forced into prostitution at eleven or twelve, whenever her femininity started to show.

Gibson rose heavily and retrieved a box of tissues from his desk and set them on the table in front of her. When she didn't move, Kurian plucked out a few and tucked them in her hands.

Wiping her eyes, Solitar went on. "The diary." Her gaze lit on it, stayed there, her jaw tensed. "She did write why I was…disposed of. Apparently, I wasn't the only one. Not the first, not the last. My folks didn't use birth control and apparently went at it like rabid rabbits. They couldn't afford all of us kids so occasionally they would toss one aside."

Both men made a shocked sound, their mouths popped, eyes bulged. "You're shittin' me," Gibson barked out, aghast. "They deserted more children? How many?"

One small shoulder rose then lowered. "I'm not sure, they may still be doing it. According to the book there were two boys before me and another girl after that they discarded. I remember one of the boys he was a year or so older than me. I had asked one day where he'd gone, he had suddenly disappeared. His chair stayed empty at the table. When I asked, Mom slapped me. I tried again a few days later and Daddy backhanded me and told me he'd beat my ass if I ever mentioned him again. He's really just a very hazy memory, I had forgotten him until I read the book."

Gibson waited a beat before asking, "What was his name?"

She pushed the book towards him. "It's all in there."

He stared down at the thing as if it had a rattle on its tail. He looked to her, asked, "The mark? The X? Tell me about that."

She shrugged again. "It's in there. Daddy beat all of us whenever the mood struck. Sometimes you just had to walk by him and he'd feel the need to haul off and slam his fist into your head. But I recall he beat Mom the most. Broken bones, internal damage, but she never complained."

Solitar smiled sardonically. "Said she loved him and he was the *man* therefore he had the right to discipline his family as he saw fit. I think," a blush rolled over her cheeks making them shiny pink. "She got off on the brutality. She liked it. She wrote in the book that the day he branded her with the X, it was how he had always signed his name, he had little education. His parents were migrants, he'd never learned to read and write. The sideways X with the curved line that ends in a tiny hook was his signature." She laughed drolly again.

"So, one day he marked her, literally signed his name on her cheek with a knife. It told her he owned her, and…" the blush darkened to mortification. "She loved it. The dominance, it…thrilled her." She nodded towards the book. "I actually recall it, the blood, can never forget how she bled that day. She looked like a horror film come to life." Solitar's sigh twisted with anguish. "Read it, you'll see. She was so proud of it, it's in there. That mark that was on poor Brittlyn is the same. I swear, Sheriff, it has to be someone in my family that killed her. My dad would still be young enough to do it, but he's sick, so it's more likely it's one of the brothers. Or sisters. Who knows?"

Gibson reached for the book but Kurian grasped it before he could. The sheriff shifted in his chair and glowered at Kurian. "Son," he started but stopped. He turned to Solitar and asked, "Have you heard of Martha Zabka or Jennifer Aandersson?"

She ran the names through her head. There were so many people, those from the Home, the mine, the university, the locals. Then she remembered. "Not Martha, but I read about Jennifer."

"Those were two other victims. Murdered the same way as Brittlyn, had the same sliced mark on their faces. Doc Saccomoto said the mark was done by a strange knife, left a curled sort of gouged line with a hook on the end of one of the lines."

Solitar's gaze skated from one man to the other. "Yes. I told you, the Jagdkommando. You see, it has to be someone in my family. The mark, brand, whatever it is and the weapon. Both too strange and unique to be coincidental. Also with the…" her lids lowered covering the shame, she trailed off.

"With the what?" Gibson prodded.

Solitar shifted with discomfort. Her hands folded primly, twisting again in her lap, she told them, "Brittlyn, although was on the athletic side, she kind of, well, looks like me. She's ah, taller yet still petite, small boned, blonde hair, blue eyes. What I read about Jennifer Aandersson too, sort of the same description well, I think…" Again she trailed off as the shameful red colored her fair complexion.

"Think what, Solitar?" Kurian asked.

"Well, I look like my mother although she was bigger, on the tough side, but," her voice strained she said, "I think the killer may be one of my brothers and he's…you know…killing my mom in effigy. If she did to him what she did to me, and if the same wretched horrible events took him over, or worse, when they dropped him by the roadside like shuckings from yesterday's corn, well, it's possible, you know what I mean? The news said Jennifer had been sexually assaulted so it's more probable it was a man instead of a woman."

Gibson plunked back, his spine slapping the chair, a whoosh of comprehension blew from his lungs with muttered expletives.

They sat silently again for a few minutes letting her words wrap around and sink in. Then, Kurian asked her, "Would you recognize your brothers, especially the one near your age if you saw him?"

Her eyes closed, Solitar shook her head. "No. I've thought about it, tried to remember what he looked like, what Dad looked like, any of my brothers or sisters, but no. I was too young, it was too long ago. I remember more the haze of the incident than the actual boy." A chill trembled through her, her eyes watered again. "Gosh, Hubie's going to be devastated. He and Brittlyn, they were dating, it was new."

Gibson moved his bulk on his chair, the cushion scrunched and the wood creaked.

Kurian asked, "Could the killer be this Hubie fellow?"

Solitar's brow creased confused. Gibson's forehead wrinkled.

"The killer. Your brother. Could it be Hubie?" Kurian said.

"I-" Her mouth dropped then clamped closed. She considered his suggestion. Then, "I don't think so. He's from Tennessee and he talks about his family, his little sister just got engaged. He's shown us pictures, no," she shook her head, blonde hair flailing across her back and shoulders. "His mom came out for his birthday a few months ago."

"We'll check him out, he could have faked things, had someone pose as his mother, we have a better hook with that receipt for the Lote Maestro Tequila," Gibson tugged on his belt while Kurian grabbed the book and rifled through it.

While flipping pages, Kurian said to Gibson, "Be easy enough to check out. You'll have to review all the people involved with the mine not just the locals, check alibis."

"Yes, I know," Gibson replied. Noticing Kurian stop flipping and lowered his head to read intently, Gibson asked, "Find something interesting?"

Chapter Seventeen

Kurian's gaze flicked to Solitar then to the page in front of him. He read out loud, " 'Oh, I hated to leave me little boy Gareth that day. My oh my, the lad was just as handsome as his da, me beloved Jack.'" Kurian commented, "She drew a happy face. I can picture the woman sitting at the table penning in this book shaking her head with an affectionate smile and a sad sigh as she writes."

He read on, " 'La, me Jack has a wicked wicked temper he does. He knows he's sick, a verra evil man he is, when we're in our cups we laugh and he calls himself Jack the Ripper.'"

A strangled sound came from Solitar as she lowered her head with the weight of familial shame weighing it down.

Kurian read on, " 'Yeah, one day he was so angry. He'd beaten a hooker to death and slashed her blinkin' throat and the bobbies almost caught him. I made the mistake of scolding him and he took that knife his da had gived him and he signed his name on me cheek. It was an odd X, you know, his signature. He couldn't never spell good like me. Gor, how it hurt, how it bled. But, secretly I looved it. Me man had branded me, made me his. What a ghastly scar it was for awhile there. Jack looved it though. Said it gave me a rakish look, said it made him hot, like I was a bloody wild woman! Heavens-' "

Gibson interjected, "Hell, I can swear I hear her girlish giggle as she writes."

Kurian agreed, "*Ja.*" After a quick glance at Solitar he said, "Here she writes that she misses her boy Gareth so much. 'Lad had me own corn silk blonde hair and vivid blue eyes, little Rosilita was even fairer than us. Should have kept him and drowned Rosilita then but Jack said Gareth was bigger and ate more. Prolly have to dump Rosilita soon enough as I'm pregnant again. The older children get so jealous when I'm knocked up. Me ma sent a letter the other day. Gor how I hated that hovel we lived in in East Jaywick, Tendring district of Essex back in bloody England. Squalor it were. Discolored, double-level crummy houses squashed right up against another with weeds as high as a coon's ass, trash on the sidewalks and broken down cars littering the streets. That old field up at the end of the street with rats and snakes, made me big brother Drew walk me through to get to school.

'Ewie, so glad when me uncle snatched me when I was eleven and hid me on his boat to America. He pretended I was his daughter even though I shared his bed. Had to find papers to make me legal. Uncle Warrick was insane with jealousy the day I runned off with me Jack Karelli. But so handsome and charming me Jackie boy was.'" Kurian looked to Solitar and said, "Your real name is-"

"Rosilita Karelli," she supplied. "I know. She recorded the dates of most of the births and Rosilita's matches my age. I read the book so many times I pretty much have it memorized. When she had her babies and later when they dumped us they did it while on travels so the law wouldn't come after them for missing children."

"You ah, want to sign your deposition with, ah, Rosa- ah, what was-"

Solitar spoke over the sheriff. "Rosilita Karelli. No. I am Solitar Lyonne now. My degrees, everything I am is Solitar Lyonne. Rosilita Karelli is dead."

"Ah," Gibson paused. "When we catch the killer, if it is in fact your brother, Gareth Karelli, you'll need to testify to this book and all, and you'll be recorded as Rosilita Karelli."

Her eyes widened, Solitar said, "But you don't know that it's him for sure. It could be any one of the brothers. My mother, Angelina, wrote," she skipped a breath, said with a small rasp, "that they dumped several of us and drowned, um, one baby. Plus there were other siblings it looks like they kept. Even a couple of babies after me," she remarked bitterly. Her body curled into itself, her head tucked down, a tear fell on her clasped hands. "They started getting money from the State for the children so they started keeping their little cash cows."

"I need to contact the American police to pick up those bastards." Changing the subject, Gibson asked Kurian, "You get anything new on Serug Partay? Did you dead end at his body and the tequila receipt?"

Kurian's gaze jumped from Solitar to him, he gave a curt shake of his head as if to say they would discuss it later. In private.

Gulping several hiccups of air, "Did you say Lote Maestro Tequila?" Solitar asked, her voice wavering weakly.

The men shared a glance. Gibson said, "Why do you ask?"

Fiddling with her fingers, Solitar sighed. "Daddy gambled. On anything. Horses, dogs, football games. I recall some but most of this is in the book. When he won big, which of course wasn't often, that's what he'd buy. He'd pour tiny shots of it and say, 'Yes, Maestro for the Maestro, Master for the Master.' I remember because he would drink for days and repeat that jingle endlessly. Otherwise he'd settle for Jose Cuervo. Mom wrote all that in the book," she inclined her head to the diary.

Kurian closed the book and pushed it towards Gibson. Gibson said to Solitar, "All right. Is there anything else you can think of that can help?"

She silently shook her head. Then replied, "No. The diary has more information than I could ever supply. I was too young before they…" she let out a belabored exhale. "If I think of anything I will certainly get in touch with you, Sheriff."

Kurian said, "It is too much a coincidence the killer is here in Ruwenstad at the same time as Solitar. He came here because of her." He stood up and put a hand on the back of Solitar's chair. "*Oke*, let me get her home. I want a copy of that diary, I will send Colby by to pick it up, and I insist on police protection for Miss Lyonne, Sheriff."

"Huh, yeah," Gibson grunted and picked up the book. He stood as Kurian pulled back Solitar's chair and she got up. "Don't have enough personnel for that son. They even closed the school due to lack of funds to keep it open. Got the kids now down at the Mary of Sorrows Church. Can only alert the Cresh staff to keep a sharp eye out, what?" He asked as Solitar and Kurian both made snorting sounds.

"Nothing, Sheriff. You know things are pretty lax at the hotel," Kurian replied. "I will put my own men on her. Come on, Solitar, I will take you home."

Rutger had Solitar's jeep brought to the police station, they found it parked outside and they drove to the hotel.

At the Cresh, Kurian walked her to her door and told her to wait. He went inside alone to check out that no one was hiding in wait for her then told her she could come in when he cleared the room.

Solitar entered and set her purse down on the small desk with a heavy sigh.

Kurian closed the door and said, "*Oke*, this is how it will be." He waited for her to stop moving and face him. "You do not open your door to anyone but me or Rutger. I have two other men, Kristjan Kristoff and Ivar Razir. I will introduce them to you tomorrow. One of us will be with you at all times until this…perp, is caught."

"Oh but," Solitar sucked in a breath. "That's not necessary. If he's my brother he has no reason to want to hurt me-"

Kurian grasped her arms and gave her a little shake of irritation. "Solitar, for fuck's sake. If he is killing women in your mother's image he most certainly will come after you. It already appears he is here because you are, as I said, it is no way a coincidence. The murders did not start until shortly after you arrived in Ruwenstad."

"But why would he want to kill me? I suffered the same fate that he did."

"Geez, Woman, who knows what he will do? If he followed you here it is doubtful he just wants to catch up on old times. Hell, he would have contacted you for a meet if that were so."

"So why hasn't he tried to contact me then? I mean, if I am his sister and he came after me, he must want…oh, I don't know, he must want to talk to me, right?"

"Baby, who the fuck knows? The guy is clearly insane. He is raping and beating innocent women to death and branding them. Maybe he has ideas to grab you too but you tend to stay withdrawn from the public other than the mine. You do not, ah *don't* go out much and the Cresh is generally crowded with mine staff thereby you have safety in numbers. So," he stroked her arms with his thumbs as he spoke, "for now, as

101

I was saying, you do not go anywhere alone, I mean without one of my men. We have no idea who your brother could be, he could be masquerading as a local or a mine employee. We trust no one but my people."

"Just who are your people, Kurian?" Solitar stepped out of his grasp and folded her arms over her chest. Her brows drew down in a frown. "I've just realized I've asked Rutger numerous times where he works, where he's from, but he evades my questions, changes the subject. Just who…" She pierced him with a suspicious glare. "And you, Kurian. You were allowed into the ring of law enforcement at the scene of Brittlyn's murder and Sheriff Gibson treats you as a- a fellow officer when in actuality you are a mine employee. Who are you, really?"

A smile tugged at the side of his mouth. "I swear, my real name is Kurian Anastaas. For now, that is all you need to know. So-"

Solitar put several feet between them. "Wait, how do I know that you are trustworthy, you could be my brother. You are not just a simple superintendent. I should have been suspicious when they brought in an additional super tech that we did not need. Who-"

"Enough, Solitar." He reached for her but she moved back. Frowning, he said, "Solitar, if I was going to harm you, hell, girl, we have been alone. *Verdomd*, we were alone way out in the woods while I taught you how to shoot for Pete's sake. Seriously, do we look one iota alike?" She was clearly soft light to his hard dark. He loomed brawny feet taller than her dainty height.

Warily watching him, Solitar didn't know what to do. "I think you are some kind of a cop, Kurian. I don't know why you are really here. According to when Gibson said the first murder occurred, you arrived before then so I don't think you were sent here to investigate the killings. And, no, I don't think you are the killer, my alleged brother. I just don't know."

"You know you can trust me, Solitar. Gibson knows who I am, he would not have let me leave with you if he had any doubt. So, back to my instructions." His mouth twitched at her rolling eyes.

"*Ja*, my instructions that you will follow to the letter or I swear I will paddle your ass, girl. This is your life we are talking about. This freak has beaten women to death. *Verdomd*, who knows what he is capable of doing. So, you will do as I say. One of my men will be with you whenever you are not here. The doors at the Cresh are made of the finest steel. The cartel kingpin who built the place was concerned for his safety. There were other drug lords that would have wanted to fight him for his kingdom. In fact, he was assassinated by one of them, but it did not happen inside these walls."

Solitar blinked rapidly at him. She'd heard the story of the ancient assassination but with all the current murders, her own life threatened in the fields by Jared, it was a lot to take in. She just wanted to do her job and mind her own business.

One eye squinted at him. "But you want me to keep quiet about the coca fields…" Like a light bulb popped over her head, her eye rounded. "You aren't here for the killings, you're here for the cocaine. That's it, isn't it? You're here in some relation to the coca growing here. Right? Tell me, Kurian, tell me what is going on here?"

He took a long step and grasped her arm to keep her from retreating from him. "Let it go for now, Solitar. I will tell you what is going on at some point, but not now. Right now we worry about keeping you safe." He slid his hand under her jaw and cupped it, lifting it up. "I want you to carry the gun with you at all times, even when you are with me or one of my men. Don't open the door to anyone, don't go anywhere without one of us with you. Do you hear me?"

She tugged at her arm not exactly appreciating being ordered around. "I'm a big girl, Kurian. I've taken care of myself so far. I don't need-" He squeezed her jaw to stop her talking.

"You are wrong, little scorpion, don't snap that stinging tail at me. No, you have not done such a good job protecting yourself so far. Just do as I say, *oke*?" He didn't wait for her response, he lifted her chin higher and settled his mouth on hers and she was instantly swept off the planet into a maelstrom of sensation. When she weakened, her mouth softened, he pushed at her lips to spread them open, slid his tongue inside and then ground on her until he felt her lips quiver. He hugged her tight, her breasts smashed against his hard chest and he felt her turn to liquid fire in his arms.

But, it wasn't the time. She was too vulnerable, and he needed to get out and meet with his people. Reluctantly, Kurian squelched his own fire and set her from him. He smiled, a real smile for a change. Her eyes shimmered with a glaze of arousal, her tongue swirling her lips as if trying to taste him. Her chest panted, he didn't dare look down at it or her clothes would be in shreds on the floor, and they would be lying atop them.

"I, ah, have to go. Lock the door, do not open it unless it is me or Rutger until you know my other men. I will call you if I send one to you. Wait for one of us to take you to the kitchen for dinner."

Her lashes flapped up and down in disorientation and confusion at her response to his kiss. "I-I don't-"

"Just say yes, honey," he instructed with a cool smile. Holding her head he made her nod like a puppet.

She uttered a faint, "Okay."

"Good. Later, my small scorpion," he said. Setting a kiss on her forehead he strode to the door, instructed, "Lock it after me," and he was gone.

Chapter Eighteen

Kurian grabbed his motorbike after he left Solitar and took off for the city. The city wasn't a giant of industry by any leaps and bounds, it was small but sprawled widely around the main avenues of linking squares. The center of Ruwenstad was a hodge-podge of connecting streets as mom and pop businesses had sprung up like toadstools and some bigger companies took over some of them. There wasn't even a train, they used the rivers for most of their transporting of goods and supplies shipped in from the sea.

The top shelf tequila the red-headed homeless man Serug Partay bought for someone, and Kurian was determining at this point that the someone was Gareth Karelli. Karelli had Partay buy it because he wanted the entire expensive bottle and knew that it would draw attention to whomever bought it. Then he killed Partay so he couldn't finger him.

A lot to go through for a few lousy cocktails, however eventually Gareth would figure as the murders continued the cops would start canvassing, asking about anyone unusual hanging around, any unusual activity. Someone might speak up and mention the purchase of an expensive bottle of booze bought by a stranger in an indigent city thus he used the homeless guy as a smokescreen.

Kurian had worked the mines long enough that he knew the miners had money but they weren't the sort to spend their hard earned bucks on expensive liquor. Kurian figured after the bottle ran out Gareth would hit the higher, but not the super high-end bars for his drink. Killing people for buying him a bottle in a liquor store every time he wanted to binge would end up with copious amounts of dead people and ultimately there would be some mistake that would lead to Gareth.

There were only a few high-end establishments in Ruwenstad and if he was smart, Gareth would avoid those because he would be more noticeable in a small more elite crowd made up of politicians, wealthy retirees and businessmen. Visiting hunters and fishermen, any new strangers would be noticed in the town if they threw big bucks around. Gareth would not want to be noticed, that's why he had Partay buy the Lote Maestro.

He's likely finished the bottle off by now and wants more. Kurian figured he'd stick to the medium priced bars where he could blend into a large crowd of drinkers and still order a better liquor, just not uber expensive. Kidnapping, raping, beating, murdering and signing off on his victim's faces, Karelli has a huge ego. He wouldn't hit the seedy honky-tonks, after paying the big money for the Lote Maestro, Gareth has rich taste, he would think himself too good for the cheap dives and cheaper alcohol.

Kurian called his friends and gave them a description of what he thought Gareth Karelli would look like so they could cover the docks, boatyards, rental agencies for apartments and vehicles, and other places he might hang out. He had to have rented something to get around. He certainly didn't carry Jennifer Aandersson over his shoulder for miles down a city street before dumping her in that alley, or Martha Zabka out in that field, or Brittlyn down that lonely dark road. Gareth arrived before Kurian and his men so he likely was able to get his hands on a jeep.

How many natural blond, blue-eyed males over 25 could there be in a village filled with mostly dark haired, dark eyed people? Yes, he assumed Gareth's hair hadn't darkened. Angelina Karelli wrote that both Gareth and Rosilita aka Solitar, looked just like her and she had to be at least in her thirties or older when she wrote some of the later diary entries and she had gone on at length that people complimented her on her bright, natural blonde hair.

He parked in front of the Sunflower on the Green. Surprisingly, as poor as the town was they still had their golfers. Opening the door he inhaled the cool air gratefully. The Sunflower was one of the few establishments to have air conditioning. It was as good as any place to get started. He first went to the hostess to ask if she noticed any blond nonlocals, then he'd hit the rest of the staff and then the customers as they came in and curled around the U shaped bar.

"Darn it," Solitar groused holding the charger to her phone in her hand, "left my cell in the glove box." She started for the door, then paused. Kurian had told her not to leave without him or one of his men with her. "Well," she muttered, "I'll just run downstairs to the lot and come right back up. Kurian will never even know I left the room."

Her hand on the door handle she paused again. Kurian Anastaas was one of those intimidating men that frightened people just taking a glance at him. He had threatened to spank her if she disobeyed him. Spank her! Right. He wouldn't dare. She was a grown woman, no one told her what to do. On that note, she opened the door and stuck her head out.

Peering up and down the hall, she didn't see or hear a soul. *Just run down the stairs, out to the lot, grab my phone and be back upstairs in a flash*, she told herself. Making sure she had her keys, she closed the door and hurried to the stairwell.

Outside, she took a quick sweep of the parking lot, it was mostly empty, everyone should be at the mine. Her boots crunched on the gravel lot as she made her way around the side of the hotel to where she'd parked her jeep. She opened the front passenger door and took her cell from the glove compartment and slipped it into her pocket. She locked and closed the door and now to rush back inside-

"Are you Solitar Lyonne?" A deep voice from behind halted her. She turned around and two men stood near enough to block her from leaving the perimeter of her jeep.

"Um," she uttered uneasily, she didn't recognize either of them. They both appeared Hispanic with olive-toned skin, dark hair and eyes. The older man looked in his fifties maybe, he had a few grey hairs at his temples and in his goatee. Both tall, the younger male perhaps in his thirties was stockier than the elder man, he was bulky with muscles under a loose button down and jeans. The older man wore a perfectly tailored grey suit.

"I asked you a question, Woman. Are you Solitar Lyonne?" The older man spoke.

Solitar was immediately on edge. They both looked sinister, and the older man's dark voice had a dangerous shade that he didn't try to hide. Her eyes swung back and forth between the pair then beyond searching for help. Dare she scream? The younger male pushed his shirttail up exposing the gun holstered at his hip. It was a clear threat.

"Sergio, check the glove box for ID," the older man ordered.

"*Si, Jefe.*" Sergio snatched her keys from her hand and opened the jeep and the glove compartment and pulled out the rental contract. Skimming it, he muttered, "*Si, es ella, Jefe,* it is her." He tossed the contract on the seat, threw the keys at Solitar who caught them, and slammed the door so hard Solitar jumped.

The older man's lids levered down like a reptile's. His voice heavy with a Spanish accent he announced, "I am Simón Bolívar."

Tucking the keys in her pocket, she blinked at him then her eyes latched onto the gun on Sergio's hip.

Suddenly Bolívar slapped her. With a cry, Solitar's head smacked to the side, her hand went to her cheek. "Now, we begin again. You are Solitar Lyonne. You are the one that stumbled onto Jared DiCello's coca crop. I am told you are the kind that will go to the police. You have not yet. I am wondering is that because you are afraid of Jared's retribution? Or," his eyes narrowed, "are you hoping for some kind of payoff for yourself. A cut of the profits *tal vez*, perhaps?"

When she just peered over her hand at him, he raised his fist as if to strike her again. "Answer me, Woman or I will beat you to death right here. You will be nothing left but a puddle of blood and pulverized bones. Which will it be?"

Sergio stepped closer to her to prevent her from running. He was terrifying. A husky block of a man with a Fu Manchu mustache, and hair that went to his collar. His onyx eyes were cold and vicious, they hadn't stopped trolling up and down her body since they got there. "*Jefe*, we're gonna take her anyway, whaddya care why she kept her mouth shut? Come on, I'll toss her in the back seat and I can have my turn while Pedro drives. You can watch from the front if you wanna then we'll switch." He reached out to grab her.

Solitar shrank back from his hands and shouted, "Wait! Why do you want me? I don't know you, I don't know Jared, just leave me alone- I'll pretend I never saw you!"

Bolívar's laugh was deep and mean. "Jared took over the fields that idiot drug lord started. Jared and his people keep the coca crop going to feed their families and pay for electric and water and medicine. I have a much larger organization deep in the jungle. I will decimate his fields. I do not want any attention drawn to this area. Too many people already know about his fields, and now you, bitch from another country knows as well. It will only be a matter of time before the police find Jared's and then it will lead to my fields."

"So," he nodded to Sergio who reached for Solitar again. "I will kill you, that will stop the flow of info leaving Ruwenstad, then I will burn Jared's crop to the ground. I just need to keep my head down until your people play out the mine and move on. Then I can bring my production back up to warp speed. Women are flighty, they will assume you ran off with some lover, we will start a rumor. Perhaps you have an eye for our Sergio here, eh?"

"We ain't killin' her yet, *Jefe*," Sergio grabbed Solitar's arm. "Not until I get my piece. Doncha want a taste of her too? Bitch is smokin'."

Bolívar's nasty grin snaked over her body. "Oh *si*, get her in the car and get those clothes off-"

"Aahh!" Sergio howled when Solitar kneed him in the groin and then she ran. Scrabbling over the gravel she ran as fast as she could around to the front of the Cresh- A fist in her hair jerked her backwards, she screamed- Footsteps pounded up and Bolívar raced to a stop in front of her.

Panting, he slapped her hard then bent over with his hands on his knees to catch his breath. He growled breathless, "Good job, Pedro. Get her in the fucking car and let's go."

Solitar couldn't see the man who twisted his fist in her hair from behind. He clamped a hand over her mouth as she screamed again and started kicking when Sergio caught up to grab her legs.

The two men started to lift her, Sergio snarled, "Wait until I get you in the car, *puta*, you're gonna pay for that kick, bitch. I'm gonna fuck you til you bleed and then some. You're gonna beg me to kill you before I'm done with-" He suddenly made a terrible gacking sound, then there were thumping sounds and Solitar was suddenly released.

She fell hard on her butt and saw a blur as a man was pummeling Pedro then he turned and bashed his fist into Sergio's throat. Sergio dropped to his knees choking. Pedro lay unmoving with the man hovering over him.

"L- lookout!" Solitar shrieked as Simón Bolívar whipped out a gun and aimed it at the man beating his thugs. The man leapt in the air and slung his leg around kicking the gun out of Bolívar's hand.

"Fuck!" Bolívar roared at the pain and grasped his injured hand. A car raced up the lot and came to a screeching halt. Sergio stumbled and caught Solitar slamming her to the ground so hard she crashed to her knees then he hit her on her back and jolted the air from her lungs when she smacked onto her belly. He rolled her over, straddled her and strung his hands around her neck and squeezed. She couldn't suck in a breath, she couldn't even kick her legs out or hit at him.

Her rescuer left Bolívar and ran to her. Two men climbed out of the car, grabbed up Pedro, and they and Bolívar hopped into the car and they took off. Her rescuer grasped Sergio's shirt and tore him off Solitar.

She lay on her back gasping like a floundering fish trying to suck air into her flattened lungs. Her rescuer knelt beside her and Sergio jumped up and leaped into the first car and the car sped off spitting gravel before the door even closed behind him.

"You *oke*, Miss, I will call an ambulance." Her rescuer patted her arm gently. He sounded just like Kurian. Solitar sucked in a gasp of air. He rolled a beefy arm around her back and helped her sit up.

"You- you're a friend of-" she heaved and coughed, wiping the tears that spurted from her eyes.

"*Ja*, Kurian. I am Ivar Razir. You were not to leave the building. Kurian sent me to guard you. What the fuck are you doing out here?" He wore beige khakis and an army green t-shirt and boots. His dark hair was medium length with a strong jaw and nose. Scars decorated parts of his harsh face. "You put yourself at such risk, if you were my woman you would not be sitting comfortably for a week."

Solitar struggled to get to her feet but she'd hurt her knees when Sergio slammed her to the ground. Her legs buckled and she gave out a little cry. Ivar swept her up in his arms and marched to the Cresh. He carried her upstairs without nary a heavy breath all the way to her room. He set her on her feet but kept his arm around her holding her steady.

"Your key," he said with his hand out.

She fumbled her key out of her pocket and they went inside. Ivar stuck his head out the door to check the halls before closing and locking it.

Staggering on shaky legs and injured knees, Solitar made it to a chair and flopped down on it. "I, uh, thank you Mr. Razir. I don't know what I would have done if you hadn't come along. They said they were going to kill me because of Jared and the cocaine crops and-"

"*Ja*, after they all took their turn fucking you."

She had hoped he hadn't heard that part. "Listen, there isn't any reason why we need to share what happened, uh, down there with Kurian." She rubbed an injured knee. "Just, let me buy you dinner or something as a way to thank you, all right?" He didn't appear the type to accept money for rescuing a damsel in distress.

He leaned a hip against an end table and fished his cell from his khaki pocket. He dialed and put the phone to his ear. "*Ja*, K. I am here. When I arrived there were men in the parking lot assaulting her. They hit her and were shoving her in their car." He nodded.

Solitar rolled her eyes. So much for not telling Kurian. At least he left off the part about-

"*Ja*, K, said they were going to rape her, all of them before killing her. *Nee*, I do not know who they were. There was an older dude in a suit. *Nee*, she has not explained her reason for being out of her room. *Ja*," he glanced at her then switched into a different language and she didn't know what he was saying.

Ivar spoke for another minute then hung up. Curtly, he asked her, "Where is your aspirin?" He was a strapping man like Kurian, had the same dark, cold edge in his eyes and military bearing that Kurian carried.

"Huh?" Her head came up.

"Aspirin. K said pop you full of a few until he gets here and can check out your injuries."

"I am fine," she insisted, pulling her legs up in the chair curling them to the side and winced at the pain.

He nodded. "Uh huh. He said if you refused the aspirin I was to haul your ass to the hospital."

Her brows sprung up. "What? No, I'm fine. You can't-"

"Sure I can. Got you up here with no prob, did I not? Now, where is your aspirin?" He eyed her purse on the table.

"I'll get it." She moved her legs.

"*Nee*. You do not move. I said I will get it, where is it?"

She sighed. "It's in the medicine chest in the bathroom."

"*Oke*. I get them then I make you tea." He disappeared.

Staring at the empty hall, Solitar mumbled to herself, "Of course Kurian wasn't serious about spanking me if I left this room. I'm sure he wouldn't. Ivar said the same thing. Maybe in their country it was acceptable for males to discipline their females?" Oh dear.

Chapter Nineteen

Kurian was so infuriated he couldn't put his whole attention into circulating the crowd of the third bar he'd been to searching for Gareth Karelli. Someone had tried to snatch Solitar. His stomach crimped. Ivar said they had hit her, they planned to assault her and then kill her. Ivar assumed, and Kurian agreed it was probably a drug lord, a cartel perhaps. They had mentioned Jared's operation, the guy Kurian had rescued her from in the coca fields.

Damn, the woman was trouble on legs. Ivar said as he was driving in he'd seen Solitar give the one guy a knee to the nuts and ran when he crumpled, good for her, at least she wasn't totally helpless. She was small and delicate, easy quarry, maybe some of the lessons he'd given her had helped stall the abduction long enough for Ivar to rush into action.

He gave up. He couldn't concentrate on what he was doing. Images of a beaten Solitar kept floating in his vision. Ivar said she'd been slapped a couple of times and had injured her knees, but still, he had to go see for himself that she was all right.

Taking the stairs two at a time, shortly after his knock Ivar opened the door and stepped aside for Kurian to enter.

"Miss Solitar." Ivar gave her a curt bow and he left closing the door behind him.

"Oh! Hey, wait-" She pushed to get out of the chair to give her rescuer a proper thank you and goodbye but the black look on Kurian's face, and the unsubtle jutting of his chin indicating for her to stay seated gave her pause. He was angry, very, his body practically vibrated with it. "You look, ah, thirsty, Kurian. Ivar made me some tea, shall I pour you a-"

A few long strides and he was in front of her, preventing her from leaving the chair. "Solitar," his voice deep and husky, eyes narrowed to fierce slits, his mouth a harsh line, he said, "what part of do not leave this room did you not understand?"

She scooched back in the chair a bit to get away from the sting of his wrath. "Listen, Kurian," she sounded more firm than she looked with those large eyes wide, lashes flapping over them. "I think we need to come to an understanding. You are not the boss of me, I am. You can't tell me what to do. Now," she plucked at the hem of her shirt. "I do appreciate the timeliness and fortitude of your friend, Ivar, I have to admit it was quite fortuitous his arrival. And, wow, that man can fight! I mean, have you ever seen him-"

In a flash Kurian was leaning over her with his hands on the chair arms. "I will not have women I am involved with killed on my watch, Solitar," he breathed harsh air at her.

"Involved?" She inched back until her spine was plastered against the back of her chair. "We are not involved. And if we were, I still don't take orders from-"

He leaned over so far their noses were in danger of touching. "That is where you are wrong, *kwetsbare schorpioen,* my small scorpion, you are way out of your league out here and no one employed by or at the mine appears to be taking responsibility for your safety including you. For God's sake, woman, there is a serial killer on the loose who is murdering women that resemble you, you were almost killed when you stumbled onto an illicit cocaine operation, and now you were again almost abducted by a likely drug lord, or a head of a cartel.

"These men are ruthless and violent and your life is not worth a snap of their fingers. Their livelihood is not a game to them. You are not capable of protecting yourself against them, no," he held a hand up as she opened her mouth to protest. "These are experienced criminals with brawn and weapons and you are not equipped to fight them. If you think otherwise then you are wearing fucking rose colored glasses. I am not criticizing you as a woman," *well, not entirely,* "just," he took a breath, dragged a hand through his hair.

He leaned back into her and said, "There is only one of you and teams of them, Solitar, you cannot hope to fight them alone."

"I," her chest fell with the resigned sigh. "But I am alone, Kurian. It's better that way."

The sharp angles of his face softened a tad. "Why is that?"

Shifting uncomfortably in her seat she said, "I am broken, Kurian. There. That's it. I can depend on no one but myself."

"You have friends, I have seen Camara and that Picola woman, what is her name, ah, Daniela? Camara mentioned she brought you chicken soup when you were ill a month ago." He nodded. "*Ja,* I have heard both of them encourage you to go out with them. Although at the moment I would not encourage you to go out without strong male escorts, such as myself and my men."

"They are not my friends, Kurian. I don't have the...emotional capacity for friendship, for caring about another person. Look how I hurt Colby. I am wired to rules and laws, you break them you pay. Really, Colby hadn't committed a serious crime, but still, I had to turn him in. You were there, you saw how devastated he and his girl Lili-Mae were."

"Hmm." Kurian clasped his hands behind his back and rocked on his heels. "Let me see what they did to you." He bent and cupped the side of her face gently, turning her one way then the other. A nasty growl rolled from his clenched jaw at the red handprint on her cheek and a bruise on the other. He stroked the pad of his thumb over the bruise. Then he crouched and uncurled one leg and inspected the bruised knee then the other. He squeezed them lightly and looked to her with an arched brow. "How is the pain? Tell me from one to ten."

Embarrassed, she mumbled, "The aspirin has taken the sting away, the shock and fright hurt worse than the injuries. I am fine, Kurian."

He examined her for another minute to satisfy himself that she didn't need a doctor and sighed. His eyes on the bruise on her cheek, his mouth flattened to an iron line and his lids lowered, hiding the girth of his rage. Then he stood and said, "About this lack of caring you say you have. What about animals? Dogs, cats? I have seen you, you cannot deny that you give them treats."

Her eyes rounded in surprise. "I didn't know anyone saw…I mean, it's nothing. It keeps them from biting and barking at me, that's all." She moved to stand up and he stepped back, not far, just enough for her to gain her feet. "You see, I have no desire to have friends, companions, people only betray you, it's better to trust only myself. You can't break a heart if you haven't got one."

"Ah, *min schorpioen,*" a half-grin lifted the side of his hard mouth. "But you lie, even to yourself. I know what is going on. You turned young Colby in to the sheriff but you also plead on his behalf asking for leniency. You recommended he do community service in lieu of jail time or a fine he would be unable to pay. That was deliberately two-fold on your part. First was punishment, he needed that or he might do the crime again and perhaps worse. And the second part was that you are aware he has no father and his mother is quite…sickly and cannot care for him, he is mostly left on his own to fend for himself. You want him to have a conscience and…to learn responsibility. You wanted him to be accountable for his actions, become a man, a good man. A man Lili-Mae can be proud of and grow with."

Her lashes lowered covering her eyes, but her cheeks pinked telling him he was on the money.

"And," his voice softened although it was still deep, heavily accented, "Colby tells me he is doing chores for someone at the Cresh and earning much needed money." Solitar ducked her head but Kurian set his fingers under her chin lifting it. "After careful study, I have reasoned out that person to be you." He inclined head indicating the set of paints on the desk and several easels covered with cloths leaning against the wall. "So, you see, you do have a heart. You just like to keep it safely encased in stone so it cannot be hurt. You have suffered so much in your young life, it is now time for you to let yourself lean on someone with big shoulders. Develop a trusting relationship…with a man."

She raised her sad eyes up to him and saw his crooked grin. "Oh?" she said lightly, "And whose big shoulders are you referring to?" She looked to his broad shoulders then back up to his smile. Solitar couldn't help but grin at his conceit.

"You can count on me for support, Solitar. And so much more. I want to be more for you." He stroked her rounded pink cheek with his broad fingers.

Then her smile fell. "No, Kurian. I am no good for anyone. How do I get beyond my horror of a past to ever have even a normal relationship?"

His hard carved lips curved with a slow sizzle that matched the smolder brewing in his normally cold dark eyes. The eyes grew darker as heat flared in them easing the cold. "You use mind-blowing sex with someone who knows their business that is how." Kurian moved with such stealth she wasn't aware of his crossing into her threshold, his head lowered as hers raised. "Sex, Solitar, with a man you can trust to take care of you, a man who can chase those horrendous memories away." His hands lifted to curl around her upper arms, drawing her those few inches until they were a hair from touching intimately.

"I...but I don't...I can't," the murmurs of protest fell even as her lips parted and her lids drifted down.

He stroked his palms up her arms then cradled her head between his hands and lowered his head, slowly, slow enough for her to get out the word 'stop,' or 'no,' but fast enough to not let her have time to think. Their mouths linked, he slipped his arms under Solitar and effortlessly lifted her and laid her down on the sofa.

Kurian set one knee on the sofa beside her and not separating their mouths he smoothed his hands over her throat then down her arms to the bottom of her sweater. While his mouth led her, taught her, savored the taste, the scent of Solitar, Kurian raised her sweater and broke the kiss to draw it over her head, he tossed it to the floor.

Ignoring her slight whimper, he bent back down and joined their mouths. Consuming her lips with hungry gusto, the room swam with the sounds of their mouths moving together, licking, sucking tongues and their blended heavy breaths, Kurian trailed down to kiss her jaw, suck her neck, down to her full breasts molding over the tops of the lacy peach bra which he paused for a moment to admire with a sexy smile. "Every part of you, my little scorpion is pretty, so damned pretty you make my eyes, as well as other parts of my anatomy ache."

Her eyes fluttered but didn't open more than a mere heated slit, the soft moan that sifted out got him moving again. His lips sucking at her breasts he reached behind her and unclasped the bra, drew it off and tossed it. His hands took over with his mouth, squeezing, nipping, his caresses almost too rough, too hard, took her to the very edge of pain along with sharp pecks and bites, he was not a gentle lover, he strove to pull back some of his rougher handling.

Solitar swooned, her back arching, she mewed his name, "Gosh, Kurian, just..."

"Mmm," he mumbled pinching her tiny nipples and grinned against her skin at the shiver that roiled through her slender body. Cupping her breasts he ground them in his hard fingers, he pressed them together and shoved his face between them, nuzzling and biting, then sucking in a nipple so hard her hips jolted when the sensation knifed from her breasts straight to her core.

That alarmed her, the intense, unfamiliar feeling he wrought in her, she moved to get up with a whispered, "No, Kurian, I can't-"

His big palm on the center of her chest he pushed her back until she lay flat and he undid the button on her jeans. Dark hair flopping over one eye his grin an evil lopsided dent in his hard face he said, "Yes, Solitar you can. You will." One hand grasping her breast with a tight clutch, he used the other to lower the zipper then with both hands he pulled her jeans down and off and pushed them out of the way to the floor.

Again she started to sit up, her cheeks rosy, lips swollen and red, eyes pure glazed honey, she baulked, "Wait, Kurian, I- I'm not sure...I..."

"*Oke*, baby, shush," he murmured softly then pushed her back to recline on the thick cushion and cupped her over her tiny silky panties. Brushing his thumb over her woman's nub he smiled at her groan. "*Ja*, baby, you are *oke*, I will take care of you, trust me. You get past your initial fear and built-in barriers and you will see what pleasure you will revel in." He wanted to bite her panties right off her but feared scaring her with his craven animalistic behavior he was trying to keep a lid on, so he slipped them off and replaced his hand with his mouth. He wanted to absolutely ravish, devour ever scintilla of her but he moved slowly enough if she told him no, without the groans of pleasure, he would stop.

"Oh my goodness, Kurian, you can't-" Shocked, she cried out. Her body fluttered at him, he pressed her to the sofa with his palm on her pelvis holding her in place and then licked and sucked until her body was no longer tense with anxiety but now her hips reached up to him, she gasped, "More, please, more..."

"*Ja*, baby, so much more," Kurian growled, and pressed her clitoris with his thumb while carefully inserting the tip of his middle finger inside her. When she bucked and gasped, "Wait!" she tried to shift her hips from his penetration but he gripped her thigh to keep her immobile while he assaulted her womanhood with his mouth and plunged his finger in deeper, curling it, searching for her hidden hot spot and grinned when her hips writhed and the sounds she now emitted were aroused gasps and wringing whimpers.

He worked her with his mouth, his teeth, his fingers, slathering with his tongue until he brought her to the precipice, on her tippy-toes at the very peak of the steep mountain about to fly off, her moans loud, her cries tight shrieks, and he pulled back.

She lay panting, her legs spread sensuously for him, her chest heaving. Kurian watched a delicate pink suffuse over her full round breasts, and his own chest rose and fell. His pants uncomfortable with the bulging, swelling fire raging inside wanting out and at her.

Solitar's lids raised to show a lace of shimmering blue. Her panicked murmur heavy with deep need, she cried, "Kurian, please, don't stop...I...it feels so," her body trembled, she folded her arms across her breasts and shivered again.

His voice thick with desire, "I know, my little baby scorpion," he chuckled. Then he slid his arms under her and lifted her, carried her to the bed and laid her down. Standing there looking at her, he palmed his erection.

She rose to her elbows, a wrinkle in her brow, she said, "I don't under...stand?"

"I need more room and to make you ready for me, little one, you are too small, unused, I am afraid I will hurt you with my…ah, size, my strength. A bit more," he said, and leaned to the bed, but then paused in surprise. Solitar rolled to her knees and reached for the buttons on his shirt. An impish, lusty smile on her pouty lips she said, "I want to feel you against me, Kurian, you can't have me all naked and hot while you are fully dressed and cold."

His head fell back with a rough laugh. His voice husky, eyes laden with rampant desire, he said thickly, "Oh honey, I am anything but cold. I had to stop for a moment and…" the side of his mouth nicked in. "I have not been this ready to explode since a boy. You make me so…" he shook his head. She opened three buttons and he grabbed the shirt and tore it over his head and dropped it. She reached out and pressed her palms against the hair on his broad chest, her fingers clutched and stroked over it.

At her giggles and moans, Kurian reached to his belt, unbuckled it, it rasped as he yanked it out of the loops and it followed the shirt on the floor. He kicked off his boots, socks, and removed his black jeans and briefs and had to slow himself from pouncing on her and taking her in one fell swoop. Her eyes bulged huge when she saw his exposed manhood thick and hard and so ready to take her, and she shrank back from him.

He murmured quietly, firmly, "No, baby, don't be afraid of me, I will be so careful, I promise," and he knelt on the bed with one knee and grasped one of her ankles that had curled away from him as she prepared to flee. He pulled her back down by her ankle and moved between her legs before she could get out a dissent. Kurian settled his body partially on her to hold her and reconnected their mouths. He skillfully brought her arousal back up and her fear level back down. When she was responding heatedly, sweetly to his kisses, he moved his hand to between her legs and worked her back up to a frenzy until she was making throaty gasping whimpers and cries and her hips undulated to his fingers.

His thumb pressing and rippling her clitoris, he plunged a finger inside her and held it there through the sudden freezing from the intrusion and her body melted again. He licked the soft skin at her cheek where he took a small bite then down to her jaw where he nipped a little harder then down to her neck where he sucked so hard her whimper became a small sob. Her silk poured into his hand and he worked another thick finger inside her and started gently plunging them, curling them until her hips thrashed and her upper body writhed and small screams hitched up her throat and he sucked on her harder, deep rumbles growling up his throat.

He moved a hand to her breast and he squeezed so roughly, pinched her clit and shoved his fingers deep and her turbulent breath rose to a harsh sob and she gushed his name in her sharp euphoria, "Kuri*aaan*!" Her spine arched, her neck arched, her head threw back then she jackknifed and bent forward as she came into his hand that was now crushing her sex hard in his palm, the other hand twisting her nipple and she shrieked and her fingers raked into his hair. She gripped his short locks and about tore them out of his scalp, and he laughed.

She fell back onto the sheet, her body shaking, huffing and gasping and he moved quickly between her legs, pushing them wider apart with his knees. Hastily grabbing the condom she hadn't seen him lay on the nightstand when he'd removed his pants, he ripped it open and jerked it on, then he grasped his erection so full and pounding and he thrust just the head into her. Her body was still writhing and convulsing, she was so wet he pushed deeper inside, painstakingly slowly, pausing every little bit for her body to adapt to his girth.

Kurian moved carefully, she was small, so tight and unused that Orlando bastard must have hurt her so badly when he- *Ja*, not now, later he would take care of that fucker. Now he would enjoy this perfect moment with this perfect woman, Solitar. He will give to her what she needs, and relish in every sight, scent, feel and emotion of it. Pausing, he whispered, "Solitar, you *oke?*"

He braced on one elbow and brushed damp tendrils from her hot cheek. She was beautiful, so amazing he felt his heart clench, that was a first. A damned first. He pushed the fear that caused aside. Now was her moment.

Her face was contorted on the axis between pain and thrill. Her lashes flickered letting out dazed blue light. Kurian glanced down at her full creamy breasts rising and falling with rapid shallow breaths and palmed one slightly more gently than before. It was his nature to be aggressive, rough, forceful, he had to force himself to hold back, he didn't dare hurt his delicate scorpion. He wanted her to love sex, not to fear it any more. When she was with someone she desired, loved, then she- He bit back a grimace at the thought of her in another man's arms.

"Kurian," she said softly. He looked to her eyes, opened just a thin line, perspiration dampened her temples, her plush lips curved in a sensual smile.

"*Ja*, baby," he murmured, his name on her lips in that sexy sigh about undid him.

"It's...it hurt, but now, I'm good. I want...more," that last bit so shyly purred caused Kurian's groin to contract.

"Oh, *ja?* You do? Thank God," and he pushed harder until finally he was fully seated, and they both sighed. He paused again briefly to allow her to adapt and then he started rocking, almost all the way out then all the way in. When her purrs grew to lusty groans, Kurian increased his rhythm thrusting deeper, then faster. He grasped her legs lifting them to wrap around his hips then he reached under her and pulled her hips up high so he could plunge deeply, so deep she cried out. He hesitated, but it was a cry of pleasure.

Kurian wasn't going to last long so help him, he reached between them and manipulated her clit until her gasps and cries wound in a shrieking crescendo. The pink flush pearled across her chest and he lowered his head to catch her squeals of release in his mouth, they vibrated down his throat as her body shook around him, clinching his sex with crazy spasms and then he let go.

His growl fled into her open heaving lips and he pounded his now out of control ecstasy, his rhythm broken, his plunges rapid short and long strokes until he halted deep inside Solitar and his seed burst from him, coating her channel with his essence held back only by the thin rubber. A few more long, slow, then jolting strokes and he collapsed.

Feeling her soft body mesh with his, Kurian realized he was crushing her with his weight and he shifted to fall to her side with a groan. But he didn't want to disconnect, he stayed inside her, his palm possessively back on her breast. Their chests heaved with panting delight and exhaustion. Kurian never wanted to move again. He wanted to stay here with her dainty body tucked half under him, cradled in his arms.

He whispered, "You good, my little scorpion?"

Her giggle rustled against his furry chest making him smile. He peered down at her and saw her smile and his heart warmed. "Yeah, real good, Kurian."

"I did not hurt you? I tried to be careful."

Her head ruffled on the pillow. "No. At first, yes, but you made it…good for me. Thank you, Kurian."

He bent and kissed her brow. "That was the plan, sweet."

"Kurian, how about I cook you a really nice meal, just the two of us-" His phone rang loudly interrupting her.

A few curses in two languages and he leaned over the bed and grabbed his pants. Sifting his phone out, he answered it.

"K," Rutger said. "We have a spotting of Gareth Karelli. That first bar you hit looking for him, the Sunflower on the Green. You want to meet us there?"

"*Ja*, I am leaving right now." He stuffed the phone back in the pants' pocket and slid so his legs hung over the side of the bed. He grasped the condom before it could escape. "Baby, I have to go, we can-"

"Yeah, sure," she said tersely and rolled to her side facing away from him.

"I have to take care of this, I will be right back." He left and went to dispose of the condom in the bathroom. In a moment he was back. "Here." He handed her a warm wet cloth to clean up. He would have liked to do it himself but they were too new, he didn't want things to get awkward. She took it without a word, and without looking at him, she didn't move. "Solitar…" confused at her withdrawing, he bent down to her.

She rolled into a ball and said, "This was a mistake. It won't happen again. Please go."

He froze. "Huh? What are you talking about? What we shared was unbelieva-"

"You did what you said you would do, show me great sex. Well, it's done, over, you have to leave."

Shades of the last time they were together! "Fuck, Solitar, what the hell is wrong?" He reached for her shoulder but she shrugged him off and curled more tightly in a ball.

"Go away," she said, her voice muffled in the pillow.

"Damn," he let loose a few curses raking his hand through his hair in baffled exasperation. "Listen, Solitar, we need to-" his phone buzzed in his pocket, he had to go. He didn't tell her why, he didn't want to get her hopes up. Plus, she didn't remember her brother, but she might carry guilt, or fear that Gareth would be injured when they captured him. "All right, I have to go. I will call you later. Don't leave without me or one of my men with you," he ordered brusquely then leaned over and put a gentle kiss on her head and left her.

He didn't hear her sobs as he left her room and hurried down the stairs to his bike.

Chapter Twenty

When she heard the door close, Solitar rolled off the bed to her bare feet. What had she been thinking? That she and Kurian would have sex and then he would pledge everlasting love to her? What a joke. He probably even had his friend call him at that precise moment to give him a graceful way out. Kurian was sure of his prowess, his seduction skills, knowing he would get in her bed and he planned to be rescued so he had an excuse to leave right after. He got what he wanted, lay claim to being the second guy to screw the cold bitch as they called her. As soon as she mentioned cooking him dinner, like a date, he fled so fast the door almost hit him in the ass on the way out.

First Jamie, now Kurian. What was it about her that drew the cocky assholes? But Kurian didn't rape her, he didn't have to. She practically flung herself at him." Take me! Take me!" she essentially begged him. Yeah, his skills were really good, extraordinary, a master seducer. The worst thing? She had loved it. And him, she had started having feelings for the big jerk. She should have known, a harsh, dangerous man, it was written all over his hard face and cold eyes, she should have run for the hills instead of into his arms. What a damned fool. Well, she was done listening to him. She had work to do.

After a scorching shower, she scrubbed half her skin off but she still couldn't get rid of the feel of his hands on her, his manhood inside her, his mouth plundering hers, he'd been like an animal devouring its slaughtered feast. She wanted him again, dammit.

Each room had a kitchenette with a toaster oven, microwave and miniscule fridge. After nibbling a piece of toast spread with peanut butter, and sipping a cup of vanilla tea, she dressed in a dark green, short sleeved sweater and black jeans. Grabbing her purse, Solitar strode out the door in ankle boots and out to her jeep.

She stopped at Zuk Zuk's Tavern near the mine for a cup of coffee. She'd had the tea but didn't possess a coffee maker in her room and she had been in too much of a hurry to make a pot at the Cresh. Last she thing wanted was to run into Kurian or one of his stupid men. How humiliating. He was probably already hanging with them somewhere, drinking beer, watching sports on TV and regaling them with stories of his bagging the icy chief. Yeah, reams of ribald male laughter at his descriptions of her inexperience and fear before turning into a wanton whore who tried to plan a date with him. Yuk yuk, big jokes.

Inside, there were only a few patrons lingering, most were at work. She made her way to the bar to order her coffee when she stopped in surprise. Camara was in a corner booth and she was what they called canoodling with some guy. Solitar's eyes narrowed on the man. And she was taken aback. He looked like the guy who drove the car that the drug lord, Simón Bolívar and his cohorts had jumped into and raced away after attacking her. *No way*, she told herself. Not almost middle-aged, plump and cheerful Camara with a man half her age, and a crude looking one at that.

Forgetting the coffee, Solitar strode right over to the booth and stood there. They were heavily kissing, petting, the man had his hands under Camara's shirt and they were both making gushing, smacking, groaning sounds. Solitar cleared her throat. Nothing. She did it again, loud. The couple froze. Camara turned towards the sound and seeing Solitar standing there, her cheeks flamed. Quickly shifting away from the man, she straightened her clothes and ran a hand through her brunette curls. A shit-eating grin on his face, the man sat back with a cocky grin and blatantly adjusted his pants.

"Soli!" Camara coughed and primped the bottom of her messy hair. "W- what are you doing here? Is there trouble at the mine? There had been issues yesterday with the excavator transporters. One of the motormen said that a wheel seemed loose."

Solitar's gaze darted from Camara to the man.

"You going to introduce me to your friend, Cam?" The man looked like he crawled out of a movie about street-thug drug enforcers. Large yet lean with gritty muscles, he had tousled dark hair that hung in uneven strands partially covering disturbing dark eyes. His skin was swarthy, he could use a shave on his coarse face. His nose had to have been broken at least twice and his thick lips kinked up at one side in a cruel sneer. Other than that, he was relatively good looking in a tough-guy sort of way.

Camara's lips parted, her apprehensive eyes galloped to her man and back to Solitar. "Uh, yeah, sure, honey." She turned more fully towards him and gave the man a sweet smile. His eyes lowered to her mouth and his grin ticked up in a crooked smirk. He reached over and brushed the smear of lipstick off the side of her mouth. Camara said, "This is my boyfriend, Luthor." Back to Solitar, she said, "And this is Solitar Lyonne, hon, she's the chief at the mine where I work."

Solitar leaned over the table and held her hand out to Luthor said quietly, "Pleasure, Mr. Luthor," the smile did not reach her eyes. Neither did his.

He stared at her hand, then leisurely leaned over the table and shook her hand. "Sure, sweetheart. Kinda young to be a chief, ain't ya?" and he sat back studying her with a coarse leer that made her feel oily and dirty. She resisted wiping her hand on her pants.

"So," a slight stammer in her voice, Camara said, "what brings you here? I'm on a break." Luthor set his big hand on her thigh, very high that was more than polite for public view. It was an ownership touch, and he was telling people that he didn't give a shit what anyone thought, he marched to the beat of his own crass drum.

"Oh, I was just grabbing a coffee. I was heading to the mine, but I've changed my mind. I'm going to go to the police and file a report on something I came across the other day."

Camara's brows rose, and Luthor lost his grin. His expression darkened.

"What would that be, honey?" Camara asked. Luthor stiffened beside her.

One of Solitar's shoulders shrugged faintly. "I guess it will all come out anyway, and I don't think it's really any big secret. I got lost the other day and accidentally ran into a coca field, actually I realize now it's not too far from here."

"Uh…" Camara and her beau shared a glance. "Why is it such a big deal to go to the police? It doesn't affect you does it?"

Solitar looked at her like she had two heads. "Really, Cam, it's cocaine. They're growing coca plants to make cocaine. They're drug dealers for goodness sake. I don't know why I've waited so long to turn them in, but I just decided I'm done waiting." She had waited because Kurian had asked her to. He probably had his own dirty mitts involved with the illegal crop and distribution. Maybe the sheriff was corrupt too and that's why he was so buddy-buddy with Kurian. Well, enough of the good ol' boy crap, she'd make sure more than one person knew she was making the report in case the sheriff was on the take.

Camara and Luthor were looking at each other again, and Luthor's face was almost black he appeared so angry. Well, it's none of his business. "I'll see you later at the mine, Cam. Nice to meet you, Mr. Luthor." Solitar turned to go.

"Wait!" Camara shuffled inelegantly out of the seat. She straightened her khakis and blouse as she moved to her feet. "I'll come with, lend you support."

"No, I really don't need anyone-"

Camara hurried to stand beside Solitar. "Sure you do." She turned back to Luthor and smiled oddly. "I'll see you later, hon."

His shifty eyes on Solitar, he muttered, "Yeah babe, later."

"I just need to grab my coffee, Cam," Solitar told her and headed to the bar to place her order. Out of the corner of her eye she saw Camara turn to wave to the crud she left in the booth.

"So," Cam nattered nonsensically, "weather isn't too bad yet, right?"

Not big on useless small talk, Solitar mumbled something brief and unintelligible.

The bartender set her coffee on the counter and said, "That'll be a dollar, hon."

She handed him $1.50 and reached for the cup. As she did, Camara reached out at the same time to grab some napkins and she jarred Solitar's arm knocking it into the cup and the coffee spilled over.

"Ow!" Solitar snatched her hand back at the slight burn as a bit of coffee landed on her. She snagged several napkins to quickly wipe off the hot liquid.

Camara blurted, "Oh my gosh, Sol, I'm so clumsy! Bartley!" She said to the bartender who was already wiping up the spill. "I'll pay for a new cup." She lifted her purse but Bartley smiled, "No need, Cam, I'll just grab another one." He tossed the ruined cup in the trash and was back in a moment with a fresh cup. "Here ya go, Miss Solitar," he said as he set it in front of Solitar.

With an annoyed sigh, Solitar smiled abstractedly at the bartender. "Thanks, Bart." She paid for the coffee and slid a lid over the spiraling steam.

A few minutes later the pair traipsed out to Solitar's jeep. Camara was still apologizing to her when they climbed inside the vehicle. Solitar stuck the key in, turned it, and nothing happened. The engine didn't even turn over. She tried again but there was only a clicking sound.

"What's wrong?" Camara asked.

"Darn." Solitar sagged back in the seat. "Something's wrong with it, maybe the battery is dead. I'm going to have to call the sheriff or a deputy to come and take my report. Darn it," she groaned, "that could take hours, or days even."

"Don't worry, Soli, I have the warehouse jeep. I can take you."

Leaning her back against the seat, Solitar rolled her head to face her friend. "Really? You don't mind?"

"Of course not. I was coming with you anyway, what's the difference? Come on, I'm parked over on that side," she motioned towards the office shanty. The women got out and as they approached Camara's vehicle three men exited the shanty.

Laddie Lafayette, Jamie Orlando and Siggy Sigmund stopped to talk to them.

"G'day you bonza sheilas," Siggy the Australian greeted them. "Pretty ladies you are and a pretty day as well, eh?" His hands tucked in the back pockets of his dungarees he tilted his head back and squinted up at the bright sun in the cloudless blue sky. Machines ground and hummed around and inside the mine. People shouted greetings and orders to each other as they worked trooping in and out of the main tunnel.

"Soli, Cam." Laddie smiled at the women, Jamie remained mute but fixed a mean glare at Solitar, he didn't spare Camara a glance.

"Where ya off to?" Laddie inquired. His helmet tucked under one arm he pulled thick carpenter gloves from off his belt and tugged them on.

Solitar was about to tell them it was none of their business when Camara said sweetly, "Oh, we just have an errand to run. You boys heading for the mine?"

"We were off to Zuk's to grab a couple of tinnies before heading into the deep dark," Siggy informed them.

"That's Aussie speak for we're getting a few cans of beer before going to the mine," Laddie told them with an engaging grin. "Only it's early so we're no doubt grabbing sodas not beer," he added with a wink. He looked at his hands as if wondering why he'd just put his gloves on when they weren't going straight to work.

"Always the flirt," Camara said, returning a smile at the handsome Australian.

Siggy favored her with his own audacious grin making her chuckle.

Motion caused Solitar's head to turn. Colby and his friend Ritchie came around the side of the mine. They were carrying huge trash bags and laughing. The teens were starting to fill out. Both tall bean poles beyond skinny from malnutrition they were earning money from helping with the mine, as well as doing extra chores assigned to them by Kurian as well as others. Apparently they were putting their funds towards much needed food. At their heels Petey the mutt-Lab was bounding and running around the boys in circles. Colby paused to rub the dog's ear then they continued on with their tasks. They gave Solitar and the others cheerful waves as they went on their way.

Determinedly keeping her gaze from lighting anywhere near Jamie who had not yet uttered a word or a smile, Solitar said, "Yes, well, we're off, see you all later," and she trod to Camara's jeep not waiting to see if the woman followed her. Being in Jamie's orbit just made Solitar's stomach roil, made her feel dirty and tawdry, and on pins and needles fearing for when he would strike out at her next. She went to pat her purse, to feel the protection of the gun Kurian had given her then frowned. She'd left the purse at the Cresh. She stuffed a few dollars and her phone and keys in her pockets and didn't bring the purse as it didn't hold anything she really needed. Except the gun.

Kurian had told her to have it on her at all times. Like he cared. More the fool her for believing it. He had lulled her into a sense of caring and interest when he gave her self-defense and shooting lessens. All designed to get in her pants.

And now after her episode with Kurian she was feeling like the town slut. Of course that was ridiculous, women were no longer considered promiscuous these days for having sex with multiple partners. Still, the filth of the two men who'd used her clung to her thoughts, her skin, her heart. She hadn't encouraged either man and had in reality rejected their advances yet both had pursued her, and being the weak, reprehensible person that she was, she'd allowed Jamie to get away with raping her, and let Kurian use his experience to seduce her. A couple of meek 'no's and then she just let him do what he desired, she hadn't even tried to fight him.

This is what happens when she tries to be normal, let feelings seep in, let a man deliberately seduce her. Well, enough of being a weak sodden doormat. She is a strong person, she doesn't need to be kind, when did she ever care if anyone got to know her, to like her? No, she was here to get a job done and not be subject to the horny whims of strange men. No more good deeds trying to help the poor folk of Ruwenstad either. Screw them all. When has anyone ever helped her or cared about her wellbeing without having their own agenda? The bitterness of allowing herself to be interested in Kurian and letting him get close was hardening her heart all over again. This time it would stay behind its steel door where she'd put it a long time ago.

They drove out of the rocky mining area to catch the main road through the savannahs to the city. Solitar was lost in her thoughts while Camara chattered on about co-workers. "Huh, and that Gizelle, I tell you, Sol, woman cannot keep her legs together! Whenever she's in the mine with Kurian she chases after that hot hunka man like a cat in heat."

Solitar hadn't been listening but hearing his name she couldn't stop herself from asking with a pathetic interest in her voice, "Oh? Are they an item?"

"Huh," Camara made another snorting sound. "She wishes. I don't know about him, he just always looks so…severe. And, you know, dangerous. He's hot but I'd be afraid to let him spread my legs, you know? He has that, you know, rugged roughness, I think he would get off on hurting a woman."

Her cheeks flaming, yeah, Solitar knew. He'd hurt her mentally if not physically. Physically, sure, he was aggressive and tough, but he had treated her with such tender consideration. He hadn't just plowed into her, he'd made it good for her. Her belly crimped at the memory of their time in bed. When she felt heat sizzle between her legs she changed the subject. "So, ah, how long have you and, what was his name, been together?"

Camara was pretty, the coy smile and blush made her appear years younger. Both hands on the wheel she said gleefully, "Luthor and I have been seeing each other for a few weeks now."

"Where'd you meet?"

"Hmm." Camara checked her side mirror but they were the only car on the road. "Oh, the usual. The bar. He and his chums came in for a game of pool and a pitcher. I'm embarrassed to say I hit on him. I mean," she laughed, "he was sitting on it today so you couldn't see, but the man has a very fine butt." She turned her head quickly and gave Solitar a saucy grin then faced the road again, "And he looks even better without clothes!"

That was more info than Solitar wanted. "I'm glad you're happy, Cam, as far as I'm concerned I'm done with men. They're all just users. Take and leave."

Her lips parted as Camara glanced quickly at Solitar and saw the sadness leeching off her. "Oh honey, who hurt you? I didn't think you would let any of the men especially Jamie in your bed." She waited but when Solitar didn't reply, she thought for a moment then said slyly, "The only one who seemed to set you off was that Kurian Anastaas." Seeing Solitar's mouth firm, Camara went on, "It was him? You two finally did the nasty? Oh, baby, tell me all about it! Is he big all over and is he rough like I thought? Wait-" She looked Solitar up and down and said quickly, "He didn't hurt you did he? If he did-"

"No," Solitar cut her off with an unhappy sigh. "He didn't hurt me physically. No, he got just what he wanted then I offered to cook him a meal and I guess he took that as a request for date or something and," she grunted, "he couldn't get out of the room fast enough. Had a friend concoct a story to get him away. I think he planned it ahead of time so he could leave gracefully," she added bitterly, "and quickly."

"Oh honey, I'm so sorry. You finally let down your guard for once and the wrong one gets in. What a lousy bastard."

Time to change the subject. Solitar asked, "So, Luthor, are you and he-"

"Listen Soli," Camara interrupted her, "maybe you should rethink this going to the police about the coca fields. You've never experienced the abject poverty these people have. The coca is one of the few incomes they can generate here."

Solitar turned her aghast face to her friend. "Cam! Really, they are breaking the law!"

Her smile gone, Camara shrugged negligently. "Everything is relative, hon. You watch your baby starve to death in your arms and you bury him while the government keeps all the money they could give here and they all become fat politicians and business owners while the children die, and you'd change your tune. Not everything is black and white, girl, just because you had a good childhood doesn't mean everyone did."

Solitar shut her mouth. She had told Camara a bit about the foster care so Camara knew it wasn't all ponies and rainbows for her as a child. She wasn't about to share her earlier childhood with her. Who was obeying the law when she was abandoned by her parents and abused by predators and molested by her foster parents? Where was the law helping her then? "I don't understand, Cam, you don't live here, why are you so all fired up about this? Who have you been talking to?"

The skin on her neck reddened, Camara kept her eyes glued to the road. "Just general conversations, Sol, you hear talk when you're here long enough. You travel back and forth so much to the States you aren't around enough to fit in with the locals."

Humph, Solitar thought, by locals she means Luthor. The man had the looks of a sleazy drug dealer that used his fists to make people do as he wanted. And Camara was afraid of Kurian? At least Kurian shaved and combed his hair. And smelled really good, manly, virile, and he- no, she had to get him out of her mind. He had already moved on to Gizelle. He was a cheat, a womanizer, a lousy man whore.

"Listen, Sol, you need to-"

"Wait! Look Cam!" Solitar shouted pointing out the open window. "There's smoke! A lot, something's on fire!"

"So what?" Camara kept driving. "There's a ton of brush out here, lots to burn."

"No, stop the car, it's the area where the coca fields were. There are children out there, we need to see if they need help."

Camara slowed but kept going. "They don't need our help, what could we do? We have to keep-"

"I said stop!" Solitar yelled, her hand on the door handle. With the windows open the scent of burning wood was becoming overwhelming.

Cursing under her breath, Camara pulled the jeep over and came to a stop. Solitar hopped out and ran towards where she could see the banana plants she'd come across the other day. The smoke was billowing from beyond them.

She moved as fast as she could, shoving tall weeds out of her way as she tromped through the tall grass. She reached the banana trees and started working through the broad-leaved plants and thick stalks. The smoke was denser, it seeped into her throat making her cough and her eyes water. A bit further and it was as she thought, the coca fields were burning. No one was around, they didn't work in the middle of the day when it was the hottest. Most of them also worked for bare pennies in crude jobs in the city, and others performed bulk labor for the mine.

She hollered at the top of her lungs, "Hello! Help! Fire! Fire!" She repeated the words again and again but no one came.

Solitar raced back to the jeep. Camara had exited it and was standing by the vehicle with a worried expression. Solitar reached inside the open driver's window and started pressing on the horn hoping to draw attention from anyone nearby in one of the shacks they called home. A solid blaring honk filled the air then she started hitting the horn making shorter faster blasts.

Meanwhile, she reached in her back pocket and fumbled for her phone. Checking it, she was relieved to see she had two bars, enough to call. The other day she couldn't get service a few dozen feet back down the road.

"What are you doing? Stop that!" Camara shrieked with her hands over her ears. Her own phone clutched in one hand.

"I'm calling for the fire brig, Cam. There are people out there in homes, shacks they've hidden away in while they work the crops. They might be sleeping!" She had glimpsed a few shacks stashed away in the high brush nearer the mountains when Jared was hauling her towards the gorge.

"No! You can't do that!" Camara reached to take Solitar's phone from her.

Solitar fought her off and tried to dial while still pressing the horn. "What are you, crazy? People could die if that fire spreads, Camara, I have to call!"

"No, stop!" Camara slapped at Solitar's arm that held the phone. Neither noticed the black truck that pulled up behind them or the men that tumbled out and moved towards them. Crackling flames and heavy smoke was working its way over the fields, the smoke lay like a dense fog that started leaping, sparking for the sky in billowing grey spirals.

"Yes, do stop that horrendous caterwauling," a man said, "and give me the phone."

Solitar felt the phone snatched out of her hand as she was shoved away from the car. Stumbling backwards with a yelp, she caught her balance and pushed disheveled hair out of her eyes. Her heart banged against her ribs when she saw who it was.

Chapter Twenty-One

Terror ricocheted around Solitar's body when she recognized the man speaking. Someone she had hoped never to see again. Simón Bolívar. Flanking him were his bodyguards, Sergio, and Pedro the man that had grabbed her hair to keep her from escaping that day outside the Cresh. Both men carried damage from when Ivar beat them but Sergio still smirked at her. Pedro's face was still bruised, his mouth a vicious hard line, his ugly glare boding savage retribution as soon as he gets his hands on her.

She tried to take a step back in preparation to run- and she bumped into another hard body. A brief glimpse behind her and she identified Camara's boyfriend from the bar, Luthor. Her gaze swung to Camara who stood with her lips bunched, her phone still clenched in her hand. Camara's eyes went to Luthor then to Solitar. She mutely shook her head, her advice to Solitar not to fight the men. Luthor grasped Solitar's upper arms to keep her from fleeing.

"Now, Miss, ah, Lyonne," Bolívar started, his smile above the goatee was like a snakeskin oil salesman, his voice heavily accented Spanish. "I am sorry but I must insist you do not call the authorities."

"But the fire!" Solitar exclaimed. She struggled but it was in vain. Luthor was a huge knee-breaker, she assumed an enforcer for the cartel, there would be no breaking away from him. "Mr. Bolívar, there could be children in those houses!" She motioned towards where she'd seen the shacks tucked like locusts into the hillside. "We have to call the fire brig! Please, send your men to raise the alarm and get the people out before the fire reaches them!"

Bolívar wore a charcoal suit, sharply tailored and wingtips highly polished. The slight grey at his temples slicked back with the rest of his dark hair. The snaky smile never wavering, Bolívar said, "Tut tut, my dear Miss Lyonne. May I call you Solitar?" He looked briefly at Camara then frowned at Luthor.

"Cam, take a hike," Luthor ordered her gruffly.

Camara's lips parted with slight distress. "No, but, wait, Luthor honey, I wasn't going to really take her to the police station. I was just going to drive her around until I talked her out of it!"

Bolívar gave Camara an angry grimace. "And you just had to come down this road? I don't know, Luthor, about her."

Solitar felt Luthor's fingers tighten around her arms. He said gruffly, "She's all right, sir, she will do what I tell her. Right, babe?"

"Mr. Bolívar!" Solitar cried out, renewing her struggles, unfortunately drawing Sergio and Pedro's attention to her jiggling breasts. "The fire! The people! My gosh there are children out there! At least alert the families, they can start fighting the fire and get the children away. You must-"

Bolívar got in her face. "I don't *must* do anything, Miss Nosybody," he told her. He started to say more when there was sound and motion coming from the nearby fields bordering along the road. They all looked over, and the brush revealed Jared, Marlie, Laurie, all the people and more that had confronted her in the field the day she discovered the coca crop.

"Oh my goodness!" Solitar yelled. "Marlie, Jared, the fire! The coca plants are on fire! You must get the children to safety, get hoses, water-" They shuffled slowly from the fields to congregate on the side of the road. Astonished that they showed no ready moves to action, no alarm, they just stood despondent with resigned misery scrawled across their faces and slumped shoulders. Solitar fought against Luthor's hold and started to plead to them but Bolívar shook his head with his oily smile.

"They aren't going to do anything my dear, shall I tell you why?"

Her frantic gaze jumped to him, eyes wide with alarm and fright. "I don't understand." Back to the despondent throng she cried, "People, your homes, your belongings, the children, you have to-"

"Stop, Woman!" Bolívar demanded with a sharp snap. He waited until she turned her attention back to him. He stood calmly, one hand in his pocket jingling whatever was in there. "You see, ah, Solitar, there are no children. I have the children stowed away from here. They are safe, well, relatively, for now. It was I who set the fires, dear, well," he smirked, "my men actually did the deed." The slithery smile thinned to a nasty gash fenced by the goatee, his eyes narrowed in dark threat.

"I…" *What the heck?* "I don't understand. Why would you do that? Why would you set the crops on fire?" Solitar tried to catch Marlie's eye or Laurie's but both women were staring at the ground. Theirs as well as the males' expressions were… frightened… helpless, fatalistic. It was confusing. Why weren't they running to save their crops? And what about the children? "Where are the children?" she asked the gangster.

The oily smile returned. His men shifted on their feet, the crowd of farmers remained quiet with very little moving about, just sad eyes glowing in front of the mounting clouds of engorging grey smoke. Bolívar explained, "Because not only are they my competition, albeit a tiny competition, I am more worried about them catching the attention of the law. Not ours so much as I keep my enterprises more carefully hidden and protected by ruthless guards, and the police are more likely to turn a blind eye for a payout. But, people like you, Miss Solitar," he reached out to touch her face but she flinched from his hand. His smile hardened.

"People like you," he went on, "will not let it go. You will push and pull and tattle, make phone calls and send reports. You get no satisfaction here you will contact your own law, Interpol, and that my dear, I cannot allow. You see, the reason these people are standing and watching their livelihoods burn without so much as pissing on the flames is because I removed the children. They don't know where I've sequestered them. If they call the police or they try to put out the fires I will kill the children. See," he shrugged, his palms up, "their hands are tied as are yours. You run to the police with any of this and again," he sighed as if he was reluctant to have to do this, "I will be forced to exterminate the children."

He leaned into Solitar enjoying the shock and fear imprinting on her face. "So, you will climb into that little jeep there with Miss, ah, don't know her name," he shot a warning glare at Luthor, "and you two ladies will go home and pretend you were never here. You never saw the fields on fire, you did not hear the children are missing. No, you will go about your business as usual. The sooner that the Gatin Mine is worked out the sooner you all leave and we won't have to do our labors under the severe cover that we are now. Hmmm?"

Luthor held her completely immobile. Solitar looked wildly at the group seeking their help, their leap to action but they were all avoiding connecting with her. Back to Bolívar she opened her mouth to spout angrily, "You can't-"

His eyelids levered down over brown orbs turning them into mean slits and the smile was cold and foul. He cupped her chin with vigorous fingers and lifted it. "If you don't care about the children, or believe that I have them imprisoned, then you should worry about your own skin, Miss Solitar. I get even an inkling you are talking to the police, and my men," he nodded to Sergio and Pedro who were still staring at her chest, Sergio with a sick leer on his rough face, Pedro glowered with vengeance, "will hurt you, and all of the little ones."

He pinched her jaw bringing her up on her toes. "You know what I mean is, they will kill you if you talk. I will find out long before the cops arrive on our turf from out of this region or out of the country, and they will never find your body. Then there will be no witnesses and they will leave and I will just continue business as always." He squeezed her jaw so hard tears sprang from her eyes. "I would take you out right now but too many people are present, it takes only one brave soul to squeal. For now, you have a reprieve, use it well. So, keep your mouth shut and mind your own fucking business. Do you hear me?"

Solitar grit her teeth to keep from crying out in pain, she refused to give him the entertainment of knowing he was hurting her. When she didn't answer he increased the pressure until her mouth was forced open. Then Bolívar bent and pressed his open lips over her mouth and kissed her. Messy, sloppy, the musky taste of cigar, he held her taut and she could do nothing to stop his indignant assault. Finally he released her with a jolt and a harsh push, she fell back into Luthor.

Bolívar said, "I believe I made my point. Luthor," he acknowledged the thug holding her arms, "see that your woman and Miss Solitar get on their way. Ensure they go straight back to the mine. Or," he glanced up at the lowering sun, "back to the Cresh. I want to make sure these two lovely ladies make it back home safe and sound. Because," his abominable eyes slithered down her body and back up, "Miss Solitar and I will have future business to attend to. I am stirred at how good you look, and taste, and sweetheart, I plan on getting me some more. If only I had the time right now." He stepped back and dismissed them by walking away and moving into a huddle with Sergio and Pedro.

Sergio's heated gaze never left Solitar as he pawed his slick Fu Manchu with thick calloused fingers. Not when Bolívar released her, and not when Luthor escorted her back to Camara's jeep with his big hand wound around her arm, and not when the women got in the car. Solitar looked back, and Sergio was still leering at her.

As Camara drove, her hands visibly shaking on the wheel, Solitar spoke, "Luthor did something to my jeep, didn't he, Camara? You deliberately knocked my arm to spill the coffee to stall long enough for Luthor to take care of my jeep. You conspired with him to keep me from going to the police, driving around in circles for hours."

The guilty flush spoke for her. Camara's fingers were white-knuckled around the steering wheel. She had been just as scared at the presence of Simón Bolívar as Solitar had been. "Just, listen, Soli," her voice wavered, she kept her eyes on the road although they flicked repeatedly at the rear view and then to each of the side mirrors, where she didn't look was at Solitar. A car pulled out behind them, in her side mirror Solitar could see Luthor was at the wheel.

Reading Solitar's mind Camara said, "Simón Bolívar is not a man to ignore. He means what he says. Luthor has told me stories, well," her chuckle was grim, "your toes would curl the things that man has done to people, to women. He just…takes them. In front of his men, he has no modesty, no shame. He has his men just pluck some hapless woman off the street that he desires and, well, he rapes them until he's had his fill then he tosses them to his men. Sometimes one of the guys will like the girl, and he keeps her. Most of the others are…disposed of, some sent to work in brothels. All held against their will, Soli, shit," her voice shook.

"Just stay away from him, out of sight out of mind. Because girl," Camara shot her a glance of pity and said, "he made it crystal that he wants you. Your best bet is to hop on the first available plane and get the hell out of here before he comes for you. And he will, have no doubt about it, he will come for you."

Solitar didn't doubt Camara's proclamation, and a full body shiver rolled through her at the profound evil that emanated from that horrible man. He hadn't disguised his desire for her. But, she was tired of being a damned victim. Screw him, she was not running from another male. Besides, she couldn't leave the mine, it was imperative she stay and do a superb job running operations. "What's all this to you, Camara?" she asked her used-to-be friend. Well, as much of a friend that Solitar would have allowed. That was over now though, burned to bloody ashes at Camara's deceit. First Kurian using her and throwing her aside now Camara's betrayal, well, it just bred more solidly into her, as Solitar had always known, you can't trust anyone. No one. Ever.

Camara bumped one shoulder up and down. "He's Luthor's boss. Luthor doesn't take me around their places of business often. He said he didn't want me under Bolívar's radar. Huh, not that he'd be interested in a copper penny like me. It's women like you, glowing silver dollars," she briefly looked at Solitar, down her lush body and back up to her face then grimaced at the purple smudges around her jaw.

"Damn, Soli, you're going to need makeup to hide those bruises. See what I'm saying? He's a brutal, merciless beast that you need to hide from. He will hurt you a lot worse than that and love every second of it. I know you don't wear makeup, we can go to my room when we get back to the Cresh and I'll help you."

Last thing Solitar wanted was to spend more time in Camara's lying, betraying company. She sighed. "Are you on Simón Bolívar's payroll too?"

Camara's head flung to Solitar with a gasp and then back to the road. She adamantly denied, "No, of course not. I am employed by Gatin de Muur. It's just, well, Luthor is one of his, oh, I don't know what his title would be, a commando or something. I mean, I like Luthor, a lot. Look at me," she shrugged with self-deprecation, "a hot guy like that giving me the time of day? Shit, I'm not doing anything that will make him run from my arms to another woman's. And," she grinned coyly, "I think he likes me too. He's in my bed almost every night, well, sometimes he shows up really late, but he has to work, you know?"

"Sure. Where's he take you on your dates?" Solitar asked but she didn't really have to, she could see the score with that creeper thug. It didn't give her any pleasure to see the shame pinch Camara's plain face. Camara just wanted love, and sex, like any other normal female. But she was allowing that mutant to corrupt her, she was lowering her integrity just to keep a hot criminal in her bed.

"Um, well, Soli, you have to understand, Mr. Bolívar keeps them busy, he demands a lot of his employees' time. I'm lucky he even shows up at all."

"Yes, I understand. Those boys are busy, busy, busy, killing people, growing illegal crops, setting fires, destroying homes and households, kidnapping innocent children."

Camara stretched her neck trying to release some of the tension gathering there. "Come on, Soli, you don't have to be sarcastic. I can see you're bitter that men stay away from you because you're so frigid-"

"Camara! You were supposed to be my friend!"

Her face growing red with anger, Camara spouted, "And it's a damned hard job, Soli. I push you to go out and live a little. I've dragged you out shopping, out for a few drinks, I've tried to be a friend to you, but you are hard as ice, my girl. One hundred percent unlovable. No man is ever going to want you. An old maid, you'll die alone, childless, you-"

"Shut up." Solitar was surprised her voice came out so quietly when she felt a terrible, lonely storm raging inside. Camara's words were too close to the truth not to cut deep. "Just...be quiet. Please." The most important thing right now was to try to figure out where the children could be being held. She couldn't tell the police the kids had been taken therefore no one would be looking for them and they could be hurt or even killed. Plus, the poor things must be terrified.

"Humph," Camara grunted. "No skin off my nose. I'll still help you hide those bruises. They will only cause questions and you need to stay low and keep your head down if you want to stay alive. I don't want retaliation overflowing on me for being near you. I'll be lucky if Luthor comes around again even for a BJ after this shit."

Chapter Twenty-Two

Kurian raced his motorbike along the worn and cracked asphalt into the city. Thank God there were no speed limits in Ruwenstad. Too few police to monitor the vast area, and most townsfolk who had vehicles ignored the fines handed out to them anyway. He was headed to Sunflower on the Green hoping that Gareth Karelli was still there, or better yet, Rutger and his men had managed to grab the killer.

The golf course stretched wide and hilly green behind the restaurant. Just as Kurian had surmised, it was one of the higher class establishments, not the very elite. Gareth wanted nice things, but didn't want to draw attention to himself. In a place like Ruwenstad anyone with wealth would have a thousand arrows pointed at him. Women would flock and businessmen would hound him. Other wealthy patrons would have had records run on him, they wouldn't associate with the young man until they were sure he was one of their set. Wealthy, powerful. So, Gareth stayed under that elite sensor but hovered right on the sharp edge between upper-middle class and filthy rich.

Shutting off the bike, Kurian scanned the area. He saw nothing amiss. No one was running, no shouts of alarm. Cars were parked haphazardly in the lot, after all, it was still Ruwenstad with few real rules. The restaurant was gleaming white with a slanted yellow roof and awning over the front entrance. Yellow shutters braced large windows that looped around the building. The lawns were of course well manicured and lushly verdant like green velvet ribbons streaming to the sides and behind the restaurant. Ruwenstad was an uneven scale of the tiny population of ultra rich in one pan, and the other very heavy pan of the poverty-stricken residents.

Kurian strolled to the emerald green door. He wore black slacks, a black button-down with long sleeves and a white t-shirt under it, and black dress boots. He smoothed his palms over his short dark hair that had been windswept from the ride. Stepping inside, cool air eased away some of the humidity that was slowly rising every day. It was early evening and the tables scattered in the center of the room and along two walls were mostly filled. A string of patrons lounged at the bar that ran along a third wall. Servers threaded in and out with trays of food and drink. It was convivial loud with clattering plates and clinking glasses and laughter.

Landscapes of South America laced the white walls. The tables covered in navy blue tablecloths had red candles in glass bowls flickering as people gabbed and gorged around them. Suddenly Ivar was at his side.

"K, fuck man," was Ivar's greeting in a deep whisper.

"What happened?" Kurian asked him in a low voice.

"Come on, out back, the shit-storm has been contained there," Ivar said, making his way to a side door. Kurian followed him out. They made their way around the building. Several men were standing in a crooked line looking at something on the ground a dozen feet away. Shades of Brittlyn Jones, Kurian thought. Déjà vu.

He joined the men. Nodding to his friends and part of his team, Kristjan Kristoff and Jaquarius Nikolaus, "Kris, Jaq," he murmured, and jerked his jaw to Rutger. He looked down at the body on the ground while Rutger spoke. Kurian was surprised to see the deceased was a male wearing a policeman's uniform of grey and white. His black hat lay a few feet away on the tar heated from the day's sun. Glaring red holes in his white shirt ran rivers of blood that pooled around the body.

"Ivar and I decided to swing by here before starting on a few other places since you had said it was high on your list to look for the bastard," Rutger explained. Beside him Ivar's face was a block of cement, he stared off to the building as if expecting more people, more trouble. "I called you as soon as we spotted the fugitive almost right away, sitting at the bar. He should have known better and tried to hide that bright hair, a hat would have been easy enough, the stupid jerk. Just like your girl, K, boy has brilliant locks and vivid blue eyes, coulda been twins."

Kurian's one brow lifted at Rutger referring to Solitar as his girl. "And?" he prompted impatiently for the story.

"Ivar went back out to cover the rear in case Karelli made us and split. I started towards Karelli when, hell, some bitch dropped a tray, made a hell of a racket and he looked up and saw me. It was too late for me to hide it, he made me. Jumped off the barstool. He literally lifted some girl off her feet into the air and launched her at me then did another and another like they were plates or big stones or someshit. Hell, K, I had to duck them and try to break their falls and go after him at the same time. Dude is big, as big as any of us. He fled towards the back. By the time I got there he was out the door." He looked to Ivar to pick up the scenario.

"Ja, K. I heard the commotion, screams, shouts. Karelli sprung out the door and I was already running towards him. Then," Ivar scowled, rubbing the back of his neck like he could scrape the entire episode away. "This cop shows up, some rookie kid came tearing out after Karelli. I guess he was in the rear of the building snagging a smooch with his girlfriend, a server here," he gestured off to the side and that's when Kurian looked at the crowd gathered to the side. He had seen them as soon as he went through the door but he needed to hear his men's stories first.

Several *politieagents* huddled under the shade of a luxurious tree. Under the broad coverage from the hot rays and blinding glare of the setting sun, they all were holding weapons, a few raised a few inches towards Kurian and his men as if they expected them to do something unlawful. In the center of the group was a young woman weeping. A female officer had an arm around her, consoling the woman who wore a white blouse and black slacks covered with a small white apron.

"Well," Ruger picked up the tale, "Karelli slammed into this guy's partner who was having a smoke back here while waiting for his friend's liaison to end. When the officer he hit fell into a car the confused officer scrambled in a panic for his gun and the fool started recklessly shooting. His partner heard the screams and the shots and as he was already near the back he raced out and one of the erring shots hit him.

"The girl stumbled out behind him screaming, I was behind her. Karelli started shooting back, he gave the cop the second hit, I grabbed the girl and tossed her behind that dumpster and dove behind a car. At that point, that gaggle of cops," he nodded towards the officers in the huddle, "must have been nearby and they all came running with guns waving. We could do nothing, K. Everything happened all at once in split seconds. They drew on Ivar and me and told us to drop to the ground. Eventually Kris and Jaq showed and advised the cops who we were and allowed us to show our ID's."

"So, Karelli got away," Kurian said.

Jaq told him, "*Ja*. In the initial chaotic confusion and gunfire he slipped away. The cops wouldn't let Rutger and Ivar leave but Kris and I took off in the direction they said Karelli went. We," he palmed the top of his wavy dark hair, his mouth twisted angrily. "This place is near the river. Karelli had a boat. We did not. He hit the river, that Purple River you know, it has innumerable estuaries. The cops got on the horn to try to catch him at bridges, but," he shrugged, "he'll be at the ocean before anyone can catch a sight of him."

"What are the chances of us getting a boat?" Kurian asked.

Jaq shook his head. "Nil. We asked the cops. They said due to the low economy there are few to sell and fewer to rent, and those a group of fishermen have already taken into the mountains to fish the streams. We asked about buying from locals and the cops nixed that. Said people hold tightly to what meagre possessions they have. Most that have boats are commercial fishermen and need them for their living. Even a steep price won't lure them into renting or selling."

"Choppers?" Kurian asked.

Again Jaq shook his head. "Too poor of a police force here to have even one. We tried to tell one of those Keystone Cops over there to put in a call to Suriname and request an air search but they said they had to wait for a supervisor to come here to make any decisions."

"We have to leave it to the cops," Rutger said, the certainty that nothing would be coming to fruition from the crew hovering nervously under the big tree was clear in his voice. "Most of the LEO's here are either very old or very young. The middle ones tend to leave for a better land to earn a living. The elders are too old to do much physically, and the young are too inexperienced and dull. They stand around like fireplugs waiting for someone to tell them what to do."

"Fuck," Kurian's curse came out in an aggravated grunt. "I will call our authorities to advise Gareth Karelli is on the run and for nearby republics and countries to be on the alert for him and to hook up an air and sea search. Shit, he could be killing women before anyone gets a sight on him." He said to Rutger, "You guys cleared to leave?"

Rutger frowned over at the group of officers that still watched them balefully. "*Ja*, we signed our statements. They have our info if they require more. It took some effort, but we convinced them to let us go."

"*Oke*," Kurian sighed, "let's get back to what we were supposed to be doing before Rudolpho asked us to look into the murdered vics." His heart weighed heavy. Not only had they let a killer get away and to be free to kill again, he felt disappointed that he couldn't put an end to a chapter in Solitar's life. It was going to eat at her that she had a brother so close and now he was gone. He was a murderer that was raping and butchering women who resembled their mother, and was more than likely a danger to Solitar herself as he had evidently followed her to Ruwenstad, yet she had so little of her past she had to be curious to want to speak with him.

Kurian wasn't looking forward to telling her what happened, that the freak had slipped through their fingers. But, he was looking forward to seeing her. Their time in bed together had been too short. About a few decades too short. He had wanted to stay in bed with her for days, leaving only to eat. They could have stolen a few vaca days to spend together. Blast the damned phone call that had taken him away from her warm body. Well, the sooner he imparted his bad news the sooner they could get back down   to   hot   and   heavy   business.

Chapter Twenty-Three

When Kurian entered the Cresh, he heard people arguing. The voices came from the grand room where people hung out. Glossy wood beams crisscrossed the ceiling and polished wood planks with knots made up the shiny flooring. The furniture was done in white leather. In the large room there were clusters of chairs and sofas, and tables for reading, watching videos, conversing, playing cards etc. Most of the seating was grouped near the floor to ceiling windows, a few with larger furniture for bigger crowds were assembled in the center of the room. A bar along one wall had stools placed in front of it.

He found the location of the arguers. Near the wide staircase that wound up to the upper levels Solitar and Camara were speaking loudly, and angrily.

Camara said hotly, "You can't go out there, Sol, you're being a fool. Let it go. Cripes, it's none of your business and it's only going to get you hurt. Come on, let me put some makeup on those bruises before someone sees them."

"No," Solitar responded fiercely, "I must go before something terrible happens to them."

"You can't think-"

"Solitar?" Kurian moved towards the fighting women. He was surprised, they seemed to be good friends, why were they arguing like a pair of hissy teenagers?

Both woman halted mid-word and turned to him. Kurian felt his stomach take a tumble. "What the hell, Solitar," he growled stalking to the pair. He caught her arm as she spun around to go up the stairs. Holding her back, he carefully grasped her under her jaw and lifted it. "Goddamn, Solitar, what is this? What happened?"

Solitar whipped her face out of his grasp and yanked her arm from his clutch and turned to the stairs. "None of your concern, Mr. Anastaas," she snapped tartly.

He blinked and shook his head. "Solitar, dammit, what is going on? What's the matter with you?" He started to follow her but she swung around and got in his face. "No. You do not get to pretend you care about me. Save your energy, I have things to do. I'm sure Gizelle is looking for you. Stay away from me." She pivoted and ran up the stairs leaving Kurian gawking after her.

"What the hell was that?" he mumbled absently staring up the stairs. Then he looked down at Camara standing at the foot of the steps with a guilty red hue staining her cheeks. He stomped down to her. "Everything was fine a couple of hours ago. What happened in that brief period of time to not only turn her against me but cause damage to her jaw? Hell, Camara," he dragged angry fingers through his hair. "Those looked like freaking fingerprints! What-"

Again guilty color flushed Camara's plain features. "I, uh, have to be uh, somewhere. I'll see you later."

"No. You will tell me what went on, who hurt her and you will tell me right now." Kurian struggled to control his confused fury. He'd left Solitar naked and cozy and happily sated in bed just a few hours ago and now she acted like she despised him and someone had injured her, and he was not leaving until he found out what the hell was going on.

"Really, Mr. Anastaas, it's not my place to-"

"Do not give a fuck, Camara. Spit it out. You stay here until I get it all. Start talking. Now."

She saw the determined steel in his clenched jaw and exhaled loudly. "Well, I guess it won't hurt anything to tell you. You're just a Gatin slug working the mine, you won't give a shit." She explained what happened that afternoon after she and Solitar had left Zuk Zuk's.

His face grew harder and harder as she spoke. She didn't explain why Solitar was so mad at her. When she stopped talking, he glowered his rage at her, a vein pumping at his temple. "Bastard took those innocent children? Manhandled a defenseless woman? Fucking *klootzak*." Through his clenched jaw he said, "None of that explains why she is angry with me. Did she tell you why?"

Camara looked away from his infuriated blazing eyes screaming a reckoning as soon as he goes out the front door. Then she looked him square on, her lashes fluttering. "I, well, the little bit she let out, I think she thinks you...I don't know, used her. You two got it on, about time I'd say. She freezes everyone else out, I don't know how you managed to get around her shield of ice-"

"Just fucking tell me, Camara, what upset her? Why does she think I used her?"

"Um, I guess as soon as you guys...finished, she offered to make you dinner, kind of like a date I guess. And without a second look or word you ran out of the room like your tail was on fire. Something about a fake phone call or something so you could leave her without a fuss. She thinks you just wanted to bang her and acted nice to get in her pants. I mean," she shrugged, "what's the big deal as long as you both had fun? No one said anything about a commitment, right? I think she's a little inexperienced when it comes to men and relationships. Explains why Jamie Orlando took one hit and split. You know he-"

Kurian ran up the stairs.

He hurried to her room and pounded on the door yelling her name, "Solitar! Open up!" No answer, he pounded harder. "Solitar, you have two seconds to open this door or it comes down! You hear me! One, two-" He heard a jeep start up outside. He moved to a long window in the wall that faced the front of the Cresh and saw a jeep racing out of the drive. Then he saw Camara fly out the door shouting and chasing the jeep.

By the time he rushed downstairs people were filing in talking loudly, voices anxious. Seeing Hubie Hubbard he beelined to the man.

"Hubie, what the hell is going on?" Kurian quickly asked him raising his voice over the increasing din.

Hubie shoved his long dishwater blond hair off his forehead. People were arguing, a few women were crying, Cregg Trent was trying to calm folks down. Hubie told Kurian, "There are children," he huffed, "a group of farmers' children have been taken."

"*Ja.* I just heard something about that."

Tucking long fingers calloused from years of playing the guitar in the front pockets of his grungy jeans, Hubie nodded. "Yeah, some cartel asshole set fire to crops and threatened to harm the kids if they tried to put out the fire or call it in. He didn't want the cops involved in case they got wind of the cartel's own illegal crops."

"How did everyone find out about it then?"

Hubie glanced around at the hub-bub of people rushing about and shouting. "One of the farmer's wives, Marlie something decided to ignore the threats and her husband's objections and ran to the mine screaming that she thought the children might have been stashed inside one of the shafts or something. That's ridiculous of course because we were closed down today due to the meth gas that the broken fan failed to deplete. Fan's supposed to be fixed so we should be back at it tomorrow." He shook his head watching the hysterical people cry and moan.

Laddie came over and said, "Hey," to Kurian. "A few of us are going out to the mine and search the area, the shacks around it and beyond in the fields."

"I think someone would have noticed if a bunch of children had been herded into the mine or one of the tiny outbuildings nearby," Kurian offered. "Where else could they be hidden?" He was worried about Solitar but he couldn't run off half-cocked with no idea where she was headed. "Where would it look natural for a group of kids to be?"

"That would be the school, man," Hubie said. "But it's been closed due to lack of funds for over a year now. It couldn't be-"

Kurian turned and muscled through the hysterical crowd and hurried outside. He jogged to his bike and was starting it as he hopped on. The engine roared as he sped out of the lot and hit the main roadway.

Chapter Twenty-Four

"She'll get over it," Solitar muttered to herself with the image of Camara chasing down the street after her stolen jeep. "Besides, she owes me for setting me up to be caught with that monstrous Simón Bolívar." Well, she hadn't exactly set her up. Solitar was the one who ordered Camara to stop the car because of the fires, she was possibly unaware that her boyfriend was following them. But, then again, Camara was instrumental in keeping her distracted while Luthor made her car inoperative.

Solitar had ignored her rattling on and on while she waited for her coffee at Zuk's, then the coffee got spilled. She hadn't locked the door to the jeep because she had the keys and there was nothing in it to steal. It would have been easy for Luthor to disable the engine in the time Solitar was delayed at the bar.

Yes, Camara was well aware that Luthor was damaging the jeep so she couldn't drive it, but did she know Luthor was following them? It made no difference anyway at this date, the damage was done. Camara had betrayed her and that would never be forgiven. Plus, wasn't the woman dating a mobster for heaven's sake? And, she knew about the illegal crops, both Jared's and probably also Bolívar's. Camara was treading a fine line as a gangster's moll. Solitar rolled her eyes at her description. What was this, the 1920's? Solitar grew angrier as she thought about Bolívar showing up, he could have easily taken both women or killed them on the spot. If the farmers hadn't been present he would have undoubtedly harmed Solitar.

Anyway, Camara was putting herself in danger being mixed up with the criminals. Bolívar had displayed he wasn't pleased with her, he may have already told Luthor to dispose of his meddlesome girlfriend. Darn. Solitar needed to warn Camara she could be in danger herself. Huh, dumb, enamored Camara probably thought Luthor would keep her safe. Luthor's loyalty would be to his paying boss and not a hot-to-trot frump.

Fortunately Camara had a map of the area in the jeep and Solitar traced the roads that led to the one school in Ruwenstad. The road she traveled was dirt like many of them in the rural republic. Tall amber grass lining both sides of the road waved in the breeze with the dense, vine tangling jungle hulking in the distance. In more robust times the school had been located between the most populated residential neighborhoods and the city to be easiest accessed by the two school buses as well as non-farming parents dropping their kids off on their way to work. But because of that it was placed in sprawling savannas with little near it except decaying abandoned warehouses. The school itself was vacant since funding to pay teachers and electricity had all but disappeared, and the buses lay in disrepair.

Solitar was positive the children were being kept at the closed school. If they'd used a residence someone would have noticed the children being shuffled inside. The many shacks tucked in the foothills were too small and had no running water to accommodate the kids, the same with the abandoned warehouses. But, then again, the school's electric and water were also turned off, but there was room to house the children and a relatively isolated outdoors surrounding them to usher the kids outside for privy purposes without the danger of being seen.

She could see the school now in the distance. Although the lawn around it had been maintained at one time, the grass and weeds had grown a foot high blending in with the surrounding empty fields. Kapok trees, rubber, gum and palms scattered the desolate open land lending shade and homes for fauna, and hopefully cover for Solitar. She wasn't about to park out front and march right in demanding the children.

Driving up to within a half a mile, due to the winding road her jeep would be mostly undetectable from the sight of the school, Solitar parked behind the largest Kapok she could find. Sliding out, she grabbed her purse which this time she was prudent enough to remember to bring her firearm. A shiver rolled through her at the thought of having to draw it, aim, fire at a human being. Locking her purse in the glove box she held the gun in her hand.

Using the trees for concealment, she darted from one to another in a sort of leapfrog motion towards the school. Keeping slightly bent over, she attempted to stay as close to the tall grass to stay hidden for as long as possible, and prayed all the basking snakes were sunning themselves anywhere but where she was treading.

She kept her eyes on the trees to ensure no sleeping ocelot or monkey noticed her skulking by. A sudden caw jolted her pulse as a red and green parrot screeched at her and flew from a bushy branch shaking the limb and leaves with a rattle. Colorful wings spread wide, it flapped them annoyed at being disturbed and soared out of sight to a grove of thick trees for a more secluded perch.

Along the way she peered inside the few out buildings; an old shed, a garage, an empty warehouse to make sure every one of them was indeed unoccupied. Only yards from the old stone and mortar one-level building she moved slower, more cautiously, continuously scanning the land for anyone hiding and ready to spring at her. Close enough now, she could see a jeep parked on the other side of the school, behind the structure. It was deliberately parked in the tall weeds to keep it hidden from view of the road and not in the lot made up of fragmented asphalt, dirt and gravel.

A quick survey to ensure the jeep was also unoccupied, Solitar crept towards the building heading for a broken window. Most of the windows were broken from kids throwing rocks. As she neared the school, she could hear crying. Children crying. Her heart clenched at the dreadful harrowing wails. Over the crying she heard a male voice shouting at the children to stop crying and be quiet or he would hurt them. "Over my dead body," Solitar swore to herself realizing that might just be the case by time all was said and done.

Against the aging grey stone and taupe wall of the school a hummingbird fluttered around a scarlet faja lobi flower. Afraid the bird might flap against the window if she startles it, Solitar stayed still waiting for the turquoise bird with a shimmering green breast to drink its fill of nectar and fly off to another bush. All clear, she stepped to the window and slowly raised to stand straight and peek into the broken window.

She peered into a large room, apparently the gymnasium. The children were sitting on the floor, several men sprawled on bleachers watching them. Solitar recognized little Bonnie. She was crying, and a man, make that Pedro was bent over snapping at her. Her blonde hair tied back in pigtails, her puffy eyes were streaming tears and her trembling mouth was emitting gulps and hiccups and sobs.

"I wanna go home," she wailed, "I want my mommy! I want my mommy!"

Pedro raised a hand and said, "You shut up you little bitch or I'll knock those tiny teeth outta your mouth. I've had enough of you kids."

"Mister, please." Bonnie's brother Bobby tugged on his sleeve. "I gotta pee, can you take me outside?" Clearly his ploy was to distract Pedro and leave Bonnie alone.

"Git off with you, ya little guttersnipe," Pedro snarled and backhanded Bobby sending him flying across the floor. The wood sports floor still held that high polish sheen but was badly marked and scuffed, and very hard for small boys tumbling down on it.

"No!" Bonnie screamed and hit Pedro with her tiny fists. "You leave my brudder 'lone!"

Solitar pulled out her phone and held it up. "Damn," she cursed. "No bars." Tucking it back in her pocket she frantically scanned the building and a ways down she saw a door that was slightly ajar. Racing soundlessly to it, she carefully pushed it opened and stepped inside.

Pedro shouted at Bonnie and reached for her. "I've had enough of you whiny little shits. I'm gonna take one a ya out, that'll shut up the rest of you. C'mere you brat-" But Bobby leapt up off the floor and ran to him, he grabbed Pedro's leg and sunk his teeth into the man's thigh. Pedro screamed and grasped Bobby and threw him across the room again. The child landed hard and skidded. The men in the bleachers chuckled, amused at the antics.

"Good show, Pedro," Sergio called out. "I was getting so damned bore. The girl is a crybaby but the boy is a pain. I say take the boy and go bury his ass outside somewhere."

"Fuck yeah," Luthor chimed in. "Less mouths to feed. Get the fuck rid of him." He turned to Simón Bolívar who was seated next to him. "Whaddya think, *Jeffe*?" Except for Bolívar, the men were in jeans and casual shirts.

142

Bolívar was not in his ever present suit. Today he wore an expensive pullover sweater and black slacks. His shoes still held a superior shine. His black hair slicked back, a few grey strands stippled his temple as well as in his trimmed goatee. He shrugged. "What's one kid minus or plus? The peasants have them like rabbits, litters of offspring. They won't miss one and it'll settle the other little bastards down. And the parents will know to take us seriously if we dispose of one or two. Go ahead, Pedro, get rid of the pain in the ass."

Pedro left Bonnie and tromped over to where Bobby lay sprawled. His eyes wide with terror, he crab-walked a few steps to get away but Pedro leaned over to grab his shirt. "C'mon ya fucker, you and me got a meeting to attend outside."

"Get your filthy hands off him, you scumbag!" Solitar yelled, raising the gun, she held it even with Pedro's heart. Mercy, she sounded like an actor in a bad B movie. Turning so none of the men could run up on her she nodded to Bobby. "Bobby, honey, get up and get away from him, hurry."

Bolívar rose to his feet, shock and rage distorting his good looks. "What the fuck? What the hell are you doing here?"

"Hurry Bobby." Solitar ignored the gangster and wriggled her fingers at Bobby. "Get your sister and the other children and come get behind me. Hurry."

Sergio, Luthor, and another man jumped up. Solitar moved the gun their way and ordered, "Don't move! Sit down, all of you, right now. Hurry Bobby." Bobby's eyes rounded with fear and stupefaction. But he climbed to his feet and hurried to Bonnie. Holding her hand, he said to the other children, "Come on, I know her, that's Miss Solitar. She'll get us home." He turned to her, his eyes begging, '*Right?*'

"You bitch," Bolívar spat. "I'm gonna wring your scrawny neck. You're just a young git, you ain't got the balls or the experience to handle that thing, put that gun down right the fuck now or I'll-"

BANG!

Solitar fired over his head. Ceiling particles instantly drifted down like a dust shower. All the men ducked with their arms over their heads and the children started wailing. Solitar counted 14 kids. "You sit down, Mr. Bolívar," she said, "or the next one goes dead center of your chest. I know how to shoot, I have perfect aim," she lied, "and I won't hesitate to shoot you or any of you." She indicated the other men. "Now, sit down. You," she waved the gun at Pedro, "you join them. Don't make me tell you twice. I want to put a hole in your head right now for the way you've treated these kids. Go."

A black scowl on his dark complexioned face, Pedro glared at her but went and sat on the bleachers with the other men.

"Now," Solitar said, "each of you, one at a time, slowly remove your weapons and put them on the second bleacher behind you." There would be a bleacher between them and their guns, that way if they went to grab them they would have to stand up, turn around and reach up and Solitar would shoot them before they could do that. She waved her gun at Bolívar who was sitting on one end. "You first, Mr. Bolívar."

143

He sat stock still, his eyes had gone blank, but Solitar knew that only hid the murderous thoughts tossing around in his head. A snarky smile raised his lips, the moustache twitched. "As you command, my dear." He lifted his sweater and removed the gun at the holster at the back of his trousers and placed it where she'd instructed.

She nodded and said, "You next," to Sergio. His face a snarl of fury, he did as Bolívar had, then settled back in his seat with a smirk. "You're not done," Solitar told him, "the gun in your boot and your knives as well." She was bluffing, she had no idea if he had any other weapons. He glared at her for a second, then sighed with a shoulder shrug and removed a small revolver from his boot and two knives from his pockets. Bolívar would assume his men would protect him, Solitar was presuming he only had the one gun.

When he was done, Solitar aimed the gun at the next guy until they were all relieved of their weapons. She looked to one of the young kidnapped boys who appeared to be one of the eldest. "Honey, what's your name?"

The boy's eyes popped from his head at being acknowledged.

"It's okay, Cooper," Bobby assured him, "that's Miss Soli, she's good peeps Colby says. An' she plays with me and Bonnie and Petey sometimes."

"Well, Cooper," Solitar said softly, "how old are you, honey?"

Cooper's gaze slid to Bobby who nodded at him then back to Solitar. "I- I'm ten, Miss."

She forced an encouraging smile when she really wanted to run and scream. "Oh, that's great, you're almost all grown up now, aren't you, sweetie?"

His eyes swept to Bobby again then back to Solitar, he nodded, his chest puffed out a bit. "Yes'm," he said.

"Have you ever handled a gun before, Cooper?"

He nodded, rust colored hair bounced on his forehead. Freckles jumbled over his ruddy nose and cheeks. "Yes'm. My daddy takes me huntin' for game. Help feed us." His gaze slew to the men then to the other children, his cheeks reddened at telling how poor his family was. But then again they all were, that's why they were in the predicament they were in. Their families were sowing coca leaves as a way to make ends meet. But they had caught the attention of a dangerous, greedy gangster who now wanted them out of business.

"That's great, Cooper, really great. See, I was right, you are almost a grown man, aren't you? Now, I want you to take that bucket over there," she nodded towards a bucket by the side of the bleachers. "And I want you to go gather up all those weapons and put them...very, very carefully into the bucket and bring it to me. You stay out of their reach, okay? Can you do that?'"

He didn't answer, his brows rose to his hairline and his mouth quivered.

"So, as a man, you can do this for me, can't you?" she asked, making her smile wider and more sincere. "Be very careful, do not get close to those...men. Just, get the weapons in the bucket, be super careful of the guns and don't cut yourself on the sharp knives." The men started uttering curses and threats, Solitar said, "Next guy that opens his mouth gets a taste of lead." A nervous giggle bubbled in her throat, geesh, there was that B movie dialogue again.

Cooper looked from her to the weapons lain out on the bleachers, his skin paled. Then, silently he trod over and retrieved the bucket and did as she asked. The entire time she held the gun as steady as she could on the men that were so angry they were red-faced and panting, fists clenched, threats of dire death pouring from their raging gazes. They glared threats at Cooper, but he kept his head down, concentrating on his task.

When Cooper collected all the weapons, he hurried over and set the bucket at Solitar's feet. Solitar could only pray the men had turned them all in, although she highly doubted it. She wouldn't have if she'd had additional weapons hidden on her person and someone demanded them. She wasn't in any position to search them and she couldn't let one of the children get that close to them to do so. She just had to hope for the best.

After Bobbie gathered the other crying children, all under the age of 10, Solitar asked him, "Are there any more men here, Bobby?"

Shaking his head, blond hair wafting, he wiped his runny nose and the tears off his cheeks. "No, Miss Soli. That mean man there," he indicated Bolívar who sneered at the boy's finger pointing at him, "he sent two other men to town to check on...pro-ah, por, uh..."

"Progress?" Solitar helped him.

"Yeah." Bobby nodded and swiped his hands on his jeans. "He tol' 'em to make sure Pa don't talk to the police and stuff. I think they coming back, Miss Soli."

"Okay, honey. Now, listen to me." She motioned for the children to come close. "Bobby, I want you to take all the kids and go outside. Wait for me out by the front door, okay? Don't let anyone wander off, you hear me?"

Bobbie just blinked big frightened eyes at her for a moment, then he tersely nodded and turned to the other kids. "Come on, you heard Miss Soli, let's go." He grabbed Bonnie's hand and tugged her with him as he made for the door. The other children, just as scared and flummoxed ambled after them.

Then she said to Cooper, "Wait, Cooper, I want you to stay by me. You're my extra pair of eyes. Do you know what that means?"

"Um..." His lips pulled in, the freckles wrinkled across his stub nose. "You want me to watch the mens to make sure they don't jump you. Right?" He looked up at her, his nose scrunching, worry in his young voice he asked, "Aren't we gonna leave too?"

"That's right, honey. Don't take your eyes off them. Yes, we're leaving too, right now." Solitar swung her arm around as Sergio made to stand up. "Do not move, Mister, I have no problem shooting you between the eyes the way you've treated these children and their parents. You sit back down." They glared at each other but when her finger moved over the safety, Sergio flopped back down hissing a string of Spanish curses.

"Now," Solitar said, "I am leaving with the children. If you try to follow us or stop us I will shoot you."

"Hell, *puta*," Pedro jeered, "we all rush you, you can't get us all, one of us will get you."

She let a sneer curve her lips. "Oh yeah? Maybe, but most of you will die before that happens. You want to be the first? Just try it." Squinting an eye at each of the men who glowered darkly at her, she said, "Well? Any takers?" She waited, holding her breath.

Bolívar leaned back and set his elbows behind him on the bleacher at his back. He casually crossed his legs as if he hadn't a care in the world. "Go on, *guapa*, pretty girl, you run with those babies. The city is closer than the neighborhoods but it's still miles away. You won't get far before we catch you. And when we do…" his brows wriggled at her.

"I get first peck at you, bitch," Sergio growled fiercely cracking his knuckles, his machismo had been badly bruised getting bested by a woman.

She didn't let him see how his goading scared her. She was terrified. There were two vehicles and not enough room to fit all the kids. Besides, she didn't have the keys to the men's jeep and as much as she wanted to try to get their keys and give it a go, there would be too many opportunities for one of them to get to her while she tried to obtain the keys. If she sent a child to pat them down one of the thugs could grab him or her and use them as a hostage, forcing Solitar to lay down her gun.

"Okay, Cooper," she said to the child. "Now I want you to hold my waistband and lead me out of here, tell me when we reach the door. I have to watch the men." Cooper tucked his fingers in the back band of her jeans. Picking up the heavy bucket of weapons, Solitar carefully walked backwards, never taking her eyes off the men, she kept her gun trained on them while Cooper guided her to the exit.

"We're at the door, Miss Soli," Cooper told her.

"Okay, you hurry over to the other children," she said. As soon as she heard his footsteps pedaling away she ran because she knew the second she was out of sight the men would be up and running after her. She burst out the door, relieved to see the kids were huddled nearby. She jogged over to the mobster's jeep and shot out one of the tires then headed for the children. When she shot the gun the loud bang started them crying again. She had to ignore their wails and get them to safety.

In the midst of the wailing children, Solitar rushed over and shoved the bucket of weapons into a thick bush, hiding it. As soon as she went to join the children, Cooper and Bobby ran to the bush and dug in. Both pulled out a gun.

"Children," Solitar said, "I don't think you-"

The boys ignored her. Stuffing the guns in their waistbands, which looked outrageous, the big guns with the little boys' pants, they strode over to merge with the group.

"Okay, kids," she said with one arm waving, "we're going to hurry to the road. Walk fast, everyone, but don't run." She didn't need a child to trip and break a leg or something. She hustled them onto a path that was overgrown with weeds but used to be the stone walk from the parking area. Her shoulders hunched as she heard the men exiting the building.

She flung around with the gun up and they all came to an abrupt halt. "Stop or I'll shoot," she commanded. "Don't test me, I'm dying to take one of you out," again she lied. Last thing she could imagine would be having to shoot a human being. An unarmed human. Which would mean nothing if one of them got his hands on her, he wouldn't need a weapon. More than likely they had knives still somewhere on their bodies. Apparently though, she felt a wave of relief, they didn't have any guns or they would have shot at her and the children by now.

The crooks, impotent for the moment, stared after the flock of children and Solitar as they hurried away from them. She moved the kids along and when they reached her jeep she shot out a tire on that too.

"Miss Solitar," Bobby asked with a quivering lip, "why'd you do that?"

"Keep moving kids," she urged them. "I don't want them to be able to hot-wire it and come after us in it. Unfortunately, there isn't enough room on the jeep for all of us, none of you can drive, and I'm not leaving anyone here. We stick together."

"Okay." Bobby bit his lip and nodded.

Chapter Twenty-Five

Solitar felt like a mother duck herding her panicked ducklings from horrifying danger as the big bad wolves chased after them with snarls and howls hungering to massacre them. Bonnie and another girl, Ruby were the youngest and had the hardest time keeping up. Bobby pulled his sister along. Solitar went to pick Ruby up and carry her but her brother Cooper beat her to it. He swung the little girl on his back like she was a clinging monkey.

The group scurried down the dirt path, the thugs right behind them but the men were careful to keep out of gun range. They kept the winding road and trees between them and Solitar's weapon, but they were moving closer and closer using the natural landscape to conceal their bodies.

Solitar despaired as she caught up one of the smaller children's hand to pull him to keep up. There was no way they could make it to the main road. She checked her phone, no bars. Discouraged, she shoved it back in her pocket. She didn't have to tell the kids to hurry, they knew what was at their back. When Solitar had arrived at the school Pedro was on the verge of taking Bobby out back, and even the youngest child knew that would have been the last they'd see of him. And the men were all viciously angry now, they could just kill most of the children in retaliation and keep one or two as a hostage. They were all in lethal danger, and hideously aware of it.

The sun was hot, the humidity growing oppressive dragging the children down in their exhaustion. They'd tromped miles, but Solitar knew they had many more miles to go. Then she heard one of the children scream, it curdled Solitar's blood and clamped her stomach in terror. She had been staying at the back of the group to keep everyone moving and making sure they didn't lose any of them, she ran through the kids up to the front and her brain froze.

One of the children, Sammy, a four-year-old stood with his hair on end, his eyes popping out of his head. On the path just feet in front of him, a mountain lion had emerged from the brush and appeared to be about to pounce on the child. The lion's head rolled back as he let loose a tremendous roar exposing huge sharp teeth, he leaned back on his hind legs to power off them and charge the boy.

"Oh my-" A terrifying chill flew up her arms popping the tiny hairs along them. Solitar drew the gun, her hands shook so badly, she couldn't hold the aim-

BANG!

Solitar jumped out of her skin! As did all the children. Cooper was sitting on his butt. The kick of the gun he fired knocked him right on his ass. He was shaking his head, the gun was on the ground next to him. He put his hands to his ears. He'd missed the wild cat but the shot had scared it and it disappeared into the scrub.

Solitar rushed over to him and crouched down. "Honey, are you all right?" Her voice came out in a cracked choke.

His hands on his ears he blinked at her. "What?" he shouted, his ears were ringing.

She smiled broadly. "You did good, Cooper, you saved Sammy. The animal is gone."

"B-but I m- missed," Cooper gushed his words, his eyes rounded at the bush where the cat disappeared.

"Doesn't matter. I froze, you didn't. You're our hero, honey."

"Yeah." Bobby grinned at him. He offered Cooper his hand and helped him to his feet. "You're our dang cowboy, Coop, a true blue hero just like freakin' Jesse James!" The other children huddled around the boy praising him. Sammy wobbled over and threw his arms around the thin adolescent.

"Hero, Coop," Sammy uttered, hugging the boy.

Solitar could hear the hoodlums hiding in the bushes rumbling, sounding as if they were confused at the shot but were considering rushing the children. "Come along, kids, we have to keep moving." She waved her hands at them to get them going.

They made it another few miles when Sammy dropped to his knees, his body slumped. They had no food, no water, and they were just small children. Solitar glanced anxiously around. She could see the thugs darting behind trees, slips of black blobs they blended into the woods. Fortunately there was enough open space surrounding them the thugs couldn't sneak around and head them off or come at them from the side, but they were staying right on their heels.

The despair was overwhelming her, the children might have been better off if she'd stayed out of it. At least they were being fed and not in danger of becoming a wild beast's dinner. The mountain lion hadn't been spotted again with his yellow-brown body and tawny eyes gleaming in the burgeoning dusk. But that didn't mean he was gone, or that there wouldn't be others.

Then again, Pedro was about to murder Bobby when she had appeared, so at least her presence prevented that. For now. She just had to get the children somewhere safe that- what was that?

Something glinted, glare of the sun beaming off. She squinted, peering through the grass and trees, and, yes! A hunk of grey jutted within the jade bushes. A structure! "Come, children, hurry," she told them, guiding them to the building.

It was a hunter's lodge, or a shepherd's shack, whatever, Solitar jogged to the door, and turned the knob, the door opened. "Quickly, kids, inside," she ordered, gesturing for them to enter the building. The children stumbled inside, a weary Cooper lowered a tired weepy Ruby to her feet.

Inside, Solitar realized it was a vacant house. Looking around, she saw dirty beige walls, no furniture, windows lent light into the living room, kitchen and the three bedrooms. There was a fridge but it was empty. She turned on a faucet but nothing came out. The cupboards were bare. The children collapsed on the floor. Everyone was dog-tired, hungry, thirsty, scared. Ruby and Sammy whimpered their hunger, Bonnie snuggled under Bobby's arm sniffling. Each child's fatigued gaze was on Solitar.

"Um," she murmured, wishing for the words of encouragement to come, tell them to have faith. But who could help them? No one would know where they were. The children were missing and no one was going to be worried that Solitar was gone. She was the only one who'd thought about the school as a hiding place to stash the children. The police weren't looking for them because their parents couldn't report them missing or Bolívar would start sending their children's bodies to them one-by-one.

Suddenly a shot rang out! A bullet broke through the front window shattering it! They either found the bucket of guns or reinforcements had joined them. "Everyone get down!" Solitar screamed. The kids flattened themselves on the floor and started crying.

"That was a warning, *chica*," Bolívar's accented voice called out. "Put your gun down, Miss Solitar," he jibed, "come out with all the *niños* and we won't hurt you."

"Miss Soli, no, you can't," Bobby's young voice trembled. Solitar was on her stomach, she saw the terror razing the child's face. He had tucked Bonnie under him.

Solitar pushed to her hands and knees and crawled to the door. She crept up the wall to peer out the broken window. She could see the men crouching behind trees, the sun glinting off the metal of their pistols.

"Miss Solitar!" Bolívar shouted although he sounded pleasantly calm. "You have three seconds and we are coming in. We have the building surrounded and we are now armed." He took a breath and then demanded, "Come the hell out now!"

"Stay down," Solitar told the frightened children. Whimpers and sobs rebounded the room. She lifted her arm and put the gun to the broken window, and fired a shot.

"You bitch!" She heard Sergio shout.

"That's the way you want it, *puta*?" Bolívar hollered, the anger slamming away his calm. A flurry of bullets tore through the window, the children screamed. Solitar covered her ears ducking her head. And a volley of bullets breached other windows in back rooms.

Cooper jumped up and ran out of the room and they could hear glass breaking and his gun firing. Bobby climbed to his feet, kissed his baby sister on her head, whispered, "Stay down," and he ran off to another room. More glass breaking and gunfire sounded.

Her heart in her throat, Solitar stuck her gun back out the window and fired several shots. She screamed, "Leave us alone! We are armed too!"

A barrage of gunfire struck the house, shattering windows and splintering wood as the bullets struck the walls. The children covered their ears and flattened themselves to the floor, shrieking.

Solitar fired out the window until the gun clicked, empty. Dropping to the floor, she crawled across the floor to the first bedroom and saw Cooper firing, but his gun was only making clicking sounds. He was out of bullets too. His horrified expression took Solitar's breath. The next room Bobby turned his strained face to her, tears streaking down his cheeks.

Solitar said quietly, "I have to surrender, they'll kill us if I don't."

"No, Miss Soli," Cooper cried, "they will kill us anyway. We have to fight!"

"But we don't have anything to fight with, Cooper. There's nothing here," her arm swept the room indicating the complete emptiness. "We have a chance of at least some of you surviving if we give up." She knew she wouldn't survive this. Sergio, Pedro and Bolívar would all use her ruthlessly, violently, brutally assaulting her, before killing her. "No, I have to-" A scream reverberated from the living room. The trio raced down the hall to the room.

The men had broken in! A man Solitar didn't know had a gun to Ruby's head. His long black hair was tied back in a bun. The little redheaded girl was wailing, "Coo-Coo help me," she cried to her brother. Solitar grabbed Cooper's arm stopping him from rushing to his baby sister. She held her arm at her side, the empty gun in her hand. They didn't know it was empty, maybe she could bluff.

"Put the gun down, *puta*, we counted your bullets, you are out. Now, come to me." Bolívar's menacing grin was filled with shiny white teeth. He ordered, "Get her, Sergio. You get first taste. Luthor, Pedro, round up those little bastards. Call Suarez to bring the trucks so we can haul them back to the school." When Solitar didn't move, he said to the man holding Ruby, "Luis, shoot the girl."

"No!" Solitar cried. Bending, she set the gun on the floor and raised her hands. Sergio hurried right to her and grabbed a handful of her hair. Twisting her head at a painful, awkward angle, he forced her to her knees. "Mine, bitch, you are mine first. If you survive me, then Pedro is waiting next." He snatched her head back so she was forced to look up at him, then he twisted viciously and she cried out at the pain of her hair ripping from her scalp.

"Please," she huffed, tears eking from the corners of her eyes. "Please don't hurt them, I'll come peacefully, I'll do whatever you say."

Sergio jerked her head hard, snarled in her face, "You don't have a choice, bitch, your time here with those *mocosos pequeños*, little brats, is done." He started dragging her to the door. He said to Bolívar, "I'm takin' her around back. I wanna grab some branches to whip her, maybe stick up her fuckin' ass for making us work so hard. I want a hard rocky ground under her back, make her suffer as much as possible." He looked to Pedro and said, "Give me a couple hours, bro, then you can have you some." He gave him a wink.

Pedro's face was a hard mask of sociopathic savagery. He didn't say anything, just let his gaze slide down Solitar's body like a rancid tongue.

With a grin, Sergio wrenched Solitar to her feet, still holding her hair with it wrapped around his fist, he shoved her forward to the exit. Last thing she saw was the men pushing the crying children together in a cluster and moving them towards the door. Their sobs and frantic wheezes a symphony of bone chilling fright serenaded her out the door.

"We're goin' round back where we can have some privacy, don't need the little ones watching us now and getting any ideas, eh?" Sergio pushed her out the door and started to the path that led to the rear of the building. They could hear the others coming out behind them, the men cursing and complaining, the children crying.

"Okay, bitch, around this corner and we-"

"Let her go, fucker," a familiar voice rang out.

Solitar felt a buzz in her belly. Although Sergio gripped her hair in a tight grasp, she veered her eyes to the side and a thrilling warmth frizzled through her body. Kurian was there. He had a gun in his hand, and although he had a face of iron, he was   clearly   angry.   Very.   Wrathfully   so.

Chapter Twenty-Six

"What the hell-" Sergio swung her around in front of him. He snatched his gun from his belt and put it to Solitar's head and froze when he saw not only Kurian aiming a gun at him, but so were Rutger, Ivar, and his other men, Kristjan Kristoff and Jaquarius Nikolaus. And they weren't all of the rescue posse. Jared DiCello and his friends, Gregor, Cesar, Brandon, Thomas and Frankie were jumping from jeeps and striding to join Kurian and his crew. Rage didn't dent the avowed hell in the men's expressions, Bolívar had taken their children and they were beyond rage. Jamie Orlando had hitched along with the farmers, he slipped from a truck and joined the furious throng.

"Hold it right there," Bolívar commanded. His gun was drawn as were Pedro, Luis, and Luthor's. "You fuckers move and Sergio first takes out the skirt and then the children." Grinning confidently, he said, "You are at a detriment. We have the woman Solitar dead to rights, eh, Sergio? His gun is at her temple. One of you moves and she buys it."

He was right. Kurian and his team were at a disadvantage. They had only just arrived and hadn't had the opportunity to swarm the building, take up shielded stances, they didn't have the element of total surprise. His gaze blazing black steel, Kurian said nothing. He had called Rutger on his way to the school to advise where he thought the children were being held. They'd had to track the footprints of the children along the dirt road until they found everyone here at this structure. His eyes to Solitar, he hid the wince at the fear on her face and the pain of her burning scalp, and the gun Sergio held pressed gleefully, brutally shoving into her temple.

Bolívar taunted, "Ah, you do grasp your shitty position. Now, none of us wants a gunfight. People on both sides will lose. That includes your men, the woman, and the wee children. You may perhaps get one of us. But, we will be triumphant, I guarantee. Thus, you will lower your weapons," his grin sharpened with his arrogance. "You, Mister, ah?"

"Anastaas. Kurian Anastaas," Kurian replied.

"Uh huh." Bolívar studied him carefully. "You are police, are you not? Do not try to deny it. Either police or some sort of military special ops, eh? It is written all over you, the daring, the lethal skills, the confident deadly menace. You and," he glanced over at the other men with Kurian. "Those four, they are with you. Not those," he indicated Jared and the farmers. "They are simply poor peasants. You," he sneered at Jared. "This is all on you. I told you I would burn you out and raze your homes and families to the ground if you did not desist with the crops. I," he pounded his fist on his chest, "I am *El Jeffe*, the boss, the king. I own the coca fields, the cocaine that comes from Ruwenstad and spreads to the States and other countries." He tilted his head to Kurian. "To the Netherlands."

Kurian didn't twitch a muscle at his pointed comment.

"We would have worked for you," Cesar spoke up. "We would have done anything to feed our families."

Only Bolívar's eyes shifted to Cesar, he kept his head aimed at Kurian. "Ah, but I did not need, nor want you bumbling hillbillies on my payroll, and your crops are too puny, you do not have the rich soil that my fields are blessed with. I told you to stop harvesting lest you draw attention to me and my operation. You did not. So I burned you out and took your children to ensure you did not fight the fires." Back to Kurian, he commanded, "Put your weapons on the ground, all of you right now or we will kill the woman and start picking off the little ones. You might get us, but you will be the cause of many of the children's deaths." Huddled in Pedro and Luthor's control, whimpers came from the frightened kids.

Kurian paused, but then he and his men obliged, as did the farmers.

"Okay," Jared stepped forward. "We will do anything you say. Just give us our children and we will disappear. You will never see or hear from us again, I swear." He glanced at the other farmers, they all nodded their acquiescence.

Bolívar said, "Ah? You do not think it is too late? Won't you go to the police once you have your children back?"

Jared shrugged. "We can't explain that you burnt our coca fields and kidnapped our children without incriminating ourselves. No," he shook his head, "we will do as I said. We're gone. Vanished."

"Hmm," Bolívar pondered Jared's declaration. "And what about punishment for making me have to go through all this- this snatching and holding and threatening and chasing. Gods, man, we just spent an entire day chasing after the *puta* and your children. Then we had to indulge in a gun battle, which," he bumped one shoulder with a grin, "I must say we actually did enjoy, mainly because we won. However, we've had to endure your whiny, sniveling spawns, we had to feed them, watch them shit. And our humility tarnished by the likes of a mere woman, a very young woman," he said of Solitar. He nodded to Kurian. "What are we to do with him and his men?"

"Hell, I don't know." Exchanging a glance with Kurian, Jared stuffed his hands in his jean's pockets. "We just want our kids and to be allowed to leave with them and go find a peaceful life somewhere."

Bolívar said, "I think we broker a deal. I will allow you to take your kids and *vámonos* but, I need something done about these fuckers," he motioned to Kurian.

"I can handle that for you, Mr. Bolívar," Jamie Orlando said, coming forward, "just give me the woman," he glanced at Solitar. Sergio still cruelly gripped her hair forcing her neck to arch and her head yanked back. He dug the barrel of the gun into her temple. "As long as I hold her hostage the cops can be manipulated." Jamie said to Sergio, "Give her to me and you can take out these assholes."

Sergio's mouth pinched in an angry line, dark brows daggered down. "Fuck no. She's mine. Just shoot the cops, get rid of the yokels and their bratty *mocosos* and we'll go on as we were."

Bolívar considered Jamie's proposition. "What you say has merit." He looked at Solitar with disappointment. "I did want my taste of the *chica*, but, for expedient's sake, ah." His attention went to Kurian. "I don't want no cops on my tail, son. What you say we let you go, I presume you are in Ruwenstad to investigate the murders of those young women, you have no care for me and my enterprises." His smile wide, he said cheerfully, "*Si*, that's it boys. We let everyone go, farmers, kids, cops, we keep the bitch as collateral and everyone is happy."

Jamie shook his head and insisted, "No, give me the girl, I will ensure she stays secreted away. I have a place in Suriname, no one will find us. You need to control the cops, not kill them because more will come looking for them, this is the only way."

"You think we can control a bunch of *policía* with the captivity of one simple female?" Bolívar's eyes narrowed at Jamie. "But how do I know I can trust you? How do I know you are not a cop or one of the farmers and will let her go as soon as we are gone?"

"No, no, I'm with the mine. Listen," Jamie inched closer with a patronizing smile. "I am just as shady as you, my friend. In fact, I wouldn't mind joining your operation. I have connections in the States that can route your product. In fact, I've been working with," he paused, his eyes shifting from Jared to Kurian, "uh, let's say I have a contact that has dual citizenship with the Republic of Kedolamer here in South America and the United States, I've been working with him to, ah, fuck up the mine."

Jamie glanced at Solitar's gasp. "Yeah, sugar, you were right. I've been allowing the impure remnants to run off into the river and cause the pollution. We needed to get the mine shut down. We were hoping to get into the coca business here. I'd heard about the old fields left from that assassinated cartel and knew the fields still existed. But my partner and I needed the mine to implode before too many people started roving around the land here and discovering the crops. We could easily pay off the random hunter that came across them, but the damned miners were becoming adventurous with hikes and fishing and the like."

He said insincerely to Bolívar, "I apologize to you, sir, we weren't aware that you had your own operation going. However, with my contacts I can exponentially raise your income from the sale of the cocaine."

"What are you saying, *implode*?" Kurian asked with a sharp tone.

Jamie turned to him with a smirk. "Just like I said. Implode as in explode from the inside out."

"Oh Jamie, what have you done?" Solitar cried.

He looked at her, his lip curled with ire, his eyes suddenly heavy with lust. "I told you I'd get you back, sugar. One simple nonconsensual act of sex and you run into hiding." He ignored Kurian's growl.

"Well," Jamie went on, "my partner and I deliberately broke the fans to allow the methane gasses to rise. Ultimately they will cause an immense explosion and the ceiling and walls will come tumbling down just like fucking Jericho, ultimately shutting down the damned mine. Then all the Gatin staff will split back to the States and we can get on with business. So," he turned back to Bolívar, "my name is Jamie Orlando, now that you see how dastardly I can be, don't you want me on your team? I can be indispensible."

Bolívar regarded him thoughtfully while pawing at his greying goatee. "People will die in the explosion, that will only bring more investigators."

"The mine has been closed due to the broken fans, no one has been working inside for a couple of days," Jamie explained. "The investigators will assume the gases caused the explosion and won't need to come out and verify it. The mine will stay closed and everyone will just go away. A closed mine is a money pit."

"Fuck," Jared cursed, "those boys, Colby and Ritchie went to explore the mine in search of the children. They had an idea they'd been stashed there."

"Mr. Bolívar please!" Solitar shouted in panic. "You have to let these men go and stop those boys! You can't let them die! Oh my God," her eyes pleading she struggled against Sergio's painful grip.

Bolívar's shoulders rose and lowered with negligence. "What do I care about two young hicks? No one will bother to look for a pair of missing teens in this shithole of a town. Pedro, usher the children to their fathers. Luis, gather the cops or whatever the hell they are together and group them over by the road so we can get them on the trucks when they arrive. Sergio," he said, "give the *chica* to Orlando."

Sergio tightened his grip in Solitar's hair. "No, *Jeffe*, you said I could have her!"

Kurian allowed himself and his men to be assembled with the farmers and the children. He surreptitiously bent and whispered to Cooper. Cooper nodded.

His smile indulging, Bolívar said, "Come now, *mi amigo*, I will buy you a dozen *prostitutas* to replace her."

Shaking his head adamantly, his black hair flopping back and forth, Sergio barked, "No, I want this one. I want to punish her. At least let me have some time with her before I give her to that fucker." He dug the gun into Solitar's temple so hard he was making a dent, her head was forced to a severe slant.

Bolívar crossed his arms over his chest and nodded. "That sounds agreeable for everyone. Go on, take her inside, use one of the rooms. You have until Suarez comes with the trucks."

"*Jeffe*," Luthor said, "a couple of the *niños* have weapons."

"So what? They have no bullets. Let the little *chicos* be big men with their dangerous guns, eh?" Bolívar grinned at Bobby and Cooper. "Maybe you will grow up to be terrible desperados like me, eh my children?"

Before Bolívar could change his mind, his gun still to her head, Sergio started dragging Solitar back into the house. Bolívar said to Jamie, "You don't mind if he has his pleasure with your woman for a few moments, do you?"

Jamie's cheeks sucked in, he blew them out, his brows lowered. "I suppose not as long as I get to keep her. We all have to make some concessions here. Prove we are viable businessmen." He turned and gave the mobster a cold smile.

Bolívar clapped him on the shoulder with a wide grin. "There you go, boy, on board. Let's steer the group to the road and await the trucks. Unless you want to dally here and listen to your woman's screams from Sergio's...ah, lovemaking?" He chuckled at the grimace on Jamie's face.

"Fuck no." Jamie's tongue poked out in revulsion. "I only want to hear her screams from what I do to her. He better leave her functional, Bolívar, I don't want her carved up in pieces. Especially her face. And her insides."

"Ah my young friend, Sergio is a savage brute, we will have to wait and see. Come along," Bolívar moved towards the collection of men and children starting for the road. "I think it's best to eliminate the police. Pedro is diligent, no one will find their bodies."

A loud cracking sound broke from above bringing everyone to a sudden stop. Cooper had thrown his gun at a rotted tree limb, snapping off, it instantly fell landing on Sergio's head. He yowled and put his hands up to stop whatever was hitting him. It wasn't enough to knock him down but it was enough for Solitar to break away-

That was all Kurian needed. Solitar out of Sergio's grip and a huge distraction. He and Rutger, Kris, Ivar and Jaq bent and swiftly snapped up their guns and started firing. Kurian's bullets went straight and sure right into Sergio's chest. The gangster grunted then stumbled backwards and let out a moan before tumbling to the ground where he lay still on his back.

Rutger took out Bolívar, Ivar did Pedro, Kris had Luis, and Jaq shot Luthor. Luthor spun as the bullet slammed into his heart and he dropped like a rock. Bolívar, Pedro and Luis all screamed and tumbled to the ground like bags of solid dung.

Aghast, Jamie turned and ran for the jeep Luis had come in. But Kurian wanted him. He sped after the traitor and just as Jamie reached the jeep, Kurian grabbed his shirt collar and threw the man to the ground. Then he jumped on him and went wailing, his fists flailing like windmills pummeling so hard so fast Jamie could do nothing but curl in a ball and try to protect himself. Which was useless as Kurian let the story Solitar had told him of her rape fuel his fists.

Sergio and Luthor were dead but Bolívar, Pedro and Luis were only injured. Rutger and Kris disarmed them and put them in restraints while Jaq commandeered the farmers. Ivar hurried to Solitar. She had been knocked to the ground when Sergio tossed his arms up.

Ivar knelt beside her. "Woman," he said surly, "are you injured?"

"No," she replied, shaking her head as he helped her to her feet. "Just stunned, bruised, we have to get to the mine!" She tore her hands from Ivar's steadying grasp and ran to the jeep. He sprinted after her.

Kurian stood, kicked a broken, unconscious Jamie in the kidney and then hurried after them. Ivar had pushed Solitar out of the driver's side and into a back seat and cranked up the engine.

They were rolling when Kurian jumped into the open back to land beside Solitar. Ivar slammed his boot to the gas pedal, flooring the vehicle- it fishtailed then they tore down   the   road   towards   the   mine.

Chapter Twenty-Seven

The jeep bounced and rocked over the uneven dirt roads spitting a cloud of dirt and gravel behind them until they reached the tarred roads the miners had created to drive in the heavy equipment. Kurian glanced at Solitar sitting next to him. He reached his hand out to touch her, but her face was remote ice, and she hadn't once looked at him or said a word. Cuts and bruises covered her soft skin, dirt smudged the creamy complexion.

Her sweater had been half ripped off by Sergio's roughness, and her black jeans were torn and dusty. Yet she sat regally as fear for the teenagers' doom weighed on her. She had just been through a nightmare yet her thoughts were only of Colby and Ritchie, and whoever else could be in the mine that was about to explode.

"Solitar," Kurian began but she cut him off.

Without looking at him she said, "I know you came for the children, but, I thank you for saving me as well." She tilted her head but still didn't look at him. "How on earth did you manage- how did Cooper-"

He told her, "I noticed he and the other boy, the little blond guy both had pistols. Bolívar had stated they were empty but it sounded like it was not he who had given them to the boys. I saw the bullet holes in the house, shit, baby, what hellfire did you guys go through? How the hell did you manage to get those kids away from that drug lord? And, for your information, I came for you, Solitar."

Her lips pressed tightly at the remembrance of the bullets flying everywhere striking the windows, the walls, chipping flakes of stone off the fireplace in the corner. The noise, the bedlam, the screams of terror. Her fear for the children, their panic, hysterical sobs as the bullets ricocheted overhead as they lay curled like embryos on the floor.

She drew a deep breath, let it out. "I managed to surprise Bolívar and I had him and his men relinquish their weapons and then had Cooper collect them and put them in a bucket. I hid the bucket in the bushes but Cooper and Bobby went there and each took a gun. They both claimed to be experienced only, heavens," her voice shook at the memory of the shootout in the house. "Bobby is only seven, and Cooper ten, it was unbelievable. Those boys were so brave."

Kurian then did pat her hand, he left his hand on top of hers. "I cannot imagine, my love, the fright you were in."

She nodded. Her long hair tumbling dirty and messy over her shoulders as a shiver rippled across them. "Yes. It was…horrible. Bolívar shot at us from outside, Cooper and Bobby each ran to a room and returned fire as did I from the living room. But," her breath expelled in a tight sound. "We ran out of bullets. Bolívar and his men were counting them. They moved in when they knew we were out, but oddly, Bolívar allowed the boys to keep their weapons. Told them the guns made them men. What a joke."

Kurian twined their fingers as she spoke, he moved their clasped hands to his thigh. "Ah, the joke was on the gangster, the chump. Serves him right. His macho foolishness was his undoing. Bested first by a single young female and then by a pubescent boy. Although, if our ruse had not worked I had Plan B and C."

Her smile humorless, Solitar said, "Yes, a stupid brutal man. Thank God. Explain your Plan A that involved a ten-year-old child?"

Chuckling, Kurian explained, "Once I saw the boys with the guns and I saw how comfortable they were holding them, not like they were toys or squirt guns kids played with, and, knowing they basically spent their lives running the fields, streams, woods, and the sheer destitution of their families I figured they were more or less competent hunters. I was sure they could throw rocks and use slingshots with expertise.

"I asked Cooper if he could throw his gun and hit that dead tree branch. He said he could. Apparently he is a baseball star wannabe so he has done a lot of practice throwing at birds and squirrels. We had to wait until Sergio was directly under it. Each of my men had their thug assigned to them to take out. We use a special sign language to communicate furtively. The thugs were watching us to make a move, but they thought the children were harmless." Kurian laughed.

"The boy was as good as he claimed. Hit that damned branch and dropped it on that bastard." He shook his head still chuckling. "I didn't really expect it to work. Maybe a slight distraction if that, we were ready to do more, but that had been sufficient."

She tipped her head and regarded him with a small shy smile. "That's an understatement, but you're right. It saved us all. The boy is a hero. Twice today actually. He shot at a mountain lion that was choosing little Sammy as his lunch while we were on the path to the main road."

Lines around Kurian's eyes and mouth dug in at the thought of the danger they had been in. The peril Solitar had faced. "You," he said, cupping her face and gently lifting it to connect their eyes. "You are the hero, Solitar. You went out to the school, alone-"

"If you were my woman I would tan your hide into next year," Ivar grunted from the front seat.

160

Kurian's mouth lifted in a grin. "Anyway, you managed to seize a dangerous drug lord and his thugs and confiscate his weapons and his hostages and lead them to relative safety."

She smiled gloomily. "But it wasn't enough. Maybe if I had grabbed more of the guns-"

"Baby," he said and squeezed her hand. "You did what you could do. You held them off long enough until we could get there. You could not have fought them off completely, you were not equipped and you had the youngsters to look out for. The crooks would have starved you out if they could not get to you through your gunfire. Your hands were tied. And," he said proudly, "not one of the children was harmed. But," he scolded gently yet with anger, "you should have waited for me. I would have come with you, me and my men. You took a terrible chance."

"Oh, Kurian," a sob split from her clenched throat, "they were about to kill Bobby when I got there. It was horrible, so horrible. I was so afraid." More sobs broke loose.

"Baby," Kurian mumbled and drew her into his arms. Stroking her head, her hair, he caressed her back while murmuring soothing words in her ear. Calling her a brave, yet reckless hero. She wept into his shoulder, wetting his shirt. He cuddled her in his strong embrace, his lips at her ear until she remembered earlier. When he'd up and left her. Got what he wanted, got his bragging rights, and dumped her.

Solitar pushed from his arms. "I'm fine," she said with a sniffle then shuffled across the seat to get as far from him as she could.

Frowning, Kurian said, "I don't know what got twisted inside that gorgeous head of yours, Solitar, but we have to talk."

"There is nothing to say, Kurian. You got what you wanted, now, when we resolve…the pending incidents at the mine, I plan on never having to speak to you again."

His brows thrust up. "What? Solitar, I did not come for the children, I came after you. I-"

She turned her back to him. "Lies, Kurian, everything you say is a lie. Even Bolívar knew you weren't a simple miner. He called you a cop, or a military guy on a mission. Don't talk to me, please, just…" she sighed, "leave me alone."

"I refuse-"

But Ivar had turned onto the road that led right up to the mine. The jeep jostled as he raced it full speed ahead. The mine came into view, an ugly dark hole gouged into solid rock, the mountain behind it looming mightily. Their dynamiting and drilling had destroyed much of the land on the mountain and surrounding area gouging a mirrored black hole in Solitar's heart as well. She hated the damage they did to the environment with every inch of her soul. Once this was over, she promised herself, she would flip hamburgers or clean toilets, take the rest of her life to pay back what she owed the school, anything but have a part in this irrevocable devastation of land.

Ivar came to a stop and parked. The trio leaped out and started for the mine. Kurian grasped Solitar's arm halting her. "No, you stay here," he ordered.

"What? No, I'm going in, if anything happens to Colby-"

Hubie, Siggy, Camara and others rushed up to them. Camara shouted, "Where have you been, Soli? Where is Luthor? You said you were going for the children-"

Solitar paused. How complicit had Camara really been with everything? The coca, the children, the sabotaging the mine? "He's-" she broke off, "not now, we'll go into it later. Right now, does anyone know if Colby and Ritchie went into the mine to search for the children?" She glanced at the men with Camara, they looked confused.

Solitar explained to them, "A drug kingpin kidnapped Jared DiCello and other farmers' children. He set their coca fields on fire and was holding the children hostage to force Jared and the others to not fight to save the fields because the kingpin was worried they would draw attention and his own fields would get uncovered. Additionally," she sucked in a breath, "Jamie Orlando was in cahoots with someone here to corrupt the mine, pollute the river. They wanted the mine and its employees to go away to keep attention off Ruwenstad so they could grow their coca undetected and create an empire."

"Never liked that arsehole," Siggy said with a purse to his lips.

"Who was he working with?" Hubie asked. His long blond hair was tied back in a ponytail.

Solitar's eyes narrowed at him. "Well, we don't know, maybe you do?"

Hubie was taken aback. His thumb pressed to his chest he said insulted, "I don't know shit. I would never hurt children, or the mine. Hell, Woman, this is my livelihood. I sent money home so my fiancée can plan our wedding. I sure ain't idiot enough to destroy my golden goose." He jutted his jaw at Kurian and said, "We heard Anastaas was some kind of a Dutch cop looking into the serial murders. But that the fucker got away."

Kurian turned to him, "How did you-"

"Small town, cops blab." Hubie scowled. "You let the killer skip town."

Solitar turned to Kurian, her brows raised. "What? My brother? He's...gone? How? What happened?"

"Your brother is the serial killer?" Simultaneous gasps abounded.

His frown at Hubie, Kurian said quietly to Solitar, "I will explain later. It was where I had to go when I left you. I-"

"Never mind that now," Solitar said turning from him. "Did anyone see Colby go into the mine? It should have been closed but I see the gate is open?" She anxiously searched the growing crowd waiting for one of them to relieve her of her fear, state that the mine was empty.

"Yes!" Lili-Mae's strident voice broke in. The petite girl shyly but with worry creasing her face came forward. Wringing her hands as she approached them, she said, "Colby told me he was sure the children had been hidden somewhere deep inside. He said there are turnoffs and formations with natural carved rooms they could be concealed in. Secreted so far into the belly of the mountain with big rocks pushed in front of the opening their screams would not be heard. He made me stay here while he and Ritchie went inside to search."

"Oh my goodness," Solitar's voice hitched with apprehension. "We have to go-"

A thunderous explosion burst from the hole, the area over the opening shot out with flames and earth and rocks thrusting to the sky. Then a ripple of more ear-splitting explosions rent the world, the very ground shook.

Kurian threw himself on top of Solitar taking her to the ground and covered her with his body. Ivar did the same to Lili-Mae, everyone was slammed back from the force of the immense blast and hurled to the ground. Fire blazed overhead and stones and dirt, pieces of equipment, iron railings and chunks of rocks, tools, everything flung wide and railed down on them.

The blast made ears ring, the heat of the fire burning those closest to the opening. Screams and cries reverberated from the dashed people pummeled with debris. After long frightening moments, when the explosions ceased, the people slowly raised their heads. Those that could, climbed to their feet, staggering with disorientation. People from nearby, the warehouse, the office shanty, Zuk Zuk's pub came barreling out with shouts of incomprehension and horror.

More stunned moments passed before Kurian lifted slightly off Solitar and peered down at her. "Baby, are you all right? Talk to me." He smoothed the dirty hair from her bruised cheek and watched as her eyes fluttered.

She gazed up at him dazed, bewildered. "Kurian? W- what happened?"

He helped her to sit up, dust and debris drifting from his hair and clothes. He crouched and scanned the area. Stunned people were helping the injured, already the local fire brigand's sirens were wailing in the distance.

Then Solitar staggered to her feet. "Colby! We have to get to them!" she shouted, stumbling towards the burning mine. Flames surged from the charred opening. Rocks and wrecked equipment, some on fire, were strewn all over, people were struggling to stand steady. Cries of pain and screams of terror trundled from all over, thick smoke poured from the fiery hole slathering a layer of dust on everyone and everything.

Solitar continued on to the mine with Lili-Mae running right behind her screeching at the top of her lungs for Colby. Just as Solitar reached the mine Kurian grabbed her arm jerking her back. When she fought him he wrapped his arms around her. "Let me go, Kurian! Colby's in there! We have to get him!"

"Hush, baby, he could not have survived the blast." Kurian held her tightly disregarding her twisting and jerking violently in his clutch, her fists pounding on his arms to release her.

Ivar caught Lili-Mae, lifting her off her feet, he held her taut as she screamed, "*Colby! Colby!*"

A fire truck lurched into the roadway, sirens with their shrill wailing and colored lights swirling, paramedics pulled in behind them. Crews scurried off the vehicles and unhitched equipment, unwound fire hoses and hurried to the burning mine. Paramedics stopped at each injured person lying on the ground to assist them.

Kurian drew Solitar back from the flames that stroked tongues of fire out of the opening, gusts of black smoke burgeoned forth blinding them. The extreme heat and thick smoke brought tears to their eyes.

"Oh, God, Kurian," Solitar wailed shoving her face into his shoulder, "poor Colby, Ritchie, *oh God.*"

"*Ja*, baby, I know," his own anguished voice filled with pain at the thought of the teens perishing so gruesomely. He held her tightly, smoothing her sooty hair down her back.

Gulping heavy gasps of air into her dry lungs, Solitar put her palms on his chest and pushed from him. "Wait," she wiped at her tearing eyes.

"No, baby," he said, "there is nothing we can do. We need to get out of the way and let the responders do their job."

She pushed harder. "No, wait, I- there- there's a small entrance way back on the side. I had it dug as an emergency exit. It- it's far back from the central tunnel and shafts, there- there's a chance, Kurian, please, we have to try, please!"

"Where?" his voice held doubt. "Where baby? Show me." He waved at Siggy and Hubie who were covered with soot and grime, pieces of debris clung to their hair, they were brushing off their clothes. "Grab some shovels, hammers, drills, hurry, follow us."

"There ain't no entrance on the side, Kurian," Hubie said. "I've seen the maps and blueprints."

Solitar pulled at Kurian's hand. "It's fairly recent, too new to be on the maps. Hurry!"

They rushed alongside the mountain feeling the heat radiating from the rocks as they moved. A few moments of quick jogging, and Solitar slowed, pointed and said, "There, there!" There was an iron door but it was scorched and dented, clearly the explosion had reached this far. The door though was intact, it hadn't been blown open.

"Please!" Lili-Mae cried as they reached them. Ivar carried her like she was a child. He set her on her feet as the miners hastened up carrying shovels and tools.

Other miners hurried to them carrying equipment and they all went to task, bashing picks and hammers into the rock around the iron door. Kurian grabbed a pick and started hacking into the mountain. Ivar picked up a huge hand drill and started drilling along the side of the door, shards of rock spewed along with the loud hammering wail of the drill. As the men worked, Solitar and Lili-Mae and others hauled away the larger rubble.

As they toiled, some of the firefighters appeared and waded into the turmoil.

It seemed like hours had passed to Solitar, her back and arms ached, she was so hungry and thirsty there hadn't been an opportunity all day during their harrowing flight to grab some food and water. But the picture of the boys lying on the ground, chunks of their limbs blown off, their skin shredded, burned to a blackened crisp kept her moving. She shook the images from her head, it only made her stomach retch, and bring stinging tears to her eyes. This is what happened when you allowed yourself to feel for people. First Kurian humiliates and breaks her heart, now she's devastated with grief at the thought of the charming imps that may have died a grisly agonizing death.

She'd felt as helpless as the child who had been held prisoner by a pedophile then later with abusive foster families, and when Jamie overpowered her and assaulted her, but this, this was 100 times worse. Darling Colby had charmed his way into her life with his mischievousness and desire to atone for his sins and be a man. A man who walked the straight line and took care of his family. He had his whole life ahead of him, the grief and torment Lili-Mae would have to bear. And poor Ritchie and his family's heartache as well. It was all too much.

Finally the men were able to pull the battered door from the wall of the mountain. The heat so intense the door had melted into the rock. They surged together, peeling the scorching door back, it thundered to the ground when they let it drop. A cloud of black smoke roiled out, dimming all hope that anyone was still alive inside.

Lili-Mae's sobs could be heard above the male rumblings of defeat. Two firefighters pushed through the crowd, they wore their hazard suits and gas masks. The people stepped aside to let them pass. They pushed their way through the blockade of smoke and disappeared inside the smoldering mine.

Silence but for the crackling of the diminishing fires, the whooshing of the hoses shooting water, and the people shouting out front of the mountain. It would have been a pretty day, but now it was marred with soot and smoke, heat and destruction, and death. The group waited, filthy and tired, adrenalin still raging keeping them on their feet, but the dread hung heavy like the fuming cloud of smoke over them.

Solitar held Lili-Mae's hand, tears streaming down both of their agonized faces. Then…

An image materialized from the smoky doorway. A firefighter, his white suit now dark with soot carried a body over his shoulder. He moved out of the door and the men waiting hustled forward to take his burden from him. They laid the person on the ground, a paramedic rushed over and she started working on him.

"That's…" Solitar was stunned, "that's Laddie Lafayette. What on earth was he doing in the mine? He had no work to do, it was supposed to be locked up. I don't under-" Her shocked eyes met Kurian's. And she understood. "He was Jamie Orlando's partner. I can't believe it." She stood with the others staring down in bafflement at the man.

"Is the damned bloke alive?" Siggy wiped dirt from his face with a filthy handkerchief, sweat dripped off the end of his nose.

Another paramedic joined the first one to render aid. He nodded. "Barely, let's hook him up." The first paramedic had already fitted an oxygen mask over Laddie's mouth and nose, air was pumping through the tubes. Together with the male paramedic they lifted Laddie onto a gurney, a third paramedic approached to assist.

165

Solitar lurched forward and grasped the firefighter's arm. "Was there anyone else in there? Please," she gulped back tears at the shake of his head.

"I don't know, Miss, I only saw this one. Javier is still inside. I have to go back in." He shook off her grasp and headed back into the smoggy blackness.

Again they waited, and prayed. Kurian rolled his arm around Solitar's shoulders while Solitar held Lili-Mae's hand again. And they waited.

"Look!" someone shouted. The two firefighters were coming through the smoke. They had their shoulders under the arms of someone and were half-carrying, half-dragging him out, the others were there to help them lay the person gently on the ground. As more paramedics dropped down beside him, the others stepped back out of the way.

"It's bloody Ritchie," Siggy said. "Although he's covered with soot and dirt I recognize the young matey's dark hair and that flannel shirt. He had it on this morning when he and Colby stopped by the office to get paid for the errands they ran." Ritchie's body jerked as he coughed. "He's alive!" Siggy crowed with relief.

As the paramedics worked on him, Kurian knelt beside the teen. "Ritchie, son, is Colby inside? Can you tell us where?"

Ritchie pushed heavy lids up to show reddened eyes, he coughed long and hard. The paramedic shoved the oxygen mask over his face but the teen pushed it aside. He coughed, sucked in a lungful of air and said gasping, "Yeah, he- he's in there. He was fighting with," he wheezed, coughed, sucked in air and said, "Mr. Lafayette. Colby saw Lafayette breaking down fans and- and-" he gasped for air.

Spasms of coughing passed before he could speak again. "Colby knew that was dangerous. We- spent time with miners, they told us that-" He broke off in a fit of coughing. The paramedic put the mask back over his mouth. He took a deep breath then pushed it away. "Colby said he was gonna- gonna tell. Lafayette said he'd pay us to keep our mouths shut. Colby said "No fucking way," and he went to leave but Lafayette jumped him and they- they started fighting. Then- then there was this huge bang, explosion, I guess I was knocked out," and Ritchie fell into fits of gasping and coughing.

"Enough," the female paramedic decreed and attached the mask to Ritchie's head. They lifted him to a gurney and took him away.

The two firefighters stood there and removed their hoods. They wiped their eyes and started unzipping their suits.

"Wait, you still have a kid inside," Kurian told them. "You have to go back in."

One of the men shook his head, sweat flung from his wet hair. "No way, man. Anyone else still in there is fried. No one could survive. We were lucky to get these two out. We're done. I'm sorry," he said, at Solitar's wretched expression and Lili-Mae's wail of anguish.

"No, no," Solitar sobbed, approaching the firefighters, "it can't be, not Colby."

"What do you care?" Darlayne Tishcott sneered at her. She was a barmaid at Zuk Zuk's. "You threw the kid away for a lousy can of beer. Everyone knows you have no heart, no feelings, you just don't give a shit. All you care about is looking good to Garrick Miles."

Solitar quailed under the venomous outburst, her head drooped.

"You shut up, Miss, you don't know crap," Lili-Mae yelled, coming to stand beside Solitar. "Miss Soli has been giving Colby and Ritchie jobs to do to earn money. She asked the sheriff to only impose community service hours for Colby to pay for the beer he tried to steal. She said she wanted some punishment even if it was a light offense because Colby has no- no discipline at home. No one to care if he did good or bad. He needed to learn responsibility, man up, work right for a living."

Lili-Mae turned glowing eyes to Solitar. "She makes these divine paintings of folks and their pets. But she does it anonymously, she don't want praise for her work. She has the money from the sales given to charity, to the animal shelter and the townsfolk who need it the most." She smiled at Solitar, her face almost black from the swirling sticky soot.

"No, Miss Solitar is an angel, she does everything she can to help us. She's been teaching me how to cook and helping Colby with his math. She's good people, she loves Colby like I do, she-" The girl broke down into sobs. "*My Colby is gone,*" she wailed, "what am I gonna do without him! *Oh God.*"

Solitar wrapped her arms around the teen and held her tightly, her own tears wetting the girl's hair.

"Fuck this," Kurian swore. "Give me your suit," he commanded one of the firefighters.

The man looked aghast at him. "What the fuck? No way man."

"Give it to me unless you are going back in." Kurian held his hand out.

With a shrug and a shake to his head, the firefighter removed his suit, the hood and gas mask too and handed them to Kurian. Kurian donned them and started for the opening of the cave.

Solitar hurried after him, she grasped his arm. "No, Kurian, you can't. If the fireman says it's too dangerous for them, then it is for you as well. Don't do it."

Kurian shrugged from her grasp, his voice muffled, "I am not leaving a child in there to die alone." He marched up to the dark hole and disappeared into it.

Ivar said, "Outta my way, Woman," and donned the same as Kurian, he followed him into the abyss.

Biting her nails, Solitar prayed. She felt Lili-Mae's hand slip into hers. No one wanted to leave. People still bustled about in front where the brunt of the explosion had expelled, trucks and jeeps rolled back and forth, in and out of the area.

They waited.

After a lifetime had passed, someone shouted, "Look!"

Two burly figures were wading out of the smoke, between them, they carried a thin blackened form. A hush rolled over the crowd as everyone held their breath.

Kurian and Ivar gently laid their burden on the ground and quickly started CPR.

One of the miners hastened around by the front to grab a paramedic and a defibrillator.

It was only minutes before the paramedics entered the scene and took over with the firefighters working with them.

As Kurian peeled off the sullied suit, he solemnly shook his head as Solitar made her way to him. He handed the suit to the firefighter he'd borrowed it from, Ivar did the same. Everyone saw Kurian's grim shake of his head indicating Colby had not survived the explosion, and shoulders wilted with defeat.

"There's no hope at all?" Solitar whispered to Kurian.

Kurian's eyes on Colby, the boy was unrecognizable he was so covered in black soot. "Not sure. We found him trapped under a shelf of rocks. Part of the roof had collapsed on him. He was not breathing when we freed him. We gave him a bit of resuscitation, but keeping him there in the heat and the smoke was not going to help him." They stood and watched the paramedics work on the boy. Lili-Mae was standing as close to them as she could.

Time passed, people fidgeted, murmured in groups. The manager of Zuk Zuk's sent over platters of sandwiches and bottles of water for the responders and a few others. Although earlier Solitar had been starving, now her stomach was tied up in knots.

"Here, at least drink some water," Kurian handed her a bottle. He had chugged down two already and plowed through two sandwiches. Solitar had declined when he tried to get her to eat.

"Thanks," she mumbled. "Oh," she said, "they're taking him." Holding the bottle she hurried over and asked a paramedic if she could ride in the van with Colby.

The paramedic said, "No. Family only. The girl there said his family isn't here so she's going. Says she's his fiancée. Didn't see a ring but," he shrugged a shoulder, "who cares at this point? They'll only be planning a funeral. What a damned shame, so young."

"He- is he dead?" Solitar was afraid to ask, to hear the final truth.

"Ah," the paramedic was closing up his medical kit. "He flat lined. They're gonna keep trying though, they won't give up. He's young and strong, maybe..." he didn't sound convincing. He nodded to Solitar then went to board his own truck.

A weeping Lili-Mae was helped into the van carrying Colby. As soon as the doors were   closed   it   took   off.

Chapter Twenty-Eight

"I will take you to the Cresh so you can clean up," Kurian curled his hand under Solitar's elbow.

Blinking erratically, her mind tumbled about in a jumble and she was suddenly almost too weary to stand. Solitar looked down at her soiled and ruined clothes, her mouth pulled in wryly. "Yeah, I guess I need a bit of a wash. But," she said quickly, "I'm going straight to the hospital afterwards."

"Sure, whatever you say," Kurian agreed just to get her moving. He helped her into the jeep and headed to the Cresh. In twenty minutes he pulled up in the parking lot and parked. Cars, motorbikes and bicycles were parked untidily around the lot. The mine was closed leaving the employees at loose ends.

People were going in and coming out of the Cresh, several greeted each other, most gawked with curiosity at Solitar and Kurian. The phone lines had blown up already since they'd left the destroyed mine. A few gave them sad waves of acknowledgment as they learned of the hell they'd just endured, and the loss of life for a young man everyone liked.

Kurian moved around the front of the jeep to the passenger side. Solitar sat limp in her seat, her half-closed eyes blurry with grief and in slight disorientation due to the day's horrendous events. Kurian opened her door and unbuckled her seatbelt then drew her out.

They trod silently to the building. Inside, Solitar patted the pockets on her pants, and said with vague bafflement, "I don't have my key, I don't remember where I left my purse." They stopped at the front desk and Kurian slammed his palm down hard several times on the bell. It rang in loud, shocking clangs.

Still, it took several minutes before the attendant toddled out from the back. Yawning and scratching his belly, Gordy moved as fast as a sloth to the desk. "Whaddya want?" he asked. His eyes were puffy and bloodshot. In his late twenties, he was a beanpole with a gut from beer and M&M's, his favorite marijuana munchie. In his twenties, lank sandy hair dusted over the red eyes, the stands moved when he blinked.

"Please provide Miss Lyonne with her room key," Kurian said.

"Huh?" The red eyes hovered over the big tear in Solitar's sweater exposing much of her breast. "She done got one," he muttered.

Kurian reached over the counter, grabbed Gordy's wrinkled striped collar and jerked him up and over the counter pulling him onto his stomach. Ignoring Gordy's yelp, Kurian said, "We are in no mood for any shit, boy. Give the lady her key. Now. And no mouth." He glared into the red eyes that were now wide and alert.

"Y- yessir," Gordy garbled.

One last hard stare, Kurian was itching to pound someone else. He hadn't worked off all his blood lust on Jamie Orlando. He couldn't outright kill Orlando or he'd be sitting in a cell and unable then to protect Solitar from whatever other devastation was out there waiting to pounce on her. He let the kid slide to his now shaking legs. Quickly, Gordy grabbed an extra key and handed it to Kurian. Without another word, Kurian cupped Solitar's elbow and walked her up to her room.

He opened the door and ushered her inside. "*Oke*," he said, "take a shower. I am going to my room and I will be back to take you to the hospital. In the meantime, I will order room service for us." When she opened her mouth to object, he said, "You have to eat, you are dead on your feet." Then he left her alone.

On his way to his room he called Dozi Shunnar. Dozi was in charge of all things Cresh. When she answered, he said, "This is Kurian Anastaas. I would like two dinners and a bottle of wine delivered to Miss Lyonne's room as soon as possible."

"Huh," she snorted into the phone. "Where do you get the idea that there is room service here, my man?"

"My hundred dollar bill gave me the idea. How long will it take?"

Chuckling, the woman said, "What do you want?"

"Something…sturdy. Find me a nice bottle of Beaujolais. Might have to send someone to Zuk Zuk's for that."

"Gonna be at least 45 minutes, Anastaas," she told him.

Kurian gave Solitar 30 minutes before he approached her door. His hair was still damp from his shower, he had changed into black jeans and a dark brown sweater. The heat and humidity had lifted as dark clouds were rolling in and the sun was lowering cooling things off.

He knocked lightly. No answer. Muttering to himself, "She had better be in there if she knows what is good for her." He had taken her room key and with no purse therefore no money, and no vehicle, it was unlikely she had left the building. But she was ballsy when she had to be, and unpredictable. And damned reckless.

When she didn't answer the door, he used her key to open it. Stepping inside, he pocketed the key. His racing heart settled when he saw her on the small balcony. She was outside ruffling her wet hair with a towel. She wore a white robe. He hadn't knocked that loud in case she'd been sleeping, standing on the other side of the partially open balcony door she hadn't heard it. Kurian ambled across the room and pushed the glass door all the way open. "Solitar," he stated her name coolly, and hated the way her body jumped, startled and instantly frightened. It was self-preservation PTSD left over from her childhood trauma.

She turned, holding the towel to her hair. "Oh, Kurian, you surprised me." Her eyes narrowed. "Why didn't you knock? Do you have my key? Please give it to me." She moved to him with her hand out.

In his mind, so slender and graceful she looked like a Grecian goddess in the flowing white robe. His gaze lowered to the opening of the robe exposing her cleavage and it heated. Ignoring her hand waiting for her key, he said, "I have ordered food for us. It should be here in 15 or 20 minutes. Also, I called the hospital and I sent Rutger there. He said Colby is in ICU, they are working on him. Ah," he took a breath, "they used the defibrillator on him twice.

"The second time they got a pulse so they are continuing treatment. They said the CPR we performed on Colby helped gateway until they got the machine hooked up to him. Rutger says the boy is in a coma and it is hit and miss at this point. He said it will be a while before we are given any more news, and they are not allowing visitors. They sent Lili-Mae home to wait with her parents."

"Oh that poor girl, she must be out of her mind," Solitar's voice was thick with compassion. "I'm glad she has decent parents unlike Colby's. If she didn't we'd have to go get her and bring her here so she'd have someone to lean on during this distressing time."

Kurian gave her a strange look. "*Ja*. Rutger said give it a couple hours before we go to the hospital."

Solitar nodded with reluctance. "Okay. But," she glanced at the clock on the nightstand and said with determination, "two hours and I am going there."

A small smile lifted the side of his hard mouth. "We can stop and see if Lili-Mae would like to go with us."

Solitar beamed. "That would be great." Her brows lowered. "We?"

He took her hand and drew her back into the room. "*Ja*. I think there are no worries anymore about the coca fields. Both of them. Jared's operation has been destroyed. Simón Bolívar and two of his men are seriously injured and will be in custody as soon as they are well enough to be moved. I spoke with Ivar and he and our other men are rounding up the rest of Bolívar's gang."

"And Jared and his…people? What will happen to them?" Her expression sad, she said, "They were only trying to keep their families intact, keep their babies from starving to death. I mean," she looked conflicted. "They broke the law, that's wrong…but…I don't know that a person should be punished for just trying to survive when the government and no one can help them." Her face screwed up as if she struggled with the concept of laws, and good reasons to break them.

"Ah, my fierce scorpion." Kurian smiled. He wound his fingers around her upper arms and pulled her close. "You are learning that there are greys in the world. A person is not 100 % good or bad, but often a mix of both. Sometimes circumstances warrant a bit of bleeding in on both sides."

Confusion rolled through her blue eyes, her lashes fluttered rapidly as she pondered his conceptions. "I…my life has been controlled by others. I had to live by rigid rules or was severely punished. Barron and Grant kept me locked in a tiny room that they filmed me in and if I acted out at all I was…well, harshly disciplined. They only cared what money or sexual fun I could bring them. Otherwise I was just a mindless doll to use and put away. They didn't even try to learn to know me as a person, just like an empty sack I was only something to be used.

Her exhale was a harrowing scourge. "My foster families were abusive and they had no compunction with locking me in a closet if I wet the bed or cried when hit. Just for amusement, sometimes they made me sleep under the bed, you know, a child's worse fear of the bogeyman hiding under the bed ready to snatch them, kill them. I lived in constant terror. I had nothing else, no toys, dolls, I guess I wrapped the rules around me as a cloak of protection, something to own as mine," she shrugged with a mild smile, "as intangible as that was. The Children's Home, well, they were a wealth of rules and discipline. Honestly, Kurian, I knew nothing but rules and harsh penalties for disobeying them."

He rubbed his thumbs on her arms. "I think the rules helped you in the long run, Solitar, to get you through. You used them to make you strong, prop you up. Look how you excelled with your education and this job. But you fell under the weight of the endless rigid rules, they crushed everything else; life, light, love out of you. You are now learning to bend, not break, to blend the good and bad. I think you are learning to care, perhaps to love."

Frowning, she tried to withdraw from his grasp but he held her. "You don't understand, Kurian," she baulked, "I had no role model of love. I found that when I tried it, that I was hurt worse. I had to shut off that side of me. I will never be…normal." Her sigh was so defeatist Kurian's chest ached. "I am incapable of caring for another person. In fact," a bit of fire lit her eyes, "I let you in, see what a fool I am? No," she shook her head and declared, "I've sure learned my lesson. I will never care about another living soul again. I am that empty sack." She struggled for release but he shook her.

"Don't be ridiculous, Solitar. You suffered terrible terror for Colby and Ritchie's lives, and as I went into the cave after them I know you feared for my safety. You fidgeted and whined the whole way back here because you were desperate to know how Colby was faring. And what about Lili-Mae? You are worried for her in her own concern for Colby's survival."

Solitar twisted in his grip to get away, her face a map of confusion and pain. "No, you're wrong, I- I," tears slipped out, she cried, "I mean they're just kids practically, I don't wish them harm."

"And the children, Solitar for cripe's sake. You put your very life on the line to rescue them. What heartless person does that?"

She turned away, blinking back the tears. "I just did it on instinct, Kurian, it was hardly a loving deed."

He gave her another shake. "Stop it. Lili-Mae told us about the paintings. The reason why the animals kept coming to you. Not because they wanted a treat, but because they knew you. You were kind to them, petted and played with them when no one noticed. You painted them and their owners with such lively warmth to their owners' delight and hung the pictures in the local shop for the owners or others to purchase. Shit sells like hotcakes, girl.

"But, as much as you need the money to pay off that wretched school you knew the residents needed it more here and you donated it. Lili-Mae said it was you that gave Colby and Ritchie extra chores so they could earn money, and that you asked the sheriff for Colby to do community service to help him build character rather than arresting him. So," he squeezed her arms, "don't give me that mercenary bullshit. You care, you care so much it hurts. Tell me I lie, Solitar," he dared her.

One brow arched, she asked, "How come you can say the contraction *don't* easily but you don't use any other contractions?"

He blinked at her. Fighting the grin that threatened, he said, "We are having a heart to heart here and you ask me that?"

"Yes."

"Ah, I am not great with the English, and my Dutch is not the same as the natives speak here. I am working on the contractions. Rutger is always making fun of me. Like he is perfect," he said snidely.

"Speaking of Dutch," Solitar said and pulled from his grasp and he let her go. She stepped further into the room from the balcony and he followed. She noticed that oddly, his eyes were lowered and the tips of his ears were read. Glancing down she realized her robe was gaping and he appeared to be enjoying the view. She snapped the sides closed and traipsed to the desk, pulled a chair out from it and sat down. "You owe me the truth, Kurian. You are some kind of lawman. Tell me why you are really here? Is it because of the killings?" She suddenly stood up. "Speaking of, they said my brother got away, what happened?"

"Hmm," he scowled and indicated for her to take a seat again. When she did he pulled out a chair and sat in front of her. He explained about the episode at Sunflower on the Green and the officer who had been shot, and that Gareth Karelli got away.

"Oh no, how could he? How dreadful?" Her brows rose in distress. "People are going to blame me. And they would be right, it's my fault he came here." She threw the towel at the bed in shamed desperation.

"No, it is his fault, Solitar. He killed people, not you. The worse thing right now is we don't know where he is. He could be in another country for all we know and continuing his deadly rampage. I have men out searching, but so far we have gotten no word of any sightings of him."

She was quiet a moment digesting this. Then, "You didn't answer my question. Why are you here in Ruwenstad?"

Kurian sat back in his chair and settled an ankle over a knee, clasped his hands and set them in his lap. "I did not come for the murders, I was sent to find the source of the cocaine. We have had a terrible influx of it into the Netherlands and I traced it to Suriname, and more directly to Ruwenstad."

"But you didn't want me to turn Jared and his people in?"

"No, because as you said, they were desperate to feed their families. And they were a small scale. They did not distribute out of the country. No, it was Simón Bolívar I was after. I had a plan to draw him out, but," he eyed her said drily, "you jumped the gun and did that for me." Starting to get out of his chair and reach for her, he said, "Damn, Solitar, I was so afraid when you-"

She held a hand up to stop him. "No. Tell me who you are. Is Kurian your real name?"

He paused, his heated gaze sauntered down her body where his pupils dilated big and black and lusting, then moved back up to her stern glare and he sat back down with an aching sigh. "*Ja*, Kurian Anastaas is my true name. I am with the Royal Netherlands Marechaussee. It is a police organization with a military status, under the jurisdiction of the Ministry of Defense. We do special operations. Um, actually I grew up in a rebel stronghold deep in the mountains, we were cut off from normal civilization for a long time. That is why my language, accent, are different from the others. But, that is a story for another time. Anyway, I used the work in the mine as my cover, Garrick Miles was in on it. I was here only for the cocaine operation."

"But you were working with the sheriff on the murders?" She was puzzled.

He nodded. "*Ja*. A friend of mine, a general high up, has relatives here. When he knew I was here and he got word of the second murder he asked me to look into it. I was told not to get too involved, other than doing a little investigation. If he knew how involved I got I might have been ordered back home. I, and my team that came with me spent time investigating the murders when we should have been focused on the cocaine. But," he shrugged unconcernedly, "the head of the snake, Bolívar, has been decapitated. As I said, it will be a small matter to grab up the rest of his gang, and we will see that the fields are totally destroyed. So it is a success regardless of how it occurred. Unfortunately, I have not been as successful with capturing the killer of the young women."

"I see." Her mind scrambled to catch up on everything. Her brother's escape after he killed another person, the business with Bolívar, and now, finding out the truth about Kurian. Later she would ponder his thoughtful words of earlier when discussing her compassion and her comfort in rules. Maybe she could be lighter on herself, not be so darn rigid and uptight about rules and the law. She was seeing that sometimes they just had to be broken for the better good. Her gaze was on his shoulder, it rose to the neckline of his brown sweater. "So, I guess it's all over for you then, you'll be, um, heading home?"

He shifted to the edge of his chair. "It will take some time tying up all the ends. I will have to be present for Bolívar's trial unless we take him back to the Netherlands to face his charges. Regardless, I will be here a bit longer. And," he slid off the chair and took her hand. Urging her to her feet, he said, "I hope to spend every free moment with you."

She tried to resist him, but of course she was nothing to his superior strength but she put her hands out to stop him from pulling her into his arms. "I think since you got what you wanted, you can freely move onto other women. Gizelle, Cortnee, there were many women who all but threw themselves down in front of you like a red carpet."

His mouth quirked. "Are you jealous, my little scorpion?"

Eyes flashing with anger and jealousy, she denied, "Certainly not you conceited oaf-"

Against her will he pulled her into his arms. "I don't mind, baby, I like it. I like it that you are jealous of me." He laughed at the sour look on her face.

"Just so you know," he murmured, his deep voice lulling, he held her more tightly, "I have been blind with jealousy myself. Every time I had to see you feeding Rutger, then damned Ivar, I thought my head would explode. I thought of you as mine. Even that day at Zuk Zuk's when you were so horrible to Colby I could not dissuade the gush of attraction, of interest in you that sunk its teeth into my gullet and would not let go. I wanted you then. *Ja*, I craved your body, but the more time I spent with you the more I liked you and liked spending time with you. And I want more of it."

A disparaging sound came from her throat. She swallowed back the tears and shook her head. "I don't believe you. You jumped at the first excuse to run from me."

"Look at me." When she refused, he gently cupped her lower face and turned her, forcing her to connect their eyes. "Baby," he said softly in his deep rough voice. "I truly was called away. Rutger called to tell me they had sighted your brother at the restaurant bar. If it had not been so…imperative, I never would have left your warm bed or beautiful body. Hell, Woman, if I had my way we would hop back in between the sheets and never leave for a week. I was not avoiding you, or a date. I want nothing more than to start to build a relationship with you. And, little scorpion, if I thought a month ago I would ever say those words I would have asked Rutger to shoot me and put me out of my delusionary misery." He chuckled at the way her brows bunched up in perplexity.

"You…want to be with me?" Her voice was small, afraid to hope.

He sifted his large hand around and cradled the back of her head. His eyes gentle, Kurian smiled. "*Ja.* I would desire to see where this takes us. I am hoping for the long run, Solitar. I cannot imagine anything I want more than seeing your sweet face before I close my eyes at night and again when I wake every morning. Please trust me, baby, give us a chance. I have no hidden agenda."

Solitar snuggled into his hard embrace, then she straightened. He looked sincere, his tone held warmth and honesty, yet, she shook her head. "No. I can't have an affair with you and then in weeks or months you're out of my life. I…I've had too much, pain, I could not withstand that. It would be easier to not be with you at all then spend time, intimate time and- and more with you and then you're gone. No," she shook her head again, damp blonde hair swishing across her back, her expression wrenching. "I can't do that to myself. It's better if we make an even break right now instead of drawing it out." She would have to make sure she avoided him. If she saw Kurian with another woman on his arm she would die on the spot.

He refused to lighten his grip on her. "Baby, we have time to work shit out. Think about it. You hate working for the mine with every fiber of your being. Camara had a word with me one day at the office and confided in me. I think she was worried when you were so surly with me that I would cause trouble for you and she wanted to, oh, cushion your manner somewhat, ignite my compassion. She was afraid you would lose your job if you pissed me off and I was not tolerant of your...attitude."

"So what's your point? I can't leave Gatin de Muur, I owe too much money and I don't know how to do anything else." Her mouth turned down as she remembered her earlier vow that she would flip burgers rather than continue to decimate a country. A rock and a hard place, she owed so much money she'd need ten jobs to pay it back if she left Gatin de Muur's employment. Using their loophole, the Children's Home was able to compound interest daily, and she was still only eating away at the principle. Brow wrinkling in perplexity, what to do?

"Sometimes for such a brilliant broad, Solitar you can be so dumb. You get in your own way."

Her mouth dropped open at his insult. "You-"

He bent and covered her mouth with his to shut her up. It took a few long resisting seconds before he worked her into a hot noodle, by the time he leaned back she was putty in his hands. "Ah, baby, that look, *Dios* how I love that look of you. Your eyes all glazed and shimmering blue ponds, lips puffy and damp, *ja*, gorgeous. Now. Hush for a second and listen to me." He put a finger to her lips when they parted to object.

"Hush," he repeated. "I spoke to the clerk at the shop where you sold your paintings. Honey, I don't think you have any idea exactly how much money they generated. Wealthy people will pay top dollar for paintings of their beloved pets. Especially done by the exquisite artist that the clerk claims you are. She says you breathe life into the portraits, love pours from the eyes of the animals. They come out three dimensional like they're alive, not flat like a photograph.

"She thinks once you leave indigent Ruwenstad and put your stuff out there you can make a fortune. She thinks if you move into landscapes and whatever else, that you are good enough to have your own gallery opening. And, if you follow your heart into the art world, you can work anywhere. Anywhere my love, like where I live. I can easily support you until you are fully on your feet. If you really don't want to live in my country, baby, I will leave my job and go where you want. I have certain...abilities, I can get hired anywhere."

Her lashes flapped over stunned eyes, her lips parted in dismay. "I don't-" There was a knock at the door.

"Ah, food, hold that thought. Thank *Dios*, I am starving." He turned and strode to open the door. Gordy was there with a large silver tray. His face was red, he didn't look at Kurian, his gaze skewed to Solitar standing in her robe.

"Put the tray on the desk, and stop looking at her," Kurian snapped.

"Uh." Gordy's mouth slapped closed and he averted his eyes, his skin darkened further. He set the tray on the desk.

"Here, give to Dozi what is owed and you keep the rest," Kurian said, handing him some bills. "Take off."

"Uh," Gordy mumbled. Stuffing the bills in his pocket he practically ran for the door. It closed behind him.

With a slight grin, Solitar said, "You were kind of rude to him, Kurian."

Lifting a metal lid off a plate, Kurian bent and sniffed it. "The way he ogles you he is lucky I don't pluck his eyeballs out of his gawky head and toss them out the window." He smiled at her. "You see, my love? I hold the same jealousy you do. All I care about is you and me. I have no desire for another woman, I never will."

"I don't understand, Kurian," worry niggled her tone, her eyes wavered up to his then lowered to his chin. "We had a…good time, I thought, in bed. But you couldn't get away from me fast enough. I offered to cook you dinner and you barely left a smoke trail you ran away so fast."

Looking from the food to her, his mouth quirked at her description. "I explained that, apparently you were not listening very closely. I planned on spending the day, or longer if we could get away with it, with you in bed. But, the call I got was Rutger saying Gareth Karelli had been spotted at the Sunflower on the Green restaurant. You know I could not waste time getting there. As it turned out, it did not matter. He was gone before I arrived. By the time I saw you again your attitude was sour on me and you snuck out the back of the Cresh."

"I had to get to the children, Kurian, I was sure I knew where they were."

He nodded. "You were correct." His eyes narrowed in anger. "How do you think it made me feel when I saw you surrounded by those gangsters? Hell, baby, my fucking heart was in my mouth. I cannot believe you put yourself in that position. However," his anger softened, "you see what I mean by brave and caring? You took it fully upon yourself to find and save those children at great risk to yourself. There will never be a repeat of that though, I will not allow you to put me through that kind of shit again."

Her mouth dropped. "Excuse me?" Her eyes lifted to his reflecting her own anger. "I did what I had to do, no one would listen to me."

"I would have listened to you, but you did not give me the opportunity. You just up and left, sneaking out the back because you knew I would have stopped you."

She rolled her eyes. "You see? That's my point. I thought I could find the children and you wouldn't have let me go search for them."

"Damned right I would not have let you put yourself into that danger. But," his voice gentled, "I would have listened to your ideas, I would have gone to the school. I trust your brain, your common sense. Now," he set the lid back on the plate and traced back over to her like a jungle cat prowling its dinner. "There is something we need to do before we eat. I fear I cannot wait to taste the food until I have had my fill of you." As he bent his head to capture her lips, he grasped the belt of her robe and untied it.

"Kurian, what are you-" she mumbled against his lips as the robe slide off her shoulders.

"Just follow my lead, love," he whispered against her mouth and pushed the robe until it fell to the floor. She was naked, and he had never wanted anything more in his life than her under him and his hands on her.

"Little scorpion," he murmured, and scooped her up in his arms. He trod to the bed and laid her down then grabbed the hem of his sweater and yanked it over his head and tossed it. His boots, socks, jeans and underwear followed. By the time he knelt on the bed, she was smiling shyly yet her eyes were lit with pure arousal, and her arms were raised to receive him. He made his place between her legs, pushing them apart with his knees.

It was hours before they ate the cold food and then hopped in the jeep for the ride to   the   hospital.

Epilogue

"What do you think about that, Colby?" Solitar asked the teen.

He was propped up in the hospital bed. After a few months the color had returned to his ashen face, burns on his arms were healing, his lungs breathed clearer and he would be released soon. The one crooked front tooth shone in his wide grin. Someone, likely Lili-Mae because he rarely bothered, had combed his dark blond hair neatly to one side.

The room was filled. Lili-Mae was as always sitting beside his bed. Many from the mine were there, Siggy, Hubie, and Colby's partner in crime Ritchie. Also crowded in the room were Kurian and his team, Rutger, Ivar, Kris and Jaq. Sadly Camara wasn't present, she was in custody pending charges of being an accessory. They still hadn't determined how much involvement she had with the coca fields and the cocaine distribution. She had been devastated when apprised of Luthor's demise.

Solitar had tried to reach her, to console her ex-friend, but Camara had declined all efforts of contact. She undoubtedly blamed Solitar for her boyfriend's death, and she was also probably feeling shame for her own part in the events that shook the town.

Colby looked around the room, his eyes warming when they landed on Lili-Mae, he squeezed the small hand he held and they made googly-eyes at each other until Kurian cleared his throat. "Boy," he prompted the teen to answer Solitar's question.

Colby grinned at him then Solitar. "It's super, Mr. K. The lawyer you hired is suing the mine owners and they're gonna pay for my, and," he looked to Ritchie and Lili-Mae, "*our* college educations in the States. The three of us got scholarships to pay for it all. Plus, Gatin de Muur has to donate tons of dough to the Republic of Kedolamer, the city of Ruwenstad. The money will pay for seeds and plants, trees, equipment and tools for the people to grow *legal* crops. Like cocoa for chocolate, vanilla, saffron, vineyards, fruit trees, coffee, on and on. Enough to sustain us for generations. They are also footing the bill for a bunch of restructuring of the city and the residential areas. The school is open again and we now have brand new school buses."

"Yes," Lili-Mae said in her shy, quiet voice, adoring gaze steady on Colby. "It was a terrible, terrible thing that happened, but at least the end is good. Our town will flourish."

Ritchie nodded, agreeing. His dark hair was moussed into spikes on the top of his head, equally dark eyes sparkled with happiness. "Yeah, once we get our degrees, mine in agriculture, Colby's in engineering, Lili-Mae wants to be a nurse, or," he rolled his eyes at her snort, "a doctor as she claims. Anyway, once we get our degrees we're coming home to take care of our own."

Kurian said, "It is all good. Jared DiCello is also going to school. He wants to be a teacher. He said if only there was a good college in Ruwenstad people would not have to leave to get a good education. He said the first thing he wants to do is open a college here."

Nodding, Rutger added, "*Ja*, he said there will be income generated from the lawsuit that is earmarked for that and he and Marlie want to be a part of it when it happens."

"And we decided we're gonna stick around and help build the college," Siggy said, nodding to Hubie who stood next to him grinning.

Hubie said, "There is no longer a viable mine here, at least not for a while. Garrick Miles said we will be paid if we choose to hang here and help build the college. It's a win-win. By the time the college is built the mine will be ready to re-excavate. Only this time," his gaze swept to Solitar and he smiled, "it will be done with no damage to the countryside, and of course the regulations regarding waste removal will be diligently adhered to, as well as all the other safety precautions, like checking for broken fans. Like they should have been done."

"Plus, since we were so close to the pollution happening right under our noses, and not looking carefully enough into those damaged fans, we will be so much more meticulous with our rules and regs. Just like you always tried to pound into our thick skulls, Soli," Cregg Trent said.

Kurian settled his arm around Solitar's shoulder and smiled when she didn't try to move away. They had come a long way in the short time since the mine explosion. They had spent every spare minute with each other and she was more easily accepting his PDA's. At first she didn't want anyone to know that she was having relations with a co-worker, but as he had told her, he was no longer employed by Gatin de Muur.

The mine was inoperative, but Solitar was drawing a severance type of pay since she had tried to look into the pollution, and had ordered that the broken fans be fixed immediately. And Kurian had pushed her to tell Garrick Miles about Jamie's rape. Miles had been aware of other complaints from women on prior jobs regarding Jamie and he hadn't done anything about them. Therefore he was discussing a settlement with Solitar to stay out of court. Kurian's real employer was the Royal Netherlands Marechaussee so they were far from co-workers.

Once Jamie recovered enough from the damage Kurian had dealt him, he was facing court and lengthy jail time.

Solitar had learned Laddie Lafayette conspired with Jamie Orlando to sabotage the mine causing the pollution of the river as well as damaging the fans to cause the explosion. Per Solitar's orders, the fans had been fixed, but Laddie had gone back in to break them back down again. Laddie had admitted his guilt to the police. He had wanted the blight of the mines in his native town ended, and he thought he could get rich with the coca fields. After their fight the day of the meeting, he and Jamie had met to make a truce because they had to work together, then Jamie mentioned the scheme of the cocaine and Laddie had eagerly, greedily jumped on board.

It had been Jamie who had damaged Solitar's jeep. He had been telling the truth to Bolívar that he wanted to capture her and keep her prisoner in a place no one could find. But he hadn't known she had gotten lost that day she collected the samples. By the time he found the jeep he was too late, she was gone. He broke into the jeep and stole the samples so no one would figure his true plot.

Colby had seen Laddie enter the mine and he was suspicious as he had been told there would be no operations there until it was confirmed the gas was completely cleared and it was safe to enter. He and Ritchie followed Laddie inside and Colby confronted him. Then the two started fighting when Colby said he was going to report what Laddie had done. Unfortunately, there was enough methane gas still in the tunnel and when Laddie had shut the fans back down again the gas exploded taking down the mine and trapping all three of them.

Laddie and Ritchie both survived but they spent a few weeks in the hospital before Laddie was arrested and is currently standing trial for his devious deeds.

Kurian had been encouraging Solitar to paint and work towards eventually being showcased in a gallery. He had also been working on her to come home with him when his job in Ruwenstad was completed. The only worm in the apple was Gareth Karelli's escape. There still had been no word on where he'd run to, where he was hiding. Where he would strike next upon some poor unsuspecting woman that had the bad luck to resemble Solitar's mother. Unfortunately, Solitar would not be safe until he was captured. He'd followed her to Ruwenstad for a reason, there was no comprehension why he did, and what he would have done if he had gotten his hands on her.

They had also discussed searching for Solitar's other siblings. She and Gareth weren't the only ones abandoned, and there were siblings that had been kept in the family as well. They all deserved to know about one another, even if they had no desire to meet. Time would tell regarding mending the riffs in the Karelli homestead.

"Come," Kurian whispered in Solitar's ear. "I have had enough of keeping my hands off of you today, let's head back to the Cresh."

Solitar turned in his arm to smile up at him, her eyes made it all the way up to his and her body sizzled at the scorching look in Kurian's gaze as he looked down at her. The side of his mouth turned up in a sexy, designing smile. "You've had your hands on me all day, Kurian." It was true. He touched her whenever he could, her shoulder, her arm, he held her hand, stole kisses when heads were turned.

He whispered near her ear, "Ah, but you have not been naked all day, my love." His leering grin made the sizzle turn into a full-fledged burn at her core. "I have yet to pry your agreement to marry me out of you. I think that would be best done in bed.

You are much more amenable to what I ask of you when you are beneath me. Or when you are on all fou-"

"Shush," she quickly set her fingers against his grinning lips. As her cheeks bloomed rosy, Solitar said, "Well, hey everyone, we have to be going, we'll see you later at Zuk's." She slipped from Kurian's grasp and moved to Colby's bed. Leaning in she kissed him on his forehead and patted his arm warmly. "We'll stop in tomorrow and bring you those comic books you wanted, Colby." She touched Lili-Mae's arm and said, "Later, honey." She was rewarded with Lili-Mae's toothy grateful smile.

Lili-Mae shyly laid her head on Colby's shoulder. "Okay Miss Soli. Bye Mr. Kurian." Her lashes fluttered at the still dangerous looking man except when his eyes were on Solitar.

"*Ja*, later kids. You big kids too." Kurian grinned at his friends and waved as he ushered Solitar quickly away before she had to say sayonara to every single one of them.

Outside, he hustled her to the jeep and opened the passenger door. Sliding in, Solitar frowned. "How come I never drive?"

Getting in the other side, he answered, "Because my pet, you are the world's worse driver. You have one foot on the gas and the other on the brake pedal at the same time going back and forth the entire time. You floor the gas then slow to a snail's pace, and when not driving with one tire in the gutter you take your half out of the middle of the road. And, you get lost."

"Well," she harrumphed, crossing her arms over her chest. "I didn't have anyone to teach me. I could only watch bus drivers and others to learn. I think the man that gave me my driving test passed me out of pity, or," she giggled, "fear that I would only return again and again and he'd have to drive with me putting his neck on the line."

Kurian smiled tenderly at her, cupped her chin and stroked his thumb on her cheek. "Baby, I will be more than happy to give you any lessons you need."

Her smile lifted her lips, coquettish pink tinged her cheeks, she replied, "So far you have been quite patient and skillful in the lessons you've given me."

He bent and bussed her lips then sat back in his seat, happiness wreathing his hard features. "I have many more lessons for you, my little love. Many. And I look forward to each and every one of them. The only thing you have to say is yes."

"Yes?"

"Finally," he murmured starting the car.

"Finally?" she asked a shade bemused.

"*Ja*, you finally agreed to marry me." He turned and grinned at her then aimed the jeep to the main road.

"But I didn't-" she broke off at his smug, gorgeous, happy expression and settled back in her seat with her own contented smile.

THE END

Solitar

www.ingramcontent.com/pod-product-compliance
Lightning Source LLC
Chambersburg PA
CBHW032141170626
46808CB00006B/2324